MIGRANTE

Migrante

by J.W. Henley

A Camphor Press book

Published by Camphor Press Ltd

83 Ducie Street, Manchester, M1 2JQ
United Kingdom

www.camphorpress.com

ISBN 978-1-78869-193-2 (paperback)
978-1-78869-194-9 (hardcover)

The moral right of the author has been asserted.

Set in 11 pt Linux Libertine

Dedicated to the women of Migranteng Kababaihan sa Taiwan; to the six brave souls who perished in the October 1, 2019, bridge collapse at Nanfang'ao; and to all those of the working class who travel the world in search of a better life for themselves and their families.

Inspired by true stories of overseas Filipino workers and migrant workers from Vietnam, Thailand, and Indonesia living and working in Taiwan, as told to the author.

Acknowledgments

As with the completion of any work, there are many hands involved other than my own and many places where genuine thanks are due. First, I extend my heartfelt gratitude to Jasmine Bonang Sanchez, without whose introduction to the world of Southeast Asian immigrant labor in Taiwan this book would not be possible. And to all those who shared their stories with me, the caregivers, household helpers, factory workers, fishermen, and farmers — men and women, young and old — I thank you for your courage, your friendship, your bravery, and your honesty. You are the true heroes of this story.

I thank those in Taiwan who dedicate their lives to the fight for equal rights for all in this beautiful, progressive country — a place that deserves the official, unequivocal, unwavering recognition of the world at large for the democratic, free, and leading nation that it is. Thanks as well to Lennon and Sherry Wong of the Serve the People Association and the indomitable Allison Lee of the Yilan Fishermen's Union. You are the allies, the firebrands, the tacticians, and the freedom fighters, whatever the day at hand may call for — the lights in the darkness idealists of future generations will rally around.

In that same vein, thank you to Camphor Press for believing in my work, helping me to bring it to its best form, many a time saving me from myself as good mentors do, and for providing a much-needed and vital outlet for writers who strive to shine a light on this corner of the world.

To Professor Jose Mario de Vega, noted Filipino philosopher, political scientist, author, essayist, and radical, I thank you as well for your fruitful efforts in reading and reviewing the manuscript, correcting my rudimentary Tagalog, and most importantly for providing invaluable guidance and encouragement.

I thank my family. My mother and father, Bill and Vionne Henley, for providing an environment in which there were no limits to what I could choose to become, guiding me when necessary yet allowing me space to fall, to fail, and eventually to find my own way in the world. I thank my brother Bryce, for being yet another example, one of many in our clan, of what it means to stand upright in the world for those things you hold dear and to put forth your best day after day.

Thank you to Isa Pilapil, who provided the magnificent cover art for this work. You and Ian are inspirations to me and my work day after day, whether you know it or not, and not just because you so generously offer to pick me up from Ninoy Aquino International whenever I find myself in Manila, even when I arrive at ungodly hours of the morning. You are kind souls, possessed of the kind of uncommon talent and brainpower that, when we speak, I find myself struggling to hold up my end of the conversation for want of simply listening to the two of you introduce me to so many new thoughts and ideas.

And finally, I thank my wife, Jill Su (Su Yu-ting). You are the one who inspired me to chase my dreams, to stretch my mind and abilities to their utmost, and to fight against the encroaching darkness of the world at large and the mind within. Without you, not only would this book, and those that preceded it, not likely exist, I myself may not as well. I love you, forever and always, and as much as this book is for others, it is just the same for you.

For anyone I may have inadvertently neglected, I truly apologize. My mind is a cluttered thing at the best of times. I hope I have and will continue to do you proud. Until next time.

Read. Refuse. Resist.

— J.W. Henley

Foreword

THIS is not my story. That is, to state the obvious, I am not a migrant worker from the Philippines. I was not born and raised in a Manila slum, though I have visited many, and count the residents of some of the city's cemeteries and underprivileged areas as friends, co-conspirators, and collaborators. I did travel overseas for work, leaving my country behind at age twenty-two, but it was not under duress, nor was it a journey undertaken due to economic necessity or lack of opportunities in my native land. It was something I did because I had the privilege of making the choice to do so. My background is that of a white middle-class Canadian, of Ukrainian ancestry on my mother's side, English and Dutch heritage on the side of my father. I was never poor. I was never exploited. I never knew hunger, or what it was to be taken advantage of or discriminated against due to the color of my skin or the name of the country embossed on my passport. And yet, this is a story that came to me.

More accurately, I should say that this story was brought to me. It was given to me by a woman named Jasmine Bonang Sanchez. It was early 2015. Jasmine, a woman I had never met before nor shared any mutual friends with at the time, sent me a message via Facebook.

She had found my name on the *Taipei Times* website. Back then I shared a weekly music column for the *Times*, covering mostly metal and punk, styles firmly within my wheelhouse, when it came my turn to fill the half-page of space near the back of the arts section. Jasmine, a caregiver for the elderly, had put on some punk shows back in her native Philippines prior to coming to Taiwan for work, she said, and wanted to meet up for a chat. About what, it wasn't quite clear in the beginning. Maybe music, I thought. She merely asked that I show up at Taipei Main Station the following Sunday and meet her in the cavernous hall of the main concourse to talk. Intrigued, I agreed; and when Sunday came, I stepped out of my apartment and was soon introduced to a new world.

Jasmine wasn't alone waiting for me at the station. With her was a crew of women, at least a dozen in all, there among the throngs of migrant workers from Indonesia, Thailand, Vietnam, and the Philippines, thousands of men and women of all ages enjoying their lone day off for the week. These, I would later learn, were the relatively lucky few, granted one day of freedom every seven days. It wasn't so much a chat that Jasmine and her friends wanted. Caregivers and domestic helpers all, they wanted their stories to be heard and told. Jasmine, sensing in me what was perhaps a kindred spirit of rebellion due to my background as a metal and punk vocalist, concert promoter, and writer, thought that I should be the one to hear and to tell.

One by one the women poured their hearts out to me, recounting tales of abuse, exploitation, heartbreak, and humiliation. They spoke of having room and board taken out of their paychecks, only to be given a bare patch of floor to sleep on, perhaps a blanket to stave off the winter cold. They recounted having their passports illegally seized by their employers or their brokers, rendering them unable to leave freely if they so wished, of being locked inside their rooms at night by their employers. And they opened my eyes to the fact that, in the eyes of the law, they were seen as second-class, below the Taiwanese themselves, underneath those largely white white-collar expats. These Southeast Asian "migrant workers," I found, were granted far less protection by the state mechanisms that allowed me, a Western expat, to change jobs relatively freely, to quit with little in the way of repercussions, and if necessary, to launch a lawsuit in the event of a serious trespass against me. None of those privileges afforded to me, I learned, were open to them, or were at least made far more difficult and even dangerous to access, simply because of where they were from, and the regional sociopolitical and economic circumstances they were born into — things that, like most people on earth, they felt largely powerless to control.

As they said all this, these things that were heartbreaking to hear, let alone to say out loud, and to a stranger no less, they did so with courage, dignity, and a sense of determination. Their numbers gave them strength, and in being there together to support one another, they were certain that this was a beginning — a means of finally wresting the power from a system explicitly tooled to render them powerless against it. This was the start of their personal revolution, and they wanted me to chronicle it.

I was touched by their bravery and moved by their revolutionary spirit. And when the feature based on their recollections broke in February, it was viewed tens of thousands of times. Yes, this was a beginning. A humble one, but a first step nonetheless. A step toward changing something at best deeply flawed and at worst innately sinister – the laws, or lack thereof, put in place to ensure that the migrant workers of Taiwan, the *migrantes*, remain faceless, nameless, shunted far out of sight, further out of mind.

In the months and years that followed, there were more stories to tell, spreading the word about a terrible thing happening in Taiwan, this otherwise wonderful country I've come to call my second home. From meeting mostly female caregivers for the elderly and infirm and domestic helpers, I came to be acquainted with the stories of many male *migrantes* – fishermen and factory workers with their own recollections of being treated as human chattel, bought and sold, regarded by their employers as something less than human.

The impacts of the ensuing features in publications from Taipei to Hong Kong to the United States varied, as they do. Hits fluctuated, comments went up and down. I wanted to find a way to make a broader impact. That's when the idea struck: I could turn all those stories I'd heard – all those words of being mired in modern-day indentured servitude – into a book. A work of fiction, rooted in the hard, brutal facts of the world the migrantes live in from day to day. All those words of those who possessed the will to make themselves heard, I could put them into another form, express them through composite characters to get the world's attention. But should I? Because, after all, this is not my story.

I did some soul-searching. Obviously, the best person to write this book would be someone who had been through the same trials the men and women of Taiwan's migrant worker community had survived. But to this point, the time of this book's publication, that book – one dealing specifically with the plight of migrant workers in Taiwan – does not yet exist. It may one day, and on that day it should become the book of record. But because that day has not yet arrived, I decided, with compassion and respect for the men and women of the *migrante* world, to write it myself, and donate the whole of my portion of the proceeds to migrant worker advocacy groups so as to further their push for equal rights under the law.

This is not my story, but I have done my utmost to write it as accurately and insightfully as I can. Being a male author, I decided it best to write from the male perspective, and weaved together a tale of a man, Rizal, who grows up in the Navotas City Cemetery in Metro Manila (a place I also visited in the course of my journalistic endeavors) and who goes to Taiwan to join the fishing fleet Having a male protagonist was an ethical choice, made to write from a perspective that, at least in terms of gender identity, is closest to my own.

Furthermore, I wanted to take on the story of a fisherman for the sheer danger these men face in earning a living for themselves and their families, whom they may not see for months at a time, if not years. Even in developed nations, working as a fisherman is among the most dangerous jobs. Fishermen are up to six times more likely to die on the job than those doing the work deemed most dangerous on land, according to a study published by the U.K. Maritime and Coastguard Agency. Add to this the dangerous level of neglect and bureaucratic dehumanization that goes hand-in-hand with the governing of migrant fishermen around the world, and you have a group of hundreds of thousands for whom death is a very real possibility each and every time they put to sea. While this tragedy is not wholly preventable given the volatility of the sea, the risk could be lessened would those in power simply see the men (and at times women) staffing the ships that go out, sometimes for months on end, less as human capital and more as simply human, possessed of lives as worthy of protection as any and all.

Hopefully, the genuine care and concern I have for those whose words have formed the basis for this work shines through in the chapters ahead. I can only stand in humility and awe of their courageousness, and hope that these words will contribute to change for the better in their world. I typed these words, but they do not belong to me. They are the words of the *migrantes*, some of the strongest individuals I have ever had the honor to know. This is their story, and I — we — now pass it on to you. Take it, share it, and join their revolution. We are better together, and best when our unique stories from our disparate corners are known and understood.

— J.W. Henley
January 11, 2019
Taipei

MIGRANTE

Chapter One

His name was Datu, and Rizal was afraid of him. "Datu Death," the children called out, mocking the bent old man with their cruel songs and chants. It was strange for Rizal to be afraid of someone who was only named for death. But then, even Rizal's own mother had long told him he was an odd boy, much different from the rest.

Yes, it was very odd indeed to fear a man named for death when death itself was all around Rizal and everyone he had ever known. It was in the places they lived. Its earthy scent was on their clothing. It clung to their skin like layers of days-old sweat. Death was their vocation. Their way of life. Rizal himself lived with the remains of eight bodies in a broken mausoleum he shared with his mother. Ashes in urns. The remains of an old Chinese family that had forgotten its departed. A family come to ruin, Rizal's mother told him when he was young and afraid. The ghosts would not haunt them. They would be happy, she whispered on those nights when her son shook with fear of the nightmares to come. The spirits would be pleased someone was there to care for them, in their place of eternal sleep.

Unlike his mother, Rizal had not spent the whole of his childhood in the cemetery. She had returned to the place where she herself was born to an unwed teenage mother, some forty years ago in the middle of the Marcos dictatorship. It was where she had grown up during those years of fear and suspicion, never knowing so much as the name of her father. In her late teens and early twenties the cemetery was remembered as the place she had managed to escape through marriage to a man only slightly better off than she – a man who with his honeyed words and handsome face had made a teenage mother of her as well. For a while, she had hope. She believed in her heart that the worst years, those of hunger and death, were those she had endured early in life, when she was young and strong enough to rise above them – struggles she prayed her infant son would never know. But she would be forced back to the cemetery, during a time when her husband was yet again unemployed and drinking away his afternoons and nights, estranged from his wife and son, living with an old girlfriend, another fooled by his way with words and good looks. Rizal's mother and Rizal himself were quickly pushed back into poverty's grip by the man's selfish ways. Rizal would come to see his father as more of a mystery than a man: a well-worn curse of the Manila slums.

Rizal was about five when his mother packed up what she could carry and took him to a place she had hoped he would never know. He was grown enough then to understand what death means, innocent enough still to be confused by the question of what comes after the soul parts from the body. Now, more than fifteen years later, Rizal told himself he feared no one in the burial ground. Well, almost no one. The man who broke the tombs with his rubber mallet; who pulled the ragged bones out, their paper-brown parchment skin crumbling and flaking; who spoke tenderly to the corpses as though they were still alive — Rizal feared him more than any other being, living or dead, in the Navotas City Cemetery.

Rizal saw him coming, walking slowly in an ocher cloud of sun and dust with the same slight limp he had since Rizal was a boy. That walk. It reminded Rizal of a *maganang kumain*. The older boys used to tell stories of them coming out at night. Living corpses stalking among the rows of steadily sinking tombs, those resting places that disappeared little by little into the soft earth dredged from the plastic-coated depths of Manila Bay. The living dead, dragging one foot behind the other, feasting on the drunks and the junkies. Whenever a user was found dead, usually a man or a woman from outside the cemetery, it was never the rats that had torn the flesh from the cheekbones, leaving patches of bloodstained bone exposed through ragged holes in the bloated, stinking flesh. It was always the work of a *maganang kumain*. Although Rizal was not a boy anymore but a man, of sorts, the old stories stayed with him.

Rizal was on his way back from the tap, the only source of water for the hundreds living in, on, and around the graves. "Funeral water," they called it, in the way only the poor could make light of something deadly. Funeral water, as in, "Go ahead, take a sip. It's your funeral." Much as their senses did against the harshness of life, the insides of the people living in the cemetery seemed to harden against any water-borne diseases pulled up out of the well. Dengue-spreading mosquitoes thrived in the stagnant puddles and ditches throughout the grounds. The summer before, even the barangay captain's child, two years old, was taken fast by the sickness. But the well water, for now, was safe. So they hoped, so they believed. And seemingly by the powers of faith alone, so it was.

Rizal had waited until the odious liquid from the well filled his five-liter jug for his first of many trips back and forth that day. The container was heavy, straining his slight, ropy arms. Ducking below the gnarled branch of an acacia tree, moving down a row of narrow rectangular tombs stacked one on top of the other, much higher than Rizal was tall, he set the jug down, rubbing his tender muscles. This row Datu had already been to. The front of some of the tombs were broken open along the partially sunken bottom row, the brittle, dusty remains exhumed. Soon, maybe even that same day, there would be more funerals. The grim processions were quick. A half-hour to inter the dead – to say truncated and always inadequate last goodbyes as the grave keepers mixed their cheap, sandy cement and readied their rusty trowels. There were always more bodies to seal up behind cinder block walls and mortar. More work for Datu the gravedigger and others like Rizal, men who sporadically shared the old man's trade when the work was enough to feed them all.

Datu, the most experienced of the gravediggers, was the only one never short of work. For every body he pulled from a tomb, those that went unclaimed after their five-year term expired and would not be moved to a permanent home in another cemetery, another twenty pesos in his pocket. A pittance to put the bones in an old rice sack, the family name written on the side with a black felt marker when he could borrow one from the cemetery office. For every mass grave he had to dig, wide and deep enough for ten, bodies from families too poor to afford even an apartment tomb or a bone box, 250 pesos for the day's work. For every new corpse shoved into those apartment tombs made recently vacant by a family's inability to pay, a new marble marker and ledge on which the family of the newly deceased would place candles or a modest bouquet of wilting lilies to replace the old ones, Datu could make a thousand pesos or more. Then there was the caretaker work, looking after the tombs for the families of the dead. Fifty pesos per tomb every month. Datu had an entire row to himself, 150 tombs or more. Rizal thought of his own empty pocket and the handful of tombs he swept, and just for a moment he envied the old man.

In Navotas even the dead could not escape the indignities of life. And the poor who lived in the cemetery, they knew that the ways out were lessened day by day. Yes, God would watch over them. The Lord would work in his own mysterious ways, and in his own time. But he would not make them rich. Nor was it certain he would deliver them from their hardship. To grant a man or a woman riches — to free them from suffering simply because they prayed for such — this was not the way of the Almighty. He would give and he would take. In the meantime theirs were lives to be enjoyed in brief moments when possible, endured when not. Pain their payment for being pure — untainted by money. For the rich, money was something else. It was their ticket to salvation, a legacy they could use to purchase a one-way ticket past the purgatory the people of Navotas lived in day after day, straight to the rich man's paradise.

Mama is waiting.

Rizal bent down, wincing at the ache in his back. He picked up the jug. Water was business. It was money in their pockets, if only for a while as he waited for his own work to pick up again. The sun broke above the base of the tall, stoical statue of Santa Maria. Most every morning Rizal saw the golden rays of the morning's early light bend as if by miracle around her robed feet, enveloping her outstretched hands. It meant the beginning of a new day. The start of another, just like the one before, and the countless before that. It might have been beautiful, once, seeing the statue bathed in a glow like the embrace of the Lord, the hands beseeching those passing beneath them to go about their lives with the peace of God and the love of Christ in their hearts. Now Rizal noticed only when he happened to be looking in that direction instead of down at his torn cloth shoes, watching drops of sweat cascade from his nose to the dust and broken bits of stone seal scattered on the ground.

Mama is waiting.

Perhaps she had customers already. To keep them waiting would make her angry. Rizal stepped over a man passed out against the blinding white tomb stacks covered in oyster shell ash, an empty bottle of Tanduay rum resting near his limp hand. The man's pockets were turned out. A slash ran down his cheek, the blood dried in short, curving rivulets. A penalty for the thieves finding his pockets empty. Rizal turned left, first looking around the corner to see if Datu was coming. The row was empty, with only a few mangy dogs pawing at insects in the reddish-brown soil. Rizal quickened his step and made for home.

Home. For Rizal it had always been a place he felt small; where the suffocating smells and the whirling dust kept him down on the threadbare floor mat, Mama barking at him from behind her bubbling pot at which she stood from morning till night.

"Such a lazy boy. Always lying around. Letting his mother work all day while he just flops there pretending to be sick. *Susmaryosep!* What I would give for a hardworking son!"

Rizal stifled his cough as he walked through the entrance. The mausoleum was of two levels. The ground floor was where they slept, where his mother worked. It was swept as clean as it could be, though there was no keeping up with the dust. The upper level, that was where the urns were kept. Eight of them, his mother said. Rizal had never bothered to count.

The mausoleums were for the remains of the rich, either of the past or of the present. The dead of the rich would never endure the shame of being torn from their resting place, bones left to bleach in unsorted piles in the glaring sun then dumped unceremoniously into Datu's old rice sacks. In structures both stately and decaying the remains of the rich were housed, and there they would always remain. Rizal rarely went up to the second level, nor did his mother. Every morning she lit eight candles lined along a plywood mantle for the eight souls, saying a rosary for each, snuffing out the flames before long. Candles were a luxury they could ill afford to replace, but respects must be paid. And every morning she uttered a prayer of thanks for sharing their home with her and her son. Then she set to work.

"*Anong nangyari?* What took you so long, Rizal? Mrs. Pilapil has already come and gone. She couldn't wait any longer. *Sayang!* What is your excuse this time?"

Rizal set the water down next to his mother's portable propane stove, his dark brown eyes avoiding her fiery glare. She snatched up the jug, drawing dust into the air. Rizal fought the itch at the back of his throat, putting a hand over his mouth. His mother poured water into her pot and turned on the gas. Blue-orange tendrils of flame licked at the bottom of the pot. The blackened copper began to glow. Though he stood above it now, Rizal always saw the copper pot from below, the viewpoint of a child, when it appeared in his thoughts and dreams.

"Well?" Rizal's mother eyed her son, tearing the top from a pack of noodles. She plopped the yellow-white brick into the steaming pot. "What took you so long? *Hay naku!* Out with it!"

He hesitated, eyes moving between his mother and the doorway that had never had a proper door, only a rectangle of rotting particle board they moved into place each night before going to sleep. A pair of cinder blocks at the corners would provide at least some resistance if the junkies decided they wanted the stove. There was little else to steal. Rizal watched his mother's eyes glow hot, the rising steam sticking to her round cheeks. She stirred the pot, ignoring the bursting bubbles landing droplets of scalding water on her scarred forearms. She pulled the wooden spoon from the pot and he knew there was little time to waste.

"I saw him today," he whispered, lowering his eyes to the ground.

"*Sino?*"

Again Rizal looked around the room. To the thin mats they slept on at night. To the transistor radio his mother let him listen to for an hour each night when their spaghetti wire patch into the power lines held. The same wiring had caused fires in other mausoleums, taking life and possessions with equal cruelty. His mother put both hands on her hips. Time was short. If he didn't offer an answer soon she would bring the spoon down on his head. He had to tell her.

"Datu."

"*Ano ba yan!*" Rizal's mother threw her hands up, turning her back to him. She whirled around again, marching toward him, the end of the spoon pointed at his nose. "When are you going to grow up, Rizal? When are you going to give up these childish games? He is a man, just like you. How many times do I have to tell you? There is no such thing as *maganang kumain. Sus!* You and your friends. Grown men running around like little boys. Datu may be old and poor, but at least he has something to do. What do you have, Rizal? Do you have a job? Do you have money in your pocket? No, you have nothing. Twenty-two years old and still living off your mother. I could die from shame."

Rizal turned his back to her. He started shuffling slowly toward the open doorway.

"And where do you think you're going?" his mother yelled. Even as she called after him she lumbered back behind the stove. White foam bubbled up over the side of the pot, water splashing down onto the ground. She lowered the level of the flame and the foam settled.

"I'm going to find Kidlat."

"*Ganon?*" she scoffed after him. "Why am I not surprised the two laziest boys in all of Navotas would find each other today. Go on. Don't worry about your mother. She'll take care of everything. Run along. Play your childish games."

Her scolding continued as Rizal walked out the door. Outside, children ran about, playing their innocent games. Boys and girls much like Rizal, raised by their mothers, wondering after absent fathers. Rizal remembered little of his father. Fuzzy images from when he couldn't have been more than a toddler boiled up in his subconscious now and then. When they did he saw a handsome man with gray in his stubble and Tanduay sewn into his gruff laughter. Tired, reddened eyes, surrounded by lines owing to long hours carrying fish from the boats down at the port and the *shabu* he smoked to keep him awake during his twelve-hour shifts. There were memories of the handful of times the old man had held his boy on his knee. The few times his mother had let the broken old drunk return to the family home only to shoo him back out again, beating at his backside with the same frazzled straw broom she used to sweep away the leaves from the gutters before a storm. How old could Rizal have been the last time he had watched his father stumble out the door, cursing back over his shoulder? Rizal's mother never said what became of the man. Rizal knew better than to ask. It wasn't that he didn't want to know. More that he knew the answer was better left unspoken.

So he did what the people of Navotas did best. Rizal carried on.

Some of the children in the cemetery had doting parents, both a mother and a father. Others were left on their own by alcoholics and *shabu* addicts. They were already fending for themselves at five, six, seven years old, surviving by taking *atang* – offerings of food for the deceased – placed on the graves of the newly dead. Those children left to live by their own cunning were old before their time, orphaned by drugs and drink, abuse and murder. They lived off whatever they could scrounge and what little the people around them could give. They slept on top of the stacks of apartment tombs, out in the open or under the branches of the acacia trees that had burst up from beneath the cracked and broken footpaths. Each night the children bedded down, knowing that the dawn to come could be their last. Many a morning brought news of another friend gone forever. So too, they knew, the next one gone could be them. And in knowing that any day could be their last, there was a strange peace. Death for those who had known life only in the cemetery was no mystery: it was a presence, a hand on their shoulder, guiding them through a life untouched by that deepest of human fears.

The whole place was crumbling in one way or another. Whenever Datu exhumed a body and a fresh corpse was not immediately interred, one of the orphans would inevitably take up residence in the vacant grave. At times a seal would simply fall, pushed loose by a creeping root or toppling down due to the lean of the row caused by the steady sinking of the structure into the muddy brown soil. Knocking the seals down simply to watch them shatter was a favorite game of the vandals Navotas seemed to have in abundance — a constant headache for the caretakers paid a few pesos a month to watch over and care for the graves. The money, if it came at all, was paid on All Saints Day — a day when the cemetery families had to clear their belongings from the mausoleums they lived within so the families of some means from outside could pay their respects. A day of remembrance for the rich. A day of reminders for the poor that the place they lived was not — would never be — their home.

If there was one thing Kidlat was good for, it was chasing such bleak thoughts from Rizal's mind. Kidlat had been one of those children left to their own quickness and cunning, doomed to a shorter lifespan than most in the bayside slum. Kidlat slept on the roofs of the tombs, riding out the summer storms in those that were vacant or using his gift for words to talk his way into another family's mausoleum, scrap metal shanty, or tar paper shack. Even when the weather was good, it was not unusual to see the boy emerge from someone else's home in the morning, a smile on his face, a few wayward grains of white rice affixed to his gaunt cheeks, sucked in by years of cheap gin and methamphetamine.

"*Anak ka nang puta!*" The words were slurred, but there was no mistaking the source. Rizal looked up. There was Kidlat, squatting atop the stack, a wrinkled plastic bag between his fingers. A small, dark pool hung in the bottom of the bag. Gasoline cut with water. Some of the boys pooled their cash to buy what little they could. They took that small amount and mixed it up with water so they could mete it out evenly without spilling precious, pure drops. Pure gasoline left them incoherent and drooling. With the water they could at least talk, even if the words did come slowly and strange.

When Kidlat couldn't get his hands on gas, there was always Rugby, the cheapest shoe polish money could buy. Easier to steal than gas. Foul-smelling, brain rotting stuff that left many a ghetto child of Manila with the mental capacity of a toddler. Not as strong a high as gasoline, nor as bad for the mind, but a weak buzz was better than no buzz at all, and as for the consequences, they may as well never have existed to begin with. Not in the slums, where lucidity was a nightmare, intoxication a dream. Rugby, the only high cheaper than gasoline or *shabu* or glue – spray paint when the boys really got hard up.

Kidlat brought the bag up to his nose for a huff. He breathed deep, eyelids closing in momentary bliss. When they opened again his words came like motor oil poured slowly out of the pan.

"*Pakshet*, Rizal, I could hear your mother chewing you out from here."

Kidlat reached down as Rizal climbed, extending a hand to his friend, smirking. His eyes were glazed, but his fingers were steady. Leaning back, he pulled his friend up. On top of the tombs they looked out over the rows – the gaps between the stacks their streets and avenues. Narrow thoroughfares with names only the locals knew, dubbed for the only landmarks a cemetery can have – the statues and murals of the saints watching over the gangs and the glue sniffers and everyone doing what they could to get by. Santa Maria. San Juan Diego. San Lorenzo Ruiz. Maria Street. Diego Boulevard. Ruiz Avenue. An outsider would be lost following the directions of a cemetery local. But there were no outsiders, save a journalist or two stopping by to snap a few pictures, maybe a missionary offering free Sunday reading lessons; in election years a politician making golden promises of help that never came. Navotas City Cemetery wasn't a place where you came and stayed long. Not willingly. It was a place where one was born, lived, and died. That, or a place one entered by a cruel twist of fate. A tragedy of life that Manila, and Navotas in particular, seemed to have in unlimited supply.

Kidlat leaned back on his elbows, squinting against the sun. He took another long, slow huff on his bag, offering it to Rizal. Rizal held up a hand, smiling.

"That stuff will turn you into a *tanga*, you know."

"Well," Kidlat's head wobbled on his thin neck, "what am I trying to be anyway?"

A scream echoed from one of the lanes, bouncing off the stone walls. A girl. A solitary noise. Something like a pop followed. The place was full of homemade pistols machined in back alley shops in the other slums. The gangster boys carried them, identified by the crude tattoos on the backs of their hands, near the crook of the thumb. When their *pistolas* worked like they were supposed to the shot boomed like cannon fire. When they didn't ... *pop*. Some poor girl had just won herself the chance to run away, if there was anywhere to run to. Rizal thought about who it might be for a moment, but his mind quickly drifted elsewhere. It was an everyday thing. The screams. The pops. The cannon fire. White noise. The sounds of death and rape, the moans and wails of addiction. Kidlat leaned back further, resting his head against the warm stone.

"What was it this time, Rizal? Your mama worried you'll come home with a baby in your arms again?"

Rizal shot him a look. How old would Liezel be now? *Nearly four*, he thought to himself, taking his knees up under his elbows. She was gone, his baby girl. Off with her mother, one of the few who had managed to make it out, if only to a slum slightly less bleak than the one she was born in. Liezel's mother had asked Rizal to go with her — to live with her and her own mother, not so different from his. A woman who made her way by sewing, washing clothes. Selling her body when that work ran low. She too had possessed the good sense to kick out her junkie husband, raising the mother of Rizal's little girl on her own. Now it seemed her little girl would do the same with Liezel.

Rizal knew little more than his daughter's name. The name he had chosen for her. A name that meant "a bountiful God." He had kept the pregnancy a secret until after the girl was born. When he brought her around to his mother, he hoped she would be happy to be a *lola*, maybe even welcome the child into their home. He was wrong.

How could you be so stupid! What is the child going to eat? Who will provide for her? Where do you plan to keep her? Here with us? We are barely surviving as it is, Rizal. And you expect me to feed another mouth?

On and on it went. She drove him away. For a time he moved in with Liezel's mother (he still couldn't bear to say her name, or even to think it). It wasn't long before she too threw him out, growing tired of the father of her child spending his days doing little more than rising for the time it took to fetch water for his mother or sweep the few mausoleums he tended idly, perhaps venturing to the trash-clogged *estero* nearby to gather up bottles, cans, scrap metal, and plastic to sell to the local junk shop – money he usually spent on beer or to buy an hour or two online at an internet cafe. A few weeks after the birth of the baby, Liezel's mother told Rizal she was leaving. Liezel would go with her. When he asked where, she gave him only a name: Bagong Silangan.

The name was supposed to mean "a new hope" for the people who settled there. People who had relocated from other slums in Manila, Navotas, and San Juan. Those who fled from Payatas and its Smokey Mountain rubbish dump. From the choking soot and waste of Happyland in infamous Tondo. (*You can take the boy out of Tondo, but you can never take Tondo out of the boy.*) If Rizal wanted to find her, she said, he could come and look for her in Bagong Silangan. He watched her walk away, Liezel held snug against her chest by a blue-green sarong knotted halfway down her slim back. At times he thought of venturing out to Bagong Silangang. But as the years went on, Maria Street, Diego Boulevard, Ruiz Avenue – the rows seemed to grow farther apart and closer together all at once. He knew it would only get more difficult to move beyond these familiar places. But there was nothing for him, even in a place named for hope itself. At least here, among the dead, he had his mother. He had her business and the meager living it provided them, his own work when it was there. There was the few pesos a month they made taking care of the mausoleum. And Kidlat, the boy who it seemed was forever watching over him from atop the stacks. He was there too.

Kidlat nudged Rizal lightly on the shoulder. "Hey, *baboy*, I was only joking. No need to look so sad."

Rizal smiled out the side of his mouth, pushing air through his nostrils in a poor substitute for laughter. "*Itaboy*, go find a grave to break into. I can smell the rain coming. You'll stink like a wet dog in the morning. Not even fat old Mrs. Ocampo would have you."

Kidlat leaned back on his elbows, the rough, uneven stone putting divots in his lean arms. Unlike Rizal, Kidlat laughed from his mouth.

"She would so have me. Even a wet dog can get himself a *landi* once in a while. You should try it sometime. Then maybe people would stop saying you're a *bakla*."

"Who says that?" Rizal lobbed a loose piece of gravestone in a high arc over his head. It landed on Kidlat's stomach. Kidlat took another pull on his bag of fumes and seemed not to notice. Leaning back further again he closed his eyes. Rizal's question went unanswered.

"Seriously, *baboy*, you would be amazed what some *puki* can do for you. It's like this," Kidlat inhaled from the bag again, pupils turned to empty obsidian pools, "it makes everything else go away."

Rizal tossed another stone off the edge of the stack, watching it break against the far gutter. The exertion, small as it was, wrought sweat from his forehead. His thin tank top clung to his protruding ribs. The pull of it on his skin sent a cold shiver through his body. Any sensation, even an uncomfortable one, was a welcome replacement for the fever penetrating his bones from the outside.

"So that's life?"

"Life?" Kidlat struggled to turn his head toward

his friend, lips curling into a shallow frown. Long pauses passed between his thoughts. The steady motion of the white wisps of clouds, some tinged with silver, distracted his gas-addled mind. "More like something to do.... Something fun, you know? Take your mind of all this ... shit." He leaned back again and closed his eyes. Rizal too looked up at the clouds. He remembered how they had passed whole afternoons watching them go by when they were kids. Here they were still, doing the same as grown men. Rizal mirrored his friend, cringing as the concrete bit into the back of his skull. He linked his fingers behind his head, grimacing as the surface of the tomb dug into his hands.

"I heard something the other day, Kidlat."

Kidlat's head was swaying slowly from side to side. A big dumb grin parted his lips, rays of sunlight shining on grayed teeth. "What did you hear, Rizal?" he asked listlessly. "What is there worth listening to around here?"

Rizal began to answer but was cut off.

"The only things worth listening to are the wind and the bullets, Rizal. You just need to know which direction they're coming from."

Kidlat's eyes were closed. It was like talking to a sleepwalker. Rizal swallowed what little moisture he had in his mouth. "Come on," Rizal said, deciding not to say what he had been planning to say. Not yet. "Let's go get some water."

"Kidlat doesn't need any water," Kidlat said, rising as he spoke. He patted the weighted bottom of the bag, sending halos of light swirling in its shadow. "Kidlat has everything he needs right here, *iho*." He groaned as he got to his feet, slapping a hand against his backside to knock away the white dust. "But Kidlat will go with you anyway. Who knows what trouble you might get into without him." He stumbled, teetering toward the edge. Rizal thrust out a hand to steady him, but there was no need. Kidlat righted himself on his own. "Who knows," Kidlat faltered again, unsteady on rubber legs. "You might even talk to a girl."

Slowly they made their way to the tap. Every time a woman or a girl passed by, Kidlat had to stop and say something. Each time he said something Rizal put his hands on his shoulders and steered him on, pulling him away when he turned back to slur a few more words. The girls all laughed at him. He waved an arm at each one.

"I had her last week anyway, *iho*. Nothing special," he lied into the bag, slipping on the loose stones scattering the lane. "Nothing special," he repeated.

When they reached the funeral water tap, Rizal decided to try again. There was a line, people waiting with buckets for their afternoon supply. Rizal lowered his eyes, keeping them down as he spoke to Kidlat.

"I heard something the other day —"

"Look at that," Kidlat ignored him, jutting his chin in the direction of a boy standing beside the tap. "One of the *pistola* boys is charging people for water again. What was it last time? A peso each? Forget this, *iho*. Let's go."

Rizal started to protest, but Kidlat was already stumbling away from the tap, down the lane in the direction of the sea. Others, too, broke from the line on seeing the skinny gangster boy with his palm locked on the spigot, turning it for a few seconds each time a coin was pressed into his free hand. A homemade pistol was tucked away near the small of his back in case anyone felt like testing him. People paid the toll or left with nothing.

Rizal followed Kidlat to a landing at the far end of the cemetery to the north. There a broken set of steps led down to a forgotten corner of Manila Bay. Waves lapped lightly against the concrete, at one time a launch for fishing boats, before the cemetery had extended itself nearly to the water's edge – a time when jobs on the local boats were easier to come by. The bottom steps were covered in a slippery green slime. Plastic bottles, tin cans, fishing buoys and nets, needles, and food containers all bobbed in the oil-slick water, purple and gold dancing toxic on the surface. Small, skinny children, older than they appeared, played naked in the water, splashing it over each other, laughing. Scratching at blotchy red skin, fingernails pulling at ruddy cheeks, slapping the itch away from distended bellies. Kidlat sat on the top step, bag still in hand. His head nodded into his chest, springing back up again, eyes rolling to the corners of their sockets.

"You remember when we used to play down here, *iho*?"

Rizal laughed. "Until Ma caught us and beat me all the way home."

"Rizal!" Kidlat raised up the pitch of his voice, laughing as he spoke, "how can you be such a *tanga*? Swimming in that filth! I'll have to scrub the skin off your bones to get you clean!" He swung his arms furiously, miming the broom driving Rizal's backside down the lane. He sighed. "When I came to find you the next day you said you weren't allowed to play with me anymore."

Rizal wrapped his arms around his knees. Still his mother hated that he spent time with Kidlat. She was the one woman Kidlat could never charm. The one who saw the gray in his smile for what it was. A wave came up, splashing against the second step. The children in the water laughed as fat droplets rained down on their heads. A woman came with a basket of the day's washing rested atop her head to collect her child, chiding him softly as he grumbled up the steps. The child took her hand and followed her home, unfettered by coverings of any kind.

"She was just looking out for me," Rizal reminded his friend. "Ma thought you were a bad influence."

Kidlat took another huff from the bag, smirking as the children continued to play. "*Pakshet, iho.* Maybe she was right."

Rizal looked out over the water. He thought of the scams he and Kidlat had tried to pull over the years. The get-rich-quick schemes. The time they stole a cockerel from Old Man Reyes, planning to raise it up to fight in the Sunday cock fights. The poor beast was dead within a week for lack of food. They tossed the limp body over the cemetery wall. Rizal remembered the guilt and the tears he shed. In the distance outriggers and trawlers bobbed on the bay, dark-skinned men pulling up nets full of plastic bags that carpeted the sea bottom like the concrete dust on the mausoleum floors.

"You remember we used to talk about doing that?"

"Doing what, *hipon*?" Kidlat pushed the smaller man on the shoulder again, poking a finger into his bony arm. He followed Rizal's gaze out to the boats, tipping back and forth now in the wake of a trash barge heading toward the horizon. "Working the fishing boats?" Kidlat's head reared back in laughter. "Imagine that. A *hipon* and a *tanga* like me out there on a fishing boat. We wouldn't last a day, *iho*. You'd get a leg caught in a net and be pulled down to the bottom. Then I'd have to jump in to save you and we'd both be finished. *Puneta ka*, you'll never get me out there." He dipped a foot down into the water, wrapping his long, skinny toes around the plastic torso of a headless baby doll. "Is that what you've been trying to tell me, *iho*? Did you get a job as some captain's *pokpok* or what?"

Rizal laughed again, kicking some of the green slime at Kidlat's feet. "How can I be a captain's *pokpok* when I'm already yours, *puta*?"

Kidlat managed to get hold of the doll with both feet and fling it up at Rizal. It landed in his lap along with a splash of filthy water.

"*Anak ng puta naman, oh!* Ma will kill me if I get another stain on these pants!" Rizal picked the doll from his lap with two fingers and tossed it back into the water, where the children stood laughing at him. They made for the doll as it came down, fighting over the limbless castaway. "I'm serious, *kuya*," Rizal leaned back, resting the palms of his hands on the dry, hot cement. Even the flies avoided his hands after they had touched the water. "We used to talk about getting jobs at sea. Seeing the world. Making money."

Kidlat snorted, face contorting as he realized he had upended his bag of petrol in flipping the doll at Rizal. The gas streamed down the steps into the water, painting chemical flowers for the children to play in. "The only thing those fisherman *putas* see is the boat, *iho*," said Kidlat. "They have their noses down on the deck and their asses up in the air all day. And if there is any money it goes to the captain and the owners. The crew are lucky to have two pesos to rub together after six months at sea." He tossed the bag down into the water. Some of the children came out, peeling plastic and seaweed off their bodies as they moved on all fours up the steps, barking and growling like dogs.

"Then why do so many men do it?" Rizal asked. "If it's as bad as you say, why do they keep going to sea?" The smell of gasoline wafted up into his nostrils. He breathed in, savoring the lightheaded feeling.

"Why did we used to swim in this garbage every day?" asked Kidlat, looking over his shoulder. "It was just something to do. Something better than doing nothing all day. They think having a job and being broke is better than not having a job and being poor. But what's the difference? At least if you're jobless and poor you've got time to sit around and enjoy yourself." He swept an arm across the bits of trash bobbing in the bay, laughing bitterly to himself. "Besides, who could walk away from all this, *iho*?" He turned serious then, moving to rest on his elbow, staring into the side of Rizal's pockmarked cheek. "You're not thinking of leaving me here by myself?"

Rizal took a heavy breath. The silver edges of the clouds had begun to bleed into their centers. He tasted rain. Later the bones of the dead would wash through lanes turned to torrents of dog shit and trash. "I heard of a place people like us can get work, *kuya*," he said. "They'll take anybody. All you have to do is sign and you're hired. It pays more than anything around here. You even make enough to send some home every month. All that just for being a fisherman. Doesn't it sound —"

"Too good to be true, *iho*?"

"Stop calling me that! For all you know I'm older than you."

"*Iho*, from the way you talk I wouldn't be surprised if you're older than Datu Death himself."

Rizal put a hand around Kidlat's scrawny neck and shook it lightly. "We stay here, *kuya*, and we're dead men," he said softly. "What do we have to look forward to? There's nothing for us here." He looked down at his feet, eyes then rising to meet the sun's muted rays as a cloud passed it by. "It's time to go."

"Go where? Some magic place where they turn boys who can't swim into fishermen? You still haven't told me, Rizal, where is this wonderful place?"

Rizal turned back to Kidlat, smiling. "Thailand," he said, "I'm sure that's what I heard. He said it again, "Thailand," as though by repeating it the power of its sound might transport him an unknown distance to a place he knew little about save the pleasant way the name slid off his tongue.

"Thailand, eh, *iho*?" Kidlat rubbed at the stray hairs poking out of his narrow chin. "I can tell you one thing about this Thai-land for sure." He picked up a chip of concrete from the steps and tried to skip it across the water. It bounced once off the lip of a low wave and disappeared beneath the surface.

"What's that, *kuya*?"

"At least there's no Datu Death there to chase you."

Chapter Two

"TAIWAN."

"Ano?"

"*Hindi Taylandiya.* Taiwan."

Rizal scratched his head. The florescent lighting hurt his eyes. The bespectacled man across from him had light skin (far lighter than Rizal's), a fat face, and a gray mustache. He wore a tie, as alien to Rizal as the flush toilet he had broken from the line of other potential workers to use. He willed himself to use the bathroom even though he didn't feel the need. Everything about the office building was clean and bewildering. Now the man was telling him about a country. A place he had never heard of.

"Taiwan?"

"*Oo*, Taiwan."

The man leaned back in his chair. He didn't look like anyone Rizal knew in Navotas. He clasped his hands over his belly, rubbing it like a pregnant woman caressing an unborn child. A sound stirred within his stomach and a belch escaped his lips. He chuckled, reaching to shake a toothpick from a white porcelain container on the edge of his desk. More strange things in a strange new world.

"*Pinagsisisihan*," the man apologized, "I just had lunch."

Rizal shifted in his plastic chair. The uneven legs

wobbled on the white tile floor. He watched the man groan as he got up to waddle over to a water dispenser. A row of blue plastic containers lined the wall. Each one of them was full, but the container on the dispenser was empty. The man called out through the open doorway, beckoning a caretaker inside. Dutifully the man came in, taking the empty container down, hoisting a full one up on top. Then he filled the fat man's cup for him.

"*Maaari kang pumunta*," the fat man said when the job was finished, "You can go," not bothering to thank the caretaker. Then he turned and ambled back to his desk. Rizal thought about how important he must be, having the same power over men that his mother held over him. The fat man took a long gulp of water, eyeing Rizal over the rim of his cup. "So," he said, putting down the cup to have a look at Rizal's application form, "I see you've left everything blank but your name. Am I correct in assuming this is because you cannot write?"

Rizal lowered his eyes, nodding toward the floor. He had known where to write his name only because another man, also waiting for an audience here in the office, had told him. Rizal heard the fat man chuckle.

"Not to worry, *bunso*. You are going to Taiwan to be a fisherman, not to write books. Am I right?"

Rizal raised his head. He smiled. The fat man seemed friendly enough. With his big belly and mustache, he seemed like a favorite uncle, the kind who never came without a gift under his arm, a *bibingka* to share among all the little nieces and nephews, and endless funny stories to tell. The man began writing things down on the application. He checked boxes with a quick flick of a black-and-gold fountain pen. Rizal thought of asking him what he was writing. The thought alone brought red to his cheek. He busied himself looking around the room, waiting for the end of the scratching sound made by the fat man's pen with the shiny gold clip. The man stopped and Rizal looked, blushing when he met his gaze.

"Where did you grow up, *anak*?" the man asked. "Where are you from?"

Rizal's mind raced. What to tell him? The truth? Would he know if he was lying? Rizal's eyes darted to all corners of the room. Again he heard the low, wet sound of the man's laugh rumbling in his phlegmatic lungs. The toothpick hung from the corner of his mouth, eyes staring through the top of the lenses of his glasses. He pulled the pen away from the form and leaned back again.

"It's just a question, son. There is no such thing as a wrong answer. We place people from all over. Go on, you can tell *Tiyo* Benjie."

Rizal swallowed and gave his answer. "Navotas, sir Benjie," he said softly. Then softer, "Navotas City Cemetery." Had he looked up, he would have seen the fat man's eyebrows sitting high on his forehead.

"Navotas City Cemetery?" Benjie's voice lilted upwards, chin tilting toward the ceiling. "You mean you live there, with the dead?"

"Yes, sir Benjie. I live there. With my mother." Rizal felt small. He wanted to leave, to walk out of the room and forget he had ever been there. Outside a long line of men were waiting. Men who hadn't slept most every night of their lives with the dead. Men who didn't marvel at flush toilets and wonder at the feel of tile beneath their feet. Rizal felt like a fool. He heard the fat man chuckle again. He looked to him and saw he was shaking his head, putting pen to paper once more.

"If you grew up there, working aboard a fishing boat will be no problem for you, *anak*," he said, smiling. Rizal felt his muscles loosen. His spine melted into a comfortable slouch, back sore from sitting so rigidly.

"Does that mean I have the job, sir?"

Benjie spoke without looking at Rizal, continuing to write things down. "Well, there are certain details we'll need to go over. Money matters, mostly. Nothing comes free in this life, you understand."

Rizal slouched further, this time for a much different reason. His empty stomach suddenly felt even emptier. He understood perfectly well. The reason he would not get the job, in the end, was the same reason everyone else in his situation would not. He didn't have the money to bribe the man sitting on the other side of the desk. He decided to try and reason with him.

"Sir Benjie," Rizal began, "I know nothing is free. I don't have much. But if you give me this job I promise I will repay your kindness."

"Eh, *anak*, you misunderstand me." Sir Benjie set down his pen and leaned forward, tenting his fingers beneath his chins. "I am not some *kotong* sitting here with my hand out and my eyes looking the other way. We do things legally here. But getting you set up overseas costs money. You can't expect us to pay out of our own pockets, can you? We'd have every lazy *hinayupak* from Luzon to Mindanao coming here just so they could have a free vacation. Am I right?"

Rizal began to feel more at ease.

"Of course I'm right. But don't worry about paying your way. We make it easy for you. If you don't have the money right now, you borrow what you need from us. When you start collecting your salary in Taiwan, you pay a little back each month. With all the *salapi* you'll be making over there, you won't even notice."

Rizal swallowed again and ventured another question gnawing at the back of his mind. "Can I ask, sir Benjie, what does the job pay?"

The fat man roared. "I can see *anak* is hungry! Good, that's good. A hungry man is a hardworking man. But there's no need to worry yourself with the specifics just yet. You'll learn as you go along. Besides, it's all done automatically for you. All you have to do is sign. We handle the rest. Training. Payment. Support. Anything you need. *Tiyo* Benjie takes care of his own."

The thoughts in Rizal's mind now turned to his home. Navotas. His mother. Liezel. Kidlat.

"How long will I be gone, sir?"

Benjie leaned his head to the side. "The term is three years. If you're a good worker, keep your mouth shut and your mind on your work, you'll last. Maybe even get picked up for another contract. It's all up to you. But once you sign you're committed to three years. No less. Unless, for whatever reason, you get sent back."

Rizal was of a mind to ask why he might get sent back, then thought better of it. Another concern manifested itself in his wringing hands before he put it into words.

"How much must I borrow?"

The fat man turned his office chair from side to side. It was nicer than the stationary chair Rizal sat in. *Tiyo* Benjie's chair had plush foam cushioning and wheels so he could move about the office without standing and walking.

"Don't think of it as borrowing, *anak*. Think of it as an investment in you and your family's future." His eyes brightened. He leaned forward. "Better yet, think of it like this," he pressed his index fingers together and pointed them at Rizal. "Think of it as a down payment. First and last month's rent for a new apartment, far away from the cemetery, for you and your mother. When you think of it that way, the amount doesn't really matter, does it?"

Rizal thought about it. "No, sir Benjie," he answered.

"Exactly, *anak*. You cannot put a price on brightening your family's future. And that is exactly what you will be doing by signing with us. You will work, and you will work hard. But that is why you're here, no? You want to better yourself and the lives of those around you. I can see something in you, *anak*. You're not like some of these others," he gestured out into the hallway where men leaned against the wall, chattering with one another. "I see a fire in you, *anak*. A desire to pull yourself out of your old life and start something new. I can tell you are a man who sees the big picture. You're just like *Tiyo* Benjie. You don't focus on trivial things, petty numbers. If you think small, you live small, am I right?"

"Yes, sir Benjie."

"Of course I'm right. And if you think big?"

"You live big, sir Benjie?"

"That's my boy! So, we have a deal?" He turned the contract around and pushed it toward Rizal, pointing to a line along the bottom. "All you have to do is write your name here," he tapped the line twice, "*Tiyo* Benjie will do the rest."

Rizal looked down at the blank line. His eyes scanned the rest of the contract. There were numbers here and there, some large, some small. He wished he had been able to go to school, at least long enough to learn to read. Then he would know what the numbers meant. On their own, spread out among the words, the figures were meaningless. Still he tried to decipher them. Eighty thousand. That was the largest there was. Eighty thousand pesos. He and his mother had never known such an amount. For them money came and went a few pesos at a time. A world where such sums changed hands with the signing of one's name.... His head began to spin. He heard *kuya* Benjie (he couldn't get used to that word yet – *tiyo* – though he tried) speaking to him again. He pointed to the various numbers with the butt of his pen.

This is your salary. This is the amount of your loan. Here is the cost of your fisherman's license. These are the monthly deductions: Room and board. Loan repayment. Service fee. All standard.

The numbers swirled in Rizal's head, one figure slithering into the next. *Tiyo* Benjie asked if he understood and he felt himself nod.

"Then we have a deal?"

Rizal reached out to take the pen from Benjie's outstretched hand. Then, slowly and methodically, he went about the task of writing his name.

Chapter Three

"TAIWAN."

"Ano?"

"*Hindi Taylandiya.* Taiwan."

It had been a week since Rizal sat in *Tiyo* Benjie's office. Seven days since he spelled out his name in big, clumsy letters. The letters of a child. Now he was at home with his mother, trying to explain where he was going, realizing he barely knew himself.

"And what exactly are you going to do in ... Taiwan?" his mother asked. Rizal had just brought her the morning's supply of water, reasoning it was better to tell her now than later, after the day's work left her body exhausted, her temper short. "What can you do there that you can't do at home?"

"Mama," Rizal began slowly, choosing his words, "you know there are no jobs here. You have to know someone to get hired. And *ku ... Tiyo* Benjie, he says...."

"Oh, *Tiyo* Benjie!" His mother's voice took a spiteful tone. "*Tiyo* Benjie indeed. Such a man, calling himself *tiyo.* I'm telling you, Rizal, I don't trust this *kupal.* You meet him once and already he's *Tiyo* Benjie to you? He's probably no different from the *pobre* on the street. Instead of sitting there with his hand out begging for change he uses his words and his fancy office to trick an *engot* like you into doing it for him."

"Mama, I wouldn't be begging. I would –"

"You would what?" Her words gathered enough volume to draw curious children to their open doorway. Rizal turned, shooing them away with a short, sharp hiss. "Tell me what you can do in a place where you can't speak one word of their language. Tell me what you'll eat. Tell me where you'll sleep. Did *Tiyo* Benjie tell you all that?" She slapped her ladle against the side of the cauldron, scattering droplets of boiling water. A few landed on her hand and she inhaled sharply at the pain. Rizal rushed to her with a towel, pressing it to her skin. She let him hold it there for a moment before snatching the towel away, slapping at his hand.

"I don't need you to take care of me, Rizal. Mothers take care of their sons. Not the other way around. When I'm old, then you can take care of me. Do you think I'm old?"

"No, Mama," Rizal slunk back to the rickety plastic chair beside the two-seater Formica table, unfolded every morning for the day's customers, folded up at night, leaned up against the wall so Rizal and his mother would have space to sleep. Rizal's mother took the towel away from the blisters rising on her hand, wincing at a pain she usually ignored. She turned down the flame, stirring more calmly than before.

"You don't have to go, you know. What is this *Tiyo* Benjie going to do? Come to Navotas and drag you away from me?"

"I signed a contract, Mama."

"Signed a contract?" she clucked her tongue against

the roof of her mouth, "Stupid, stupid boy. How do you know what you signed? A city filled with con men and you go and sign whatever someone puts in front of you. Have you secretly been learning to read, hmm? Is that what you and that waste of skin Kidlat have been doing all this time? That's it, isn't it? It's *him*. He put you up to it. Since the day that *ulol* sank his teeth into you he's infected you with his foolishness." She placed her free hand on her hip, staring off into the corner of the cramped room. Mrs. Pilapil ducked her head into the doorway. Seeing Rizal with his head down and his mother standing the way that she was, she quickly removed herself without being noticed. "Nothing but headaches since that boy came into your life," Rizal's mother sighed. "Headaches and heartache." She walked to the doorway carrying the cracked plastic "Open" sign to hang on the rusted metal hook outside the entrance.

"I'll tell you what we're going to do, Rizal," she said. The anger was gone from her voice, replaced with resolve. "We're going to go see this *Tiyo* Benjie," her sour sense of spite found its way back at every utterance of his name. "We're going to explain to him that you didn't know what you were signing up for. I'll tell him you're just a stupid boy from the cemetery who didn't know any better and to tear up that contract. I'll close up early today. We'll go this afternoon."

"Mama —"

"Don't start with me, Rizal. I've made my decision. We're going. That's all there is to it."

"No, Mama."

She paused partway back to the cauldron, turning

around, both hands on her hips this time. "What did you say?"

Rizal's eyes rose to meet his mother's. He swallowed a lump the size of a stone, throat dry as the ashes resting above their heads. "I said," he paused, the word to come the most difficult he had ever spoken, "no."

His mother moved toward him. Rizal's eyes hit the floor. She stood over him, he listening to her deep breaths rising and falling, thankful for the ladle being momentarily out of reach. He felt her hand on his shoulder and braced himself. Then she pulled his head to her stomach, holding him tight, running her hands softly over his dark, thick hair. He closed his eyes, fighting back tears as he felt his mother's teardrops land hot on the top of his head.

"If your mind is made up, Rizal," his mother said, voice breaking, "what is there left for a mother to say?"

Rizal put his arms around his mother's waist. "I'm doing this for us, Mama. *Tiyo* Benjie says —" He stopped himself. "They say with the money I can make over there, I'll be able to send some home to you every month. Enough for us to get our own apartment someday. No more cemetery. Our own place with running water. A stove. Our own bathroom, Mama. Your own room. A bed. Furniture. Everything we ever wanted. Just like we used to have, before Papa —" Again he stopped himself. "I can do this for us," he said, after a time. "I can get us out of here."

He felt more tears fall into his hair from above. His mother squeezed him tighter, rocking him back and forth.

"And what am I going to do without you while you're gone for so long?"

"It will be okay, Mama," said Rizal, "I promise."

* * *

"Taiwan."

"*Ano?*"

"*Hindi Taylandiya.* Taiwan."

For the third time that week, Rizal began a conversation in exactly the same way. This time he was with Kidlat. The patterns of life, the way things had a way of repeating themselves, were still lost to him.

"I thought you said Thailand."

Rizal and Kidlat were walking near the edge of the cemetery farthest from the sea. Usually they stayed away from the surrounding streets. Shaking down slum dwellers was a favorite pastime of the Navotas District Police, getting what they could out of the poorest of the poor on threat of a vagrancy charge. That word, "vagrancy," was one of the few Rizal knew in English. It was the title of his favorite song — a track on a tape he had found by the Manila punk band I.O.V. Like many of the things he found — toys, knick-knacks, playing cards — someone had just thrown the tape away, for no good reason it seemed, other than they didn't want it anymore.

Rizal used to take the tape down to Mr. Bongalos' arcade, housed under a canvas awning near the cemetery gates, the only place he knew with a cassette player. After the player broke and Mr. Bongalos replaced it with a KTV machine (five pesos for a song), Rizal would still pull out the cassette from time to time (keeping it out of sight of his mother), just to look at it. He didn't know what "punk" was. He only knew that he liked I.O.V. His favorite band, so far from anything he ever heard on the crackly transistor radio or blaring out of Mr. Bongalos' noisy new toy. He was afraid to play the tape at first. There was something about the name so foreboding and taboo. Surely it would make his mother angry if she ever found it, or worse yet heard it for herself, Rizal thought. But after that first play it was all he ever wanted to listen to. He reminded himself to take the tape with him to Taiwan. He would buy himself a new cassette player there. Then he could listen to it every day.

"Hello? Earth to Rizal?" Kidlat pulled him from his thoughts. "Didn't you say the job was in Thailand?"

"No, I'm sure I said Taiwan," Rizal lied. "You've been huffing too much gas, *tado*."

Kidlat shrugged his narrow shoulders. The street beyond the wrought iron fence was jammed with jeepneys, pedicabs, motorcycles with tinny-sounding engines, cars, and trucks. Vehicles backed up from one end of the narrow strip of land in the north of Metro Manila to the other. Rizal's mother had told him the people of the old town of Navotas used to make their way by fishing, before the city had spread out to join with the surrounding settlements. As a child Rizal had always wondered if the people used to be fishermen, why were there so many cars and trucks, so few boats?

"When will you go, *iho*?" Kidlat asked. They stopped to sit down on a standalone concrete tomb, facing the street. Night was falling over the corrugated iron rooftops of the neighborhood around the cemetery, the people there barely better off than the people living within the burial ground, living chockablock in one-room flats built from scrap wood and sheet metal, families of four, five, six, or more sleeping and living on top of one another on dirt floors and busted planks.

"Soon," Rizal answered. The sun was setting behind their backs, casting the dilapidated shacks and the vein of traffic before them in an orange haze. "Three weeks, *Tiyo* Benjie says. He told me how to catch the bus to meet him at the airport. He'll help me get on the plane. He helped me apply for a passport. It's all taken care of. He even gave me an advance on my salary so I could buy a bus ticket. He's a very kind man."

"Yes," Kidlat answered blankly, "he seems very generous."

Rizal ignored his tone. "You could still come with me, you know. Go talk to *Tiyo* Benjie. Meet me there in a few weeks. Say your goodbyes to old Mrs. Ocampo first, of course."

Kidlat chuckled, then feigned seriousness, sighing deeply. "Yes, *iho*, but then who would take care of your dear mama while you're away?" He poked a digit rapidly through a hole formed by his thumb and index finger, smiling. Rizal drove a fist weakly into his shoulder.

"You should come with me, *kuya*," Rizal pleaded with his friend again. "I could introduce you to sir Benjie. We could go to Taiwan together and *both* come back rich. I'm sure you could make enough to get out of this place."

Kidlat seemed to consider it. He raised a bottle of gin to his lips, relishing the warm burn, exhaling audibly through the nose. Rizal wondered where he got the money for it this time. "Ah," Kidlat looked down at the bottle, studying the label, "I'd only blow it on this stuff and women, *iho*." He drained the rest of the liquor in one long pull, tossing the bottle away. It clinked off a gravestone, unbroken. He spit the bitter aftertaste out of his mouth. "And besides, Navotas is all I've ever known. I wouldn't know what to do with myself out there. At least here things kind of make sense, you know?"

Rizal's head reared back in silent laughter.

"Don't laugh, *iho*," Kidlat chided playfully. "One day when you're far from here, making all that money, chasing the *putas* all over the place, you'll stop and realize you actually *miss* this place. We might be poor, but we're like a big family here, you know? Everyone looks out for each other. You'll be back one day, and you'll be happy to come back. Mark my words."

Rizal looked around. Smoke rose from the trash fires burning between the grave sites. The *maganang kumain* began their twilight march through the lanes, seeking their next hit of *shabu*. A short distance away a dealer stood on a corner, flicking a small switchblade open and closed, shaking a matchbox at passersby, letting them know he was open for business.

"The next time you see me, *kuya*," said Rizal, "I'll be taking my mother as far away from here as we can get."

Chapter Four

BENJIE was waiting for Rizal at the airport as promised. He stood there, exactly where the bus came to a stop, filling the doorway as Rizal made his way slowly down the steps, greeting him with an outstretched hand. Benjie smiled. In his hand he held a stack of booklets. A number of men, some hardly more than boys like Rizal, others far older, still others somewhere between, circled around, nodding and smiling, greeting one another, saying hello to sir Benjie like they had only just arrived. Some were smoking, staring off into space as though they had been waiting a long time. Benjie grinned at them all. He held up the booklets. Rizal, the last to arrive, looked around wide-eyed, wondering why he thought he would be the only one meeting Benjie today. Benjie spoke quickly, the pace of his words far quicker than it had been back at his office. He sounded like a different man.

"Come on, hurry up. We don't have much time. These are your passports," he waved the booklets aloft. "I will hold on to them for now, but you will need them later to pass through security and board the plane. Once I give you your passport, guard it with your life until you reach Taoyuan International. There we will be greeted by Mr. Chen. He will collect the passports from you for safekeeping. You don't want those on a fishing boat anyway. Too easy to lose, and then you'd really be in trouble. Does everyone understand?"

Ten heads nodding, looking to one another, smiling nervously.

"Good," Benjie continued. "For most of you this will be your first time on an airplane, but don't worry. It's a very short flight. You'll be there before you know it. Mr. Chen will take good care of you once you arrive."

"Sir Benjie," an older man behind Rizal spoke. His hair was thick and starkly gray, contrasting with the dark brown of his skin. His voice carried the accent of Mindanao: e's and o's swapped out for i's and u's. Sir Benjie nodded, eyes narrowing at what he seemed to perceive as the Bisaya butchery of the Tagalog language.

"Yes, yes, what is it?"

"Does Mr. Chen speak Tagalog, sir?"

Benjie threw his hands up, looking to the rest in disbelief. "Of course he doesn't speak Tagalog. Once you reach Taiwan you will receive your instructions in English and Mandarin. Most of you have at least enough English for day-to day-things, I'm sure. As for Mandarin, you'll pick it up as you go. But don't worry too much about these matters. All of you are going there to join the fishing fleet. The work is simple. You'll be able to get by with a few basic words. They don't need brains over there. They need strong backs and shut mouths. You can all give them that, yes?"

Nods all around.

"Good, then I know you won't be giving *Tiyo* Benjie any trouble. Remember, if you cause any problems, Mr. Chen has only to make one call to me and you'll be sent back to wherever you came from that same day. Am I making myself clear?"

More nodding.

"Good. Now follow me."

Together the men marched into the terminal, following Benjie's squat, quick stride. He led them to the check-in counter.

All around were swarms of people. Many walked briskly, some dragging wheeled suitcases, others with children in carriers on their back or chest. Most seemed to know where they were going. Others were in groups much like their own, following doe-eyed behind a man or a woman — a leader like *Tiyo* Benjie, guiding their first steps toward a new life abroad. There were many tearful goodbyes, new fathers leaving behind young wives and newborn sons and daughters, mothers bound for jobs overseas clutching their children one last time, their next embrace a reason to endure the coming years apart. The eyes of Rizal's bewildered platoon darted around the busy terminal, staring at a woman's flashy clothes, a businessman's new suit or gold watch. Rizal turned and in a moment of panic thought he had lost sir Benjie and the rest in the crowd. Then he saw them up ahead. With a jump he ran a few steps to catch up.

After checking in and receiving their tickets the group reached a very long line. Benjie turned around to perform a head count, face darkening as he pointed to each of them one by one, frowning rather than smiling when the count reached ten. "Security check," he shouted back at them. When they reached the head of the line Rizal watched as the men in front of him placed their packs on the black conveyor belt. It fed into a machine that seemed to eat them up and spit them out the other side. Those who had a few coins in their pockets emptied them into gray plastic trays. Then, one by one, they walked through a rectangular doorway, one that had no walls around it, only the frame.

Some passed through in silence. For others the machine made an angry sound and a security guard passed a beeping wand over their bodies. Sleepily the guard waved the wand until he found what he was looking for and motioned the man on to collect his things. Sweat formed on Rizal's brow. He looked to the other lines, the other rectangular doorways. Beyond he saw yet more lines, uniformed men and women calling travelers up one by one, taking their passports, bringing down red stamps heavily – *thump, thump, thump*, like the beat of a drum. Past the last of the lines were bright, gleaming shops, shelves filled from one end to the other with bottles of rum, whiskey, vodka, gin. There were whole sections of sweets, chocolate bars, potato chips. Rizal's mouth watered at the big bags of *chicharrón*. A nudge at his elbow told him he was next to pass through. He placed his pack on the belt. Then, with a deep inward breath, he went through the gateway. Silence. The guard waved his wand toward the conveyor belt. Tentatively Rizal collected his pack and then, looking to the security guard once more to confirm he was indeed free to go, rushed to join the rest of the group, everyone eyeing the duty free shops past passport control. Sir Benjie came through last. He quickly did another head count, taking stock of sheepish smiles and downcast eyes. Rizal too looked around and counted, confirming no man had been left behind. The count reaching ten once more,

Benjie seemed relieved, the sweat on his brow abating slightly. One by one they went through passport control, answering the questions of the humorless officers in just the way Benjie had instructed them. Then, finally, they were on the other side.

To Rizal the other side was yet another new world. It reminded him of sir Benjie's office. The shops were clean, products new and perfectly organized, some with names he had never seen. The women working in the duty free stores wore bright lipstick and makeup like magazine cover models or movie idols. Their clothes were sharp, neatly pressed, and tight fitting. Others in the group also took notice. Benjie shook his head at them.

"Come on, boys," he laughed, "they'll be plenty of time to stare at the *babae* when you get to Taiwan."

With a jerk of his head he beckoned them down a corridor, leading the group along the rows of gates on either side. Some of the men giggled and made jokes about following their teacher on a field trip. Rizal laughed with them.

On they walked through the terminal. Between the gates there were restaurants. Lines of people holding plastic trays, picking food off cooled shelves in refrigerated compartments. Families seated at tables, unwrapping perfect Jollibee hamburgers, sipping on sweating bottles of Coke, and smiling or staring ahead with blank faces. Others gazed at their phones, fingers flicking mindlessly, upward, down, sideways. Rizal nearly tripped over his own shoelace. A stout man ahead with an ample beer belly chided him.

"Come along, *anak*. Don't fall behind your classmates."

Rizal smiled nervously and tried to think of a response,

but the words caught in his throat. He quickened his step and followed in silence, looking down at the pair of shoes in front of him, the surrounding sights too much to handle at once. When they reached their gate and flopped into a row of seats, it was a relief. There was a large television nearby, tuned to GMA News. The anchorwoman on TV chattered away, the volume turned down to an inscrutable level. Rizal watched the images flashing across the screen. A landslide in the south after a heavy rain. Men and women wailing. Rescue workers digging through mud and the remains of homes, the broken, flimsy walls of a schoolhouse. Rizal looked to the man with the Bisaya accent. The man's gaze was glued to the television, images of suffering reflected in his eyes, a worried expression affixed to his dark southern features. The voice of sir Benjie took Rizal's attention away. Benjie stood in front of them, scanning along the row of shifting feet and wavering glances.

"The hard part is over," Benjie announced, beaming. "All you have to do for now is sit back and relax. Enjoy the experience, *guwapos*. Once you get to Taiwan you should be ready to work, and work hard. That's what you're going there for, am I right? Work hard, make money!"

Nods and smiles.

"*Napakahusay.* You catch on quickly, every one of you. Three-year men, I can tell. The kind of men who sign on again and again. And just remember, if it ever gets hard, think of that house you're going to buy for your mama," he eyed Rizal. "Think of your little girl finally being able to pay for her school uniform and supplies," his eyes moved to another. "Remember why you're there, each of you: to work hard for your family, to build a better life for your loved ones. That will get you through anything." He looked to the screen mounted behind the counter where a woman stared intently at a monitor, an unbroken scroll of paper belching out of yet another alien machine behind her. "Not long now, *mga ginoo.* Just a few more minutes and we'll be boarding the plane." Again he looked to Rizal. "Some of you for the first time."

The floor-to-ceiling window behind the counter gave a panoramic view of the tarmac. Rizal looked through to the planes, the vehicles zipping back and forth, following the straight and curving yellow lines painted on the concrete. He looked and found himself transfixed by the sight of their plane. He had seen planes before, high in the sky by the time they reached the north end of Manila Bay, wings outstretched like a great metal bird held in mid-glide above the statues of Navotas City Cemetery. Out of reach and nearly out of sight as most things were by the time they got there. Now, in minutes, he would be aboard one of the beasts. Taking off not just to a new place, but to a different life. A tightness seized his chest. For reasons he could not explain he felt tears building in his eyes. He jerked his head back and took a deep breath as quietly as he could. As he fought off the tears, he faked a sneeze and ran a forearm across his eyes to wipe away the drops that had escaped, smiling to no one in particular. To his relief no one seemed to notice. They were all staring out the window, held entranced by the plane, just as he had been. The tightness in his chest began to abide. He breathed easier, knowing he was not alone.

The minutes passed slowly as the boarding time drew near. Then it was as though time ceased its normal flow and froze in place. Rizal was stuck, bound in a blank space between his old life and that to come. A place where he was neither man nor child but something in between. He barely heard when sir Benjie told them to get up and get in line. He hardly noticed when he gave his passport and ticket over to the attendant, who took them both and scanned the bar code on his ticket, returning it to him with a smile. Sounds were muted as he walked down the gangway to the aircraft, the high hum of the turbines sucking everything up, drowning sights and sounds in a sea of white noise.

Rizal felt himself growing smaller: a scrawny teenager, a stunted and malnourished child, a fetus suspended in the womb. Down and down he went, the world growing in proportion to the speed of his decline. *The world*, he thought. *When the airplane door opens again, the world will never be the same. In that world I will know nothing and no one. In that world no one will know me. I, Rizal, will not exist.*

Rizal began to panic. He eyed the walls of the gangway. The small windows looking out to the tarmac, shafts of blinding light smashing through them like girders careening down from the sky. He thought of turning back. He turned his head and met the wide gaze of the man behind him. It was Beer Belly, the man who had made the crack about falling behind his classmates. He could see the jokester was just as scared as he was. Again he reminded himself he was not alone in his fear. He turned forward once more and stepped through the ovular door, greeted by the smile of a flight attendant.

She wore a blue pillbox cap to match her smart knee-length uniform with gold buttons running up and over the curve of her chest. A new kind of fear grasped his testicles with icy fingers as she reached out to him and he found himself lost. He stopped in his tracks, Beer Belly nearly running his nose into the back of Rizal's head. The flight attendant laughed, flashing coffee-stained teeth behind bright red lips. Her hand remained outstretched. *She wants something*, Rizal reasoned. *What does she want? What am I supposed to do?*

"Boarding pass, sir?" she said kindly.

Sheepishly Rizal reached into his pocket and handed his pass to her. She glanced down at the ticket, then pushed it back into his hand, lowering her chin in an effort to find his eyes. "Row nineteen, sir," she said sweetly. "You have the window seat on the right-hand side. Have a pleasant flight."

Rizal took the pass back without a word, smiling with his face still pointed toward the dark upholstered floor of the cabin. He followed the column of passengers down the aisle, looking to the right and left, counting the pairs of seats on each side as he passed them by. *One, two, three….* The column stopped and started. Rizal saw men and women opening the overhead compartments, placing their baggage within. *Eleven, twelve, thirteen….* When his count reached nineteen he stowed his backpack above, taking another look around to confirm he was doing the right thing. No one stopped him. He tried to remember what the woman in the blue hat had told him about his seat. Window, he recalled. He shuffled through the narrow gap to the window seat and looked down at the metal seat belt clasp. Then he sat, pushing the belt off to the side, eyes glued to the small window. Out on the tarmac men in bright-orange jumpsuits with vests with neon stripes crossing their chests and backs were at work. He wondered how they got their jobs. Who they knew. Who they had to pay to get hired. A feeling of envy clenched his guts and he looked away, locking eyes on the headrest in front of him. He closed his eyes and held them closed, longing for little more than silence and sleep, seized by an exhaustion of body and mind.

The next thing Rizal knew his head moved gently forward then back as the plane began its taxi toward the runway. A voice came over the intercom and the attendants moved into position, beginning the safety demonstration. Rizal looked to the other passengers. Some were already falling asleep, others reading books or busying themselves with their phones. He found the others in his group, to a man eyes locked on the women now explaining how to fasten and unlock the safety belt. Rizal reached down to retrieve his from the crevice between his seat and the cabin wall. He pushed the clasp into the lock, concentrating such that he caught only part of what was said next. Something about a bag of oxygen falling from the ceiling. The recording, played first in Tagalog, then once again in English, told them where to find the life jackets in the event of a water landing and Rizal felt beneath the seat for his. The demonstration ended with the recording once again wishing them a pleasant flight. The plane came to a stop for a moment and an electric whirring filled the cabin as the turbines picked up speed. Rizal's heart raced. The attendants took their seats. Not long after, the plane abruptly lurched forward, picking up speed as it shot down the runway. Rizal's fingernails dug into the ends of the plastic armrests, teeth clenching, eyes popping open then slamming shut again just as quickly. He felt the nose of the plane raise up off the ground, and suddenly he was at an angle. Instinctively he reached down, fumbling with the seat belt in an effort to pull it tight. The tail of the plane lifted off the runway and he felt the entire craft floating, jerking upward as the currents of air pulsed beneath the wings, his mind spinning with thoughts of how it was even possible that this huge, heavy machine filled with so many people could lift itself into the air.

It seemed a long time before Rizal willed himself to open his eyes again. When he did he saw the carpet of white clouds passing slowly below, through the window. He maneuvered his head in an effort to see through the cover, to see if he could glimpse the city, the bay, the island of Luzon. But it was gone, disappeared behind an impenetrable and silent wall. As he stared down at the clouds, they too moving farther and farther away as the plane continued its ascent, he wondered if he would ever see home again.

Chapter Five

"FOLLOW me! Come on! Let's move!"

Sir Benjie led them through the corridor toward the immigration desks. Rizal hardly remembered the landing. The screech of the tires hitting the tarmac. The way the plane had bounced once, risen up like it might not come back down, then fell again. It happened fast, waking him from a sleep that had taken him so quickly he had not realized it had taken him at all. For a moment he thought himself dreaming. But it was real. He had arrived in another world.

All through the terminal there were signs and posters and LED displays covered in symbols, the characters formed with deft, uncountable strokes, so different from the simpler alphabet Rizal could not read at home. The dark skin tones of his group were unlike those of most other people making their way through the concourse, some walking, others stepping onto moving belts, pausing to rest or keeping their brisk pace. The other faces were Taiwanese, Chinese, Japanese — a few white people here and there, like the missionaries who sometimes visited the cemetery. Some locked eyes on Rizal and the rest, looking away when they found their gaze returned. Most ignored them.

"Quickly!" sir Benjie yelled. He had catapulted into

action the second the plane touched down, collecting passports from the men, ensuring everyone had their packs, telling each to make sure that they followed him. Gone was the jovial, encouraging man who met them at the airport in Manila. Replacing him was a headmaster, corralling his group of wayward charges, proving their prior joke prophetic. This new version of Benjie spoke to the men as he would to a group of small and slightly slow children, issuing terse, monosyllabic orders. "Come," he said, wiping sweat from his brow, suffering in the high humidity of Taiwan's thick summer air. Though still indoors, Rizal could already feel a change in the air. Hot, yet slightly cooler than what he had left behind. A dampness he could taste clamped to his skin, clothes clinging to his body. He readjusted his pack on his shoulder, cool air touching the column of sweat left beneath the strap.

"We will go through immigration together," sir Benjie repeated for at least the fourth time since they landed not more than a quarter of an hour before, first calling it out the moment the plane's wheels ceased their motion. Now he flipped through the stack of passports again, counting, *one, two, three....* He looked back, doing the same through the group. *Eight, nine, ten.* He mouthed the words to himself, pausing to wipe away more sweat from his brow. The corridor opened on a wide room where columns of people snaked their way out from a row of desks. Sir Benjie led them to the far right where Rizal recognized the attendants from his flight, passing by the desk there with little more than a flash of their books and a smile. Benjie walked up to the desk and put the stack of passports down before the man. He too counted the booklets then did a quick head count, stopping to examine a sheet of paper filled with names, stamps, and signatures that Benjie slid across the counter. The officer looked and pushed the form back, pulling a red stamp from somewhere below the counter and slamming it down indiscriminately onto the pages of each booklet. In a matter of minutes it was done. "Okay," sir Benjie said with a sigh of relief. "This way to meet Mr. Chen."

They moved to an escalator that took them down to the baggage claim. Benjie hustled them past the lumbering carousels. "No need, no need," he dismissed them with a flick of his hand, picking up his stride. He led them past customs, officers eyeing them for a moment then turning their attention to other passengers as they filed by the sleeping X-ray machines. Beyond the machines a set of automatic doors slid open and shut. As they opened Rizal saw rows of people waiting behind a low glass barrier, some holding signs with scribbled Mandarin on them and what he presumed was English or other languages. His group was silent, but all around them the chattering of voices filled the arrival hall, the joyous sounds of reunion echoing off the sheer glass walls of the terminal, afternoon sunlight streaming through tinted panels. Sir Benjie's eyes darted about, searching for a sign of Mr. Chen. He stopped and the men halted along with him. A female security guard motioned for Benjie to move his group along. He took them beyond the barrier and there they stood, looking like a huddle of lost boys. Then sir Benjie's face brightened, alighting in a broad smile. "Ah, here is Mr. Chen," he switched from Tagalog to English, "*Ni hao, ni hao,*" he favored Chen with a few words in Mandarin. He thrust out a hand to the man that was met somewhat tentatively. Chen sported a crop of thinning hair combed straight back over a bald spot on the crown of his head. Dark glasses covered his eyes. Rizal studied him. He looked to be somewhere around fifty. Crow's feet birthed at the outer canthus of his eyes, lines rolling from the corners of his mouth. He returned little of Benjie's enthusiasm, tone flat and businesslike.

"I hope you've brought me workers this time," said Chen. He had a deep voice, in spite of his small stature. Though Rizal could not understand him, he noticed a few nervous smiles sprout among the others.

"Oh, yes, yes, Mr. Chen," Benjie answered, a slight waver in his words. "You won't have any problems with these."

Chen made a sound somewhere between a grunt and a murmur.

"Would you like to say a few words to them, Mr. Chen?"

Chen nodded sternly and began, addressing the men in English. "All you need to know is that you're here to work. This isn't a vacation or some kind of working holiday. If you wanted time off, you should have stayed home." Rizal looked to the others, some wearing the same look of confusion as he, others nodding, nervous smiles replaced by blank stares. "Work hard and you won't get any trouble from your captains, or from me," Chen continued. "Keep your heads down and your mouths closed. Anyone who complains will be sent home immediately. Do you understand?"

A few men nodded, Beer Belly among them. "What did he say?" Rizal asked him.

"Work hard, don't complain," Beer Belly hissed back.

Around them a few others translated for those like Rizal who didn't fully understand. Rizal turned his eyes toward Mr. Chen and nodded quickly. The others did the same.

"Good," said Chen. He turned to sir Benjie. "This lot doesn't seem very bright," he chided.

"You need backs, I think, not brains," Benjie fumbled with his words, the sweat on his brow returning. Chen chuckled.

"Anyway, plenty more where they came from, Mr. Benjie. But speak to them in your own language. Make sure they know exactly what they're here for. And be certain they know who I am."

Benjie nodded much in the same way the others who had not comprehended the message at first had. He turned to the men, some shuffling nervously from side to side, handing the stack of passports over to Chen. Chen placed them in a brown leather satchel bag and fastened its gold clasp.

"Mr. Chen is a very important man," said Benjie, switching back to Tagalog. "He is your broker, the man who has so generously arranged for you to work here in Taiwan. He is the man who decides whether you stay and earn money or go back home. So if he says work hard and keep your mouths shut, that's exactly what you'd better do. Remember why you're here, and never forget that it only takes one phone call from your captain to Mr. Chen to have you sent back. Keep that in mind when you're thinking of asking for a day off or complaining about some little problem. People work hard here, every day. We're not asking anything of you that the Taiwanese don't already ask of themselves. You're not in the Philippines anymore.

Remember that. This is Taiwan. Things are different. It won't be easy. Remember the money you're making and why you're making it. You're doing this not just for yourselves but for your families. Three years to change your lives forever. It's a once-in-a-lifetime chance. Don't waste it."

He turned again to Mr. Chen and smiled. "*Hao le*," said Chen, "the vans are waiting. Let's get them on their way."

Chen turned to walk toward the exit. Benjie motioned for the men to follow, remaining still, tapping each on the elbow as they passed by. He performed another silent head count, mouthing the numbers as the men went past. Rizal was the last to go by. Rather than tap him on the elbow, Benjie took hold of it. He glanced from side to side.

"You heard what I said? I saw you talking with your friend while I was speaking."

"No, sir Benjie, I was only —"

"I don't want to hear it," sir Benjie dismissed him with a wave of his free hand, the other clamped down on his shoulder. "It wasn't easy convincing Chen to take you, a *buwisit* from the cemetery," he said plainly, "hardly better than that Visayan hillbilly." He pointed outside to the gray-haired man from Mindanao. "It won't be nearly as difficult to convince him to send you back. Don't forget that, *bata*." Rizal lowered his eyes. He felt Benjie's hand then clapping him lightly on the shoulder. His free hand chucked him softly below the chin. Rizal raised his head and saw sir Benjie smiling. "Hey, *anak*, there's really no need for this *tampo*. As long as you work hard and don't embarrass me, we'll have no problems between us." He slapped Rizal on the back and pointed toward the exit. "Now, go and join the rest," he said. "The vans are waiting."

Feeling uneasy, Rizal walked outside into a wall of humidity. Rows of yellow taxis and black transport vans snaked their way past the numbered entrances, stopping to pick up passengers, drivers hopping from their seats to assist with suitcases and boxes covered in plastic wrapping. Directly before him Rizal saw Chen guiding the men into a pair of white vans, plumes of rust blooming above the wheel wells. Drivers sat in their seats, smoking cigarettes, blowing white clouds out of the windows. Rizal patted his pants pocket, ensuring his I.O.V. tape was still there. Chen pointed Rizal toward the van on the left. "Su'ao," he said. Rizal nodded and smiled. He repeated the unfamiliar word, his tone suggesting a greeting. Chen roared with laughter and said something to the driver in Mandarin. The driver laughed, shaking his head as he knocked cigarette ash onto the pavement with a tap of his middle finger.

Rizal smiled along with them, unsure if it was a joke at his expense or if he had endeared himself to the men with his effort to speak their language. A simultaneous feeling of warmth and dread tossed his stomach as he got into the van, the upholstery reeking of cigarette smoke and another acrid odor he traced to a white plastic cup filled with red fluid and an emulsified rind. He found the source when the driver pulled a betel nut from a small bag and spit the cud-like contents of his mouth into the cup before popping in the fresh one. There were two banks of seats in the back of the van. Beer Belly and another man sat in the second, one more man in the first. Rizal took his seat in the first row. He saw Chen get into the front passenger seat. Sir Benjie peered through the rear sliding door, smiling.

"This is where I leave you," he boomed, his voice finding its old friendly pitch and volume again. "You're in Mr. Chen's hands now," he patted the man on the shoulder through the open passenger door. Chen seemed to bristle at his touch, but sir Benjie didn't notice, face diverted toward the silent men in the back. "Get some rest on the drive to Su'ao," he went on. "Once you arrive, the work begins." His eyes scanned from man to man. "And remember, a call from Mr. Chen is never good news for me, so make sure it's not your name I hear when I pick up the phone, okay?"

Somber nods.

"Okay then. *Paalam*, and good luck." He pushed the rear door shut. Chen pulled his door closed without a word of goodbye to sir Benjie. With a nod from Chen to the driver they pulled away from the terminal, joining the line of cars queuing to exit the terminal grounds, inching their way toward the freeway. The blinding sun sat just above the upper edge of the windshield as the driver turned the van onto the road and pushed a heavy foot down on the accelerator. Rizal squinted against the light, trying to take in his new home. The roadway's four lanes were filled with cars weaving around one another, changing lanes alone and in tandem. Rizal heard the roar of the engine beneath the hood as the van picked up speed. He watched the moving dials and hands on the dashboard, regarded the digital clock face. The speed felt quicker than when he had been on the bus in Manila, the movements more severe. He held tight to his pack, clutched beneath his forearms on his lap. He looked to Beer Belly and the other three men, nearly asleep already. Rizal closed his eyes and tried to do the same. He clenched his eyelids only for them to pop back open seconds later, driven by his pounding heart and electric thoughts.

To the left, mid-rise apartment buildings zoomed past, connected by black tangles of wires sagging at their midpoints before rising up to meet the next mass of concrete, brick, and mildewed tile. Occasionally there was a break in the urban blight to reveal an expanse of rice paddies or a rock-strewn spillway, bone dry, tumbling down from the green mountains to the right. The van sped through a tunnel blasted through a rocky outcrop of the foothills, and Rizal leaned over the lap of the man beside the window to watch the lights and the smooth rounded walls go past at dizzying speed. Everything was new and wondrous and terrifying. So far removed from the cemetery and its *maganang kumain* and gangster boys selling *shabu* and sacred statues watching over lanes where there were no cars or tunnels or green mountains to be seen. Only row upon row of tombs and a sky that seemed to hang like a glass dome over Rizal's corner of the world – a world he shared with Mama and Kidlat, and for a short time with Leizel, his little girl, and her mother. These were the people he thought of and missed more than he had ever missed anything or anyone before.

At once Rizal felt very tired, body and mind heavy with a million thoughts and impulses and emotions. The driver said something to Mr. Chen, pointing to a striped plastic bag filled with four white rectangular boxes and four sets of chopsticks. Wordlessly and without looking back Mr. Chen picked up the bag and handed it back to Rizal, the only man wakeful enough to reach out and take it. Rizal could smell the rice and meat within the paper boxes, grease soaked through the bottoms. He put down his pack to make room to eat. Nudging the man beside, he handed him a box, took one himself, then passed the bag back to the groggy man behind. As the van sped further toward their destination they ate greedily, stomachs thankful for the ample portions of pork, brown hard-boiled eggs sliced in half, and piles of steamed vegetables. When he was finished, Rizal asked for the bag back. He put his empty rice box into the bag along with his chopsticks, then leaned back. Before long his chin lowered onto his chest. In seconds he was out cold.

Chapter Six

IN his dream, Rizal was a young boy, five years old. He stood beside his mother, his tiny hand in hers. They were in the cemetery, a new and bewildering place for him. A place he had been brought to for reasons his mind could not yet understand. He tugged at his mother's hand, asking her why. Why had they come to this place with its bad smells and strange people who came to meet them at the gates yet said nothing, just standing and staring? "Let's go for a walk," said his mother. And she took him through the cemetery lanes for the first time, telling him about their new home.

"The seals of the tombs bear the names of those who are no longer with us, Rizal. Do you see? Filipino, Spanish, Chinese. This is a resting place for all those who have passed."

"Passed, Mama?"

She paused. "Those who have gone away, Rizal. Old, young; we never know how much time we have on this earth. When the Lord sees fit, we are called to the kingdom of heaven. Do you understand?"

A stray dog happened by, belly swollen in pregnancy, begging for scraps. "I think so," said Rizal, eyes following the dog as it went on its way. They walked slowly after the mongrel. Rizal studied the tombs, the crucifixes cut into the stone and the words he could not read etched into the seals. Before long they were on the outskirts of the burial grounds. They stopped. Here and there were mounds of earth, covered in a patchy coat of grass. Between the mounds, burning piles of garbage smoldered. Rizal breathed the bitter smoke into his lungs and coughed. His mother patted him on the back, worry in her eyes.

"What is *this* place, Mama?" Rizal croaked. His throat ached.

"This too is a resting place, Rizal. But here, the graves have no names. This is where the poor are put into the ground when their time comes. They are buried here, many at a time, all sharing the same small space, nameless. I want you to see it, Rizal. I want you to learn from it."

Rizal looked to the mounds. He struggled to understand. There was a scent in the air he had smelled before, but never like this, never so strong. It was sweet but sickening at the same time. It made his stomach turn. He wanted to leave, to go back to the home they had lived in before. The place they had left just that morning. Rizal pulled at his mother's hand, tugging her back in the direction from which they had come.

"Let's go, Mama. Let's go home."

His mother pulled him back. She crouched beside him.

"This is home, Rizal," she whispered, drawing him close to her body, arms wrapped around him. Then softer, like a gentle wind through an open window, "We are the nameless dead now."

The sound of the van door opening woke Rizal with a start. Long late-afternoon rays bounced off the low ripples of a small east-facing harbor, bounding through

Rizal's half-closed eyelids. Holding a hand over his brow he looked out at the boats bobbing up and down, bumping against the row of black tires running along the edge of the harbor wall. The boats were mostly small and rusting, curved steel hulls rising at the bow and stern. They were tied up two and three abreast, some rows as deep as seven in the long rectangular shelter lined on three sides by narrow roads in the midst of the town. Larger vessels were moored further out toward the harbor's open end, it guarded by a breakwater and a hilly green cape rising up out of the water. To the north a white arched bridge led over a second primary harbor to the cape. At the rear and along its southern side, the smaller harbor, where the men suddenly found themselves as aliens dropped onto the strange terrain of an aquarian world, was backed by densely treed and low hills rising up behind the lines of shops and two-, three-, and four-story buildings that bordered the water. There was a temple at the closed end of the harbor. Near the temple, a convenience store, where some crewman of the harbor ships loitered in front or came out carrying bags of chips and bottles of water or tea. Along the northern road leading from the temple out toward the green cape was a Christian church, rooftop cross looming tall over all those below. Two doors down from the church, a large building, taking up the space that could have accommodated several of the others: the police station.

The decks of the boats rising and falling in the harbor were strewn with netting. Bulbous lamp lights hung along the tops of the small square wheelhouses, ragged, grease-stained laundry strung from lines running from wheelhouse to bow and stern. Rizal looked and saw men there on the decks, holding phones at arm's length, speaking words unhearable at distance, sitting and staring, scrubbing clothes in soapy plastic buckets, many shirtless in the summer heat, skin browned to the point of black. Some to Rizal's eyes were countrymen, others with traits unfamiliar. Where he looked Rizal sometimes found his stare returned, and at times those he looked upon quickly found reason to turn their eyes elsewhere. On the streets, those who appeared foreign in this new land could be seen walking, alone or in groups of two or three, some riding creaking, rickety bicycles along, wavering to the right and the left, giving way to the tour buses arriving, parking before a row of seafood restaurants serving the fresh catch and merchants selling pungent dried fish laid out on plastic trays, above them mechanical devices with circular brush arms twirling to keep away the flies.

Chen appeared at the side door and motioned for the men to come out. Slowly they slid out of their seats and moved from the cool of the interior into the blazing sunlight, lining up side-by-side on the concrete a few feet from the water's edge. Rizal stood beside Beer Belly in the line, Chen and another man before them. The men squinted and shielded their eyes with their hands. The harsh sun behind Chen and the man beside him wrapped the pair in a yellow-white shroud. Rizal thought of the statues of the saints back in the cemetery. Chen began talking, once again pulling Rizal from his thoughts of home. The men tried to follow as best they could as Chen spoke to them, using simpler English than he had back at the airport.

"This is Mr. Li," Chen indicated the man beside him. "He is your *laoban*. Boss. Captain. Understand? *Captain*," he said sternly. It was a word Rizal and the rest understood. "He say, you do. No questions. Okay?"

Nodding from the men, none more enthusiastic than Rizal.

"Good," said Chen. "Welcome to Su'ao, Nanfang'ao Fishing Harbor. Work hard. Li *xiansheng* say, you do it fast, fast, fast. Okay? You call him *chuanzhang*. Captain. He is a very important man." He gestured toward the reddish tubs in the harbor. "Owns many boats. Catches many fish. If you don't work hard, he will not be happy." Pointing a finger to his chest, he said, "If he is not happy, I am not happy. And if I am not happy," he pointed down the road they had come by, lined with seafood restaurants and shops, "you go home. Understand?" He pointed now toward Rizal. "You call Mr. Li what?"

Rizal looked down the line of men to Beer Belly and the two others whose names he also had yet to learn. They stared forward, unwilling or unable to help him. Chen moved toward Rizal, eyes narrowing behind the dark lenses of his glasses. The glasses fell on his nose as he scrunched up his face in frustration.

"You call Mr. Li what?" he repeated, louder.

Rizal's voice caught in his throat. He watched as Chen pointed to Li and ventured a guess.

"Boss?" Rizal croaked, the word crawling through the desert of his throat, emerging to the world a dried-up wretch. Chen's hand rose up and cuffed him on the side of the head. Rizal cowered.

"*Bu dui*," Chen admonished. "*Chuanzhang!*" he barked at Rizal, the boy before him turning his face away. "You call him *chuanzhang*. Captain. *Baichi*." He turned, shaking his head, laughing sardonically. Li joined him. They exchanged a few words in Mandarin, the others standing and sweating, each repeating the word in their head. *Chuanzhang, chuanzhang, chuanzhang*. Chen turned his attention back to them. "You say it," he commanded. "*Chuanzhang*."

"*Chuanzhang*," said the men, failing to grasp the word's subtle shifts in tone from one syllable to the next.

"No!" Chen shouted. "*Bu dui!*" He repeated it slowly, stretching out the rising tone of the first syllable, the rise and fall of the second. "Again!"

"*Chuanzhang*." They did the same.

"Again!"

Once more the exercise was repeated. Chen's scowl relaxed. "Good," he said, voice quieting. "Now, I must be going. Remember, if Li *chuanzhang* is not happy, I am not happy. If I am not happy," he opened his satchel bag, took out the stack of passports, waving them at the men, "you go home." He put the passports back in his bag as he walked past. The driver opened the passenger door of the van for Chen and closed it once he was inside. Then the driver got in and turned the van around. They drove away, turning right at the narrow, closed end of the harbor, passing by the temple, then disappearing, headed north on the highway toward the center mass of the sprawling seaside town. Then it was just the five of them – four greenhorn crew and their captain.

Captain Li surveyed his crew. Rizal tried not to stare, head smarting from the blow suffered moments before. He was seized by a new kind of fear, one magnified by being in a new and unfamiliar place where everything carried new and unfamiliar meanings. The captain was old, he thought. Sixty, maybe more. His face was dark brown, legs slightly bowed. He wore a weathered blue baseball cap pulled down low, hiding his eyes. There was something unsettling about him. Rizal soon realized what it was. It was his skin. It reminded him of the dead back home, the ones with a few years stuffed up inside a tomb to dry them up like a flame had been held to their flesh, just far enough away so that it didn't burn but thinned and browned the hide until such that a stern breeze might blow it right off the bones. As though on cue the wind picked up. Rizal shuddered, the vision of Li's defleshed face flashing in his mind.

"Come," Li said in English. "*Agad!*" he barked then in Tagalog, his mood changing like the rise and fall of the wind. The men quickened their steps to follow. He walked toward the edge of the harbor, feet swinging nearly as far to the side as they did forward. Still he moved quickly, the slight stoop of his back slowing him none. His hands were clasped behind him. Rizal drew close enough to see them, gnarled and calloused. He stared down at his own hands, soft and smooth.

Li stopped in front of one of the small boats, thirty feet from bow to stern, one of a few alone in place against the harbor wall. He stepped to Beer Belly and put a hand on the shoulder strap of his pack, pulling on it. Beer Belly watched in confusion, allowing the pack to slide off his shoulder. Li took it and tossed it on board. It landed with a dull thud against the deck. He motioned for the men to do the same. All at once they threw their packs aboard. Li lowered himself down from the top of the harbor wall down onto the deck of his boat. Silently he beckoned them to follow. One of the others went first, the man beside him following, then Beer Belly. Rizal was the last to board. On deck he felt the vessel rising and falling beneath his feet, almost giggling at the sensation. The trash-filled waters of the small landing where he and Kidlat had swum were calm, the water so still it was almost stagnant, moving only when a barge or ship went by, far out at sea, or when the winds were high. There the water was black and dead, the surface coated in oil, the seabed covered in a blanket of plastic. In Su'ao the sea was blue and alive.

Li grabbed Rizal by the shoulder, snapping him out of his momentary trance. He led Rizal to where a thick, frayed dock line was tied around a squat mooring. He pointed to Rizal's eyes, then to his own hands, instructing him to watch. Then he turned and loosened a winch. Rizal's eyes followed as the dock line and another at the far end of the boat slackened. Next, Li loosened the knot from the mooring and tossed the line on board with the same lack of ceremony with which they had pitched their packs. Li pointed to the far dock line, indicating that Rizal should do the same. Nervously Rizal moved to the line, struggling with the cleat before wresting the rope free with none of the ease or skill of the captain. Li shook his head, muttering something in Mandarin under his breath. He watched Rizal finish, and when he did Rizal sighted the life jackets hung on the wheelhouse wall. Eager to impress with a knowledge of safety procedure, Rizal went to take down a jacket and put it on.

The captain stopped him, pulling the jacket from his hand. "No!" barked the captain. He put it on over his head and showed how the jacket's bulk restricted his movements. "No good for working," Li explained. He pulled the life jacket up over his head again, knocking loose his baseball cap to briefly reveal his balding head. He hung the jacket back up, put his cap back on, face flushed, waddled to the wheelhouse, and went inside.

Seconds later the engine below deck rumbled to life. The boat began to pull away. Rizal grabbed hold of the low railing as the boat rocked from side to side, puttering slowly through the harbor. As they pushed past the marina Rizal's eyes turned to the expanse of open water to the east, the sun beginning to set behind them, beyond the town and the mountains to the west. He thought of how it had been back home, when he and Kidlat sat out by the landing until nightfall, the sun setting before them. There he could watch the sun drop down, lowering itself into its great turquoise bath. From his place at the stern, he watched the other three crewmen at the gunwales and the captain at the wheel in the wheelhouse. To a man their eyes were locked on the line separating sea and sky. Rizal looked back toward the land and for the first time saw the whole town of Su'ao, the twin peaks of the tree-covered cape rising like the humps of a desert camel from the seabed to protect the harbor. The white steel arch of the bridge curved above the entrance of the larger harbor, a pair of breakwaters just beyond. Passing the concrete breaks, the captain turned the wheel toward the narrow opening between a secondary pair in the distance, gentle waves lapping beyond the calm confines. Lights flashed at the ends of the breaks and Rizal saw another fishing boat navigate its way through them, this one on its way home. A third hump of rock thrust out of the water in the open sea, a white froth gathering around its edges, mist rising as waves broke upon its black crags, wearing the bottom edges smooth.

The captain pointed toward the rock and bellowed something from within the wheelhouse, gesturing to the rock, miming some sort of animal. The men struggled to hear him over the rough roar of the engine. Li gave up, dismissing the crew with a wave of his hand. He turned his attention to the wheel, maneuvering them effortlessly between the last set of breaks and onto the open ocean, where the waves were taller than Rizal had previously thought, sending the boat up and over crests some several feet tall and down into the troughs below with rhythmic pace and timing. As the boat climbed, fell, and climbed again, Rizal watched the town appear and disappear and grow smaller and smaller behind them. Eventually it began to sink down below the water's edge, in time disappearing altogether. Within the hour the island itself was gone.

Rizal looked in all directions: there was only water, the boat, and themselves, no other vessels to be seen on the undulating sea that breathed like a living thing, seething in the encroaching darkness. Li reduced speed to a trawl and emerged scowling, turning on a light above the wheelhouse to illuminate the deck as night descended quickly around them. Then he showed the men the ways of his primitive setup. A wheel mounted at the stern, strung with a long spool of line, whirred to life, letting out the main line at a slow, steady pace into the sea. Next to the wheel were racks hung with branch lines, hooks, floats, and neon glow sticks. Below the racks were buckets of bait fish, Li removing the lids to let loose a fetid stink that enveloped the deck like a thick cloud of flies. Quickly and without patience Li showed the men how to affix bait to hook, float and glow stick to branch, and then the branch itself to the main line while it flowed steadily past into the water. With speed he affixed several branches to the main and set them loose into the black water below. Then he motioned for the men to do the same, two men working on either side of the spinning wheel. The men worked slowly at first, reticently handling the sharp hooks, struggling to remember the myriad steps Li had taken to do something that to him was second nature, to them as new and bewildering as were the many forces that brought them to this moment.

"*Gan ni niang, kuai yi dian! Kuai yi dian!*" Li shouted, commanding them to speed up.

Nervously Rizal reached for a branch and in his haste felt the barb of the hook pierce a finger. With a hiss he dropped the line to the deck and tried to shake away the pain, holding up his injured hand to watch a trickle of blood flow from the wound. He held it up for the captain to see. "*Chuanzhang*," he said, pleased with himself that he remembered the word. Li put down his line. He waddled over to Rizal. Rizal looked and saw the captain eyeing his hand.

"Oh," said Li, feigning sympathy, "*hao kelian*." He raised a hand and slapped Rizal across the cheek, causing the others to halt their work and look at Li and Rizal before a glare from the captain sent their eyes elsewhere. "*Gan ni niang, kuai yi dian! Kuai yi dian!*" Li screamed louder than before, again cuffing Rizal upside the head. He pointed to the branch lines. Rizal looked down and took a line. He fumbled with it, hands shaking. With difficulty he managed to affix bait to hook, trying to steady his lip from quivering. He kept his eyes on the main line streaming by and watched the others to see if he was indeed doing as the captain commanded, fearing anything that might again draw the man's ire. The fear bled into his work but pushed him on, turning the boy's fright into the man's will to do what needed to be done.

From time to time Rizal stifled a retch, Li shaking his head and muttering under his breath. For every hook set by the crewmen Li set five or more. In the span of a few hours the oath of *gan ni niang* became a familiar refrain to the crewmen. Fear of the hand that had already crossed Rizal's cheek drove them on through their exhaustion. They finished with aching hands, pressing their thumbs into cramping palms to push out the stiffness. The main line at its end, a radio beacon was attached last by Li and he returned to the wheelhouse to push the engine to a brisker pace than the slow trawl he had kept it at while the men worked. Then he came back to the stern, pulling a small flashlight from his pocket to shine down into the water. He pointed at the small fish that flocked around the stern where bits of baitfish and blood had drawn them to their rich scent.

"No," he said, pointing at the many small fish gathered around. "No good," he spoke in English. "*Weiyu*," he pushed his mottled hands out to the sides, indicating the size of catch they were after. "Tuna."

Beer Belly knew the word and translated it for the rest of the crew. "*Tulingan*," he said. Rizal nodded enthusiastically, hoping to catch Li's eye. The old man only muttered and pointed to another line, pulling out more hooks to be set. The other two men, standing across the cramped deck from Rizal and Beer Belly, passed a look between them. One elbowed the other lightly and he spoke up.

"Boss," he said, forgetting the way in which they were instructed to address the captain. "Eat?" the man asked, shoveling phantom food from a phantom bowl into his mouth. He punctuated the request with a smile and a rub of his flat stomach. For the first time since getting in the van with the two men other than Beer Belly, Rizal studied them closely. They were of nearly identical build, skinny with long, narrow faces. He wondered if they might be relatives. Cousins, if not brothers. One was slightly taller than the other, hair a little thinner. Both wore their hair in the same style, parted neatly to the side, though now it was mussed and frayed, slicked with sweat and the blood of the bait fish. The captain turned away from the wheelhouse and stared at the pair of them. He kicked aside an empty chum bucket and moved across the deck toward the man who had dared to ask the question, tilting an ear toward him.

"*Ni shuo shenme?*" No one aboard the boat understood the words but all knew a question had been asked, one to which there was no right answer but silence. "*Zai yi ci*," the captain implored. "Again," Li said in English. "Say again."

"Eat?" the man asked again. No sooner was the word out of his mouth than the captain's quick hand found his cheek just as it had Rizal's. He caught him full and flush, the sick sound of flesh on flesh cracking through the still night air, sucking all sounds of the boat and the sea into a silent void. The eyes of the others found the deck. Li stood and stared at the man. He raised a hand as if to strike again, reared it back then held it there. The man flinched and the hand fell back to the captain's side.

"Now, working," Li said, raising the hand once again to point at the cowering man who stood a full foot taller than him. "Later, eating." He pivoted slowly to face the rest of the frozen crew, dark eyes moving from man to man. He raised his arms in question, watching as the eyes of his crewmen searched each other for an answer. None forthcoming, he gave it to them.

"Work!" he screamed, drawing the surrounding sounds back out of hiding as his boot found the same bucket again, sending it clattering with a sure-footed kick. "*Gan ni niang, kuai yi dian! Kuai yi dian!*"

The crew blinked their confusion. Li threw up his hands. He went to the wheelhouse and came back with a box of tools, dumping it out on the deck. He picked up a putty knife and pointed to the peeling paint on the deck, getting down on all fours to mime scraping the curved waves of white from the wooden planks. "Work!" he repeated. The men scrambled to grab an implement, each grabbing a knife or a scraper and got to work. On hands and knees they scraped for hours while the boat trawled its way along course unknown. Rizal rubbed his hands together and felt the layer of slime move over his skin, unable to clear it away. The smell of saury was all over him now, on his clothes, coating his hair when he raised a forearm to wipe the sweat from his brow. Just a few hours into his new life and already his thoughts were dominated by one that would not leave him. Over and over, the voice in his head repeated:

We are the nameless dead now.

Chapter Seven

DAWN was breaking when the boat finally puttered back into port. For all the lines the men had set and left to soak in the brine of the sea then hauled back aboard, removing the floats and glow sticks, untying the branch lines and hanging them back on the racks; for all the dead and mortally wounded creatures they had tossed overboard and become soaked in their blood, they had brought aboard one fat, round-eyed fish that pleased Captain Li. A *weiyu.* A *tulingan.* It had taken the five of them to bring it on deck, its white, swollen belly smacking solidly against the wooden planks. *Chuanzhang* himself dispatched the creature with a cold blow from an aluminum baseball bat. They watched the fish gasp its last, eyes chasing a diminishing light of the world as its pupils widened and finally went still. The great fish was carried by the five men into the cramped freezer below deck and packed with ice. Then, when the lines were spooled, the hooks taken off the branches and put back into storage, Li returned to the wheelhouse. "*Huijia,*" he said calmly, as though the night's work had brought nothing out of the ordinary. "Go home."

The men were hopeful, even grateful. Home meant food and a chance to get some sleep. Relief and exhaustion felled them, each slumped against the gunwale with chin pressed against chest, not even the strength to dry heave from the seasickness still tossing their empty stomachs. From time to time a head bounced up in the faintest attempt of the body to expel what fluid had built up in the belly, a pathetic belch all that could be mustered. Though the night had chased little of the day's heat from the sea and the morning saw it steadily returning, the crew still shivered with cold, soaked to the bone in seawater and sweat and blood. A flock of seagulls circled overhead, following like vultures awaiting a dying animal's final gasp.

As the boat went past the twin scarps of rock sticking out of the sea and under the white bridge, the men heard Li get on the radio, speaking yet more words unintelligible to them. He navigated the breakwater gap, then steered the boat sidelong into its berth. As it bumped the tires lining the ledge, he yelled at the crew, pointing to the spring lines and the cleats atop the rough concrete. Rizal moved as quickly as his sore limbs would allow, taking up a line on his own at the stern, Beer Belly taking the other at the bow. In spite of the rising hunger turning his thoughts to a drone, Rizal remembered to cross the lines as they had been before they set out and tied the cleat hitch successfully with only a few false beginnings.

Li emerged from the wheelhouse to inspect their work. He nodded, stern and silent. A small blue pickup truck backed to the edge of the wall. A man about Li's age in rubber boots and overalls jumped out, teeth stained with betel nut. He said something to Li, pointing to the bedraggled men and laughing. Li shook his head and replied, drawing a hearty laugh from the driver punctuated by a stream of dark red spit that landed just in front of Rizal at the wall's edge. Li made a *tsk*-ing sound. He moved to the stern and inspected the cracked and peeling white paint on the gunwale there, pointing to a few red blotches, speaking rapidly and pointing from man to blotch and back again. The driver raised his hands in contrition as Rizal wiped a large red gob from his forearm, feeling a pull on his shoulder. It was Li tugging on him again. He pointed Rizal toward the hatch blocking the hold, motioning for him to open it. When the hatch was open the four crewmen hoisted the tuna from the freezer, this time Li merely watching, standing back with his arms folded over his chest. The crew brought the fish to the stern, where the driver waited. Li pointed to two of them, seeming to tell them to stay on deck while the other two were to jump to street level to help hoist the fish.

Rizal pulled himself slowly up onto the edge of the wall, arms burning, looking into the back of the pickup to see a dirty polystyrene container packed with ice, lid tipped on its side next to the wheel well. Beer Belly took up the spot opposite Rizal and with much grunting and groaning they managed to bring the fish up, the other two men and the driver joining them to take it the rest of the way into the container. Li too pulled himself out of the boat and pointed to the crewmen and then to the back of the truck. They hopped up with the fish, fixing the lid in place, while Li took the passenger seat in the cab. The suffering engine sputtered to life, and with surprising pep the truck took off toward the open end of the harbor, away from the temple, a breeze drawing cold air from the frozen compartment up and over the men. They shivered as the truck moved quickly down the road, turning right and stopping less than a minute later at a collection of tented canvas roofs held up by thin aluminum poles next to the still water, makeshift shelters standing over rickety wooden tables. The odor of fish filled the air along with the squawks and cries of a multitude of gray and white seabirds circling above the labyrinth of stalls, some sitting empty, others manned by fishermen and women in rubber boots and overalls loading up more polystyrene boxes with ice, laying all manner of sea creatures on bedrocks of melting chips. The men waited as Li emerged and rounded the back of the truck, pointing to the soaked ground and ordering them out of the bed as he thrust down the tailgate.

"*Xialai*," Li barked loudly enough so those in the market could hear him. Several sets of eyes were drawn from their work to the four dark-skinned men hopping down from the tailgate to help Li unload his catch. As they moved the fish's awkward bulk Rizal saw more than one finger raised in their direction, hands covering words he would not have understood even if he could hear them or see them spoken. Together the four crewmen along with the driver transported the container to an empty table. The container shifted, Rizal's corner at the downward end. A stream of icy water poured from a gap below the lid, soaking his pants. Rizal stifled a groan and watched as the other crewmen held their laughter in check.

Once the container was set down a crowd gathered as the lid was lifted. Li stood beaming over his prize. Several men as old and weather-beaten as he stood round the table and pointed to the fish, then to the crewmen, talking and laughing, some slapping Li lightly on the shoulder. Rizal stood still, averting his eyes from every gaze that came his way, finding the attention unsettling. He felt something bubble up in his stomach and suppressed a belch, the ache in his gut like stones scraping against the inner wall of a shrinking pit of nerves. Around the market old women milled about, some on their own, others walking and chatting in groups, heads covered by brightly colored shawls to hold their frizzy hair in place in the thick seaside air. They stopped to inspect the catch at each table, as content to look as they might be to buy. Toward some of the catch they nodded with seeming approval, shaking their head openly at others without fear of embarrassment for themselves or causing offense to the seller. Though Rizal could not understand the words in the exchanges going on around him, he surprised himself in finding he had an idea of what was going on. The fear that had traveled with him from the moment the squealing wheels of the plane awoke him to this new reality eased slightly as he worked to convince himself this place was not so unfamiliar after all, and perhaps not so bad as he might have thought during the long, hard night. Maybe the blood of some long gone Navotas fishermen still flowed in his veins, he said silently. The blood of men from a time when there were more boats than cars; when Navotas was still a fishing village, not the slum it had become. And maybe that ancestral strength was such that it would see him through the years ahead.

The other Filipino crewmen stood still, unsure of what they should do. For the moment Li seemed content to bask in the glory of his catch. Looking around, Rizal saw no sign of another prize like theirs. The other tables were stocked with squid and octopus, red snapper. Some had strings of oysters. His knowledge of sea life was limited to that which washed up dead on the garbage-strewn patch of shore near his home. The jobs unloading the catch from the fishing boats and the cargo from the cargo ships, once held by men such as his father? Those had shifted south to the new port at the far end of Manila, many miles down the freeway in what might as well have been another continent. The knowledge Rizal's father and the burden of toil he and many others before him carried had gone, thrown by the powers that be to other fathers in other places, destined to pass to other sons. Li continued pointing to his crew, speaking to the men and women gathered around them. Laughing. Smiling. From time to time Rizal and the others smiled too, the people of the market flashing brief smiles back at them.

"Ha-lo!" an old fisherman's wife called out to Rizal. He froze, looking to Li, eyes white and wide. His head pulsed with a rising pain and he favored the woman with an awkward smile and a halfhearted wave. The crowd buzzed with modest laughter and Rizal wished there was somewhere he could run away to. A place like all those he knew in the crooks and crumbling holes of the cemetery where he had passed many an hour in hiding from Datu Death or the *pistola* boys who chased him for sport. There was no such place here. And so he stood, ignoring the smiles and chatter, waiting for the interest in them to die down so he could at long last be released from his duties and eat and rest.

Li seemed to be waiting for something. An hour passed before the crew knew what it was. A man came around with a portable scale on wheels, a chain affixed to the top for hoisting up the large catch. The man had a name tag on his shirt. He carried a clipboard, a pen stuck behind his ear. He spoke with Li as the men hoisted up the fish once again, another fisherman offering his assistance to set the chain around the tail. They held the fish up until it was in place and let it go, watching as the hand of the scale swung around and bobbed until it settled finally on eighty-four kilograms. Li clucked his tongue, pointing to the scale, speaking angrily to the man with the clipboard. The man tapped the scale with his pen, having back at Li, and for a time their words escalated until Li said, "*Hao le, hao le*," and patted the man on the shoulder, smiles returning to their faces.

A man standing beside the scale who had watched the weighing with interest then spoke to Li. They engaged in a calm back and forth before he handed Li a stack of blue bills. Li counted the money, flipping the notes over one by one with a spit-licked thumb twice over. With that he nodded to the buyer, smiling, the man returning the gratitude with a slight bow of the head. The eyes of the crewmen were on the money. Rizal stared long until he realized the captain had caught his lingering gaze.

"*Kuai yi dian*," Li pointed to the back of the truck just outside the canvas hovel. They walked back out from the protection of the torn and tattered roofs and bent aluminum poles and ropes holding the entire ramshackle complex together, into the morning sun. Rizal hoped for nothing more than the chance to rinse the stinking film from his body and wash it from his clothing. A bite of food, something cold to drink, a bed to lie down on. They jumped up into the back of the truck and it sped off again, a white cup filled with more betel nut spit flying past Rizal's head as the driver let it go out the window. The short trip was repeated in reverse, the little blue bug zooming back down the road, stopping in front of Captain Li's bobbing tub. For a moment Rizal feared the worst: they were going straight back out to sea again.

Li pointed down into the boat. The men jumped in, eyeing one another warily. A dark cover was rolling in, black clouds with linings of sunlight on their outer edges. Li jumped down with them and made for the wheelhouse. Rizal's stomach sank and he felt the vise compressing his skull tighten. Li emerged from the wheelhouse once more, holding three thin foam mats. He tossed them on the narrow benches lining the gunwales, two on one side, one on the other. He pointed to the mats, then to the men.

"*Shuijiao*," he said, drawing more confused stares. He searched his mind for the correct words in English, muttering angrily to himself. "Sleeping time," he finally managed, annoyed that he had to resort to the language. "Sleep," he repeated, heading back toward the stern. His ropy old arms pulled him up the wall and without looking back he went to the truck and got in. With the spitting of stones from the rear tires the truck sped back toward the temple, the town center beyond. Slowing slightly it rounded the corner, sped up again, and was gone from the confines of the harbor. Four men were left on the boat. Four strangers staring at one another and the three mats between them. Beer Belly quickly took a seat on the lone mat behind him. The other two men looked behind themselves and claimed theirs. Rizal, visibly the youngest, looked back to the bare bench and sat without complaint. They all looked one another over, eye searching eye for glints of personality – veiled threats or signs of friendship. Rizal did his best to hide his anxiety, not a difficult thing to do with hunger pangs and the headache pounding in his skull to distract him. He cocked his head across the deck at the two men sitting opposite.

"What do you call yourselves?" he asked. Remembering his manners, they too momentarily lost to hunger, he hastily offered up a "my name's Rizal" before they could answer.

The men stared silently for a moment. "Amado," the taller of the two said first. Then, pointing to the other, "This is Arvin."

Rizal nodded. He looked to his right to Beer Belly, sat looking down at his ragged and soaked sneakers. "You?"

Beer Belly shrugged as if to say names weren't important. "Datu," he eventually volunteered. Rizal smiled. A curious look came over Datu. "My name is funny to you, *anak*?" he asked. Rizal lowered his eyes.

"No, *kuya*," Rizal spoke to the deck. "It's just that … I used to know a man named Datu back home."

"Oh," the new Datu said, lips curling to a thoughtful frown, "was he *guwapo*, like me?" he asked, shaking his gut with both hands. For the first time the men laughed together, the sound carrying across the harbor, dying a quick death on the salty breeze. Rizal turned his attention back to the men across, Arvin and Amado, the boat tipping them slightly above he and Datu, then below as the wake of a docking vessel met them broadside.

"Brothers?" he asked. The two men looked at each other, then back at Rizal, both shaking their heads.

"Cousins," Arvin said softly. His voice was of an unusually high pitch, and Rizal realized why the man had hardly spoken a word. They sat in silence for a time, to a man unsure of what to say next, if there was anything worth saying at all.

"Anyone worked abroad before?" Datu asked quietly, quickly taking the pressure off the others by saying, "Until yesterday I'd never left Quezon City. Zabarte Road, born and raised."

Rizal saw the two pair of eyes opposite light up.

"Quezon?" said Amado, "We are neighbors." He patted himself on the chest. "San Juan."

"San Juan!" Datu's eyes flashed silver. "I used to see a woman there. Every time she would invite me to a love hotel, always the same one, on Serrano. Then she would get me drunk and rob me."

"You went there to get robbed?" Rizal asked, smiling in anticipation.

"Many times!" Datu boomed, drawing his head back.

"Why?" asked Amado.

"That was our arrangement," said Datu, waving a hand to the side. "She would get me drunk on whiskey, then when I was good and *malibog* she would drag me to the bed and *sip sip buto* until I was dry." He laughed. "Then I would lay back and pass out. When I woke up she would be gone and so would all the money in my wallet."

"So she was a *puta*," said Rizal.

Datu's face darkened, black eyebrows set against deep brown skin coming together. "A whore? No!" he boomed. "A thief, yes."

Again they laughed together, longer and deeper this time, chuckles melting slowly into silence. Amado mentioned that his father had gone overseas for work when he was young. "Where?" asked Datu. "Japan," said Amado, "he was gone for many years." Datu said he had a cousin who had worked in Taiwan for a short while, but that all he spoke of from that time were his occasional Sundays off.

Datu rubbed his bulging belly, coaxing a gurgle from its depths and exhaling with a grimace etched in the fleshy, wrinkled curves of his round face. "Do you think there's anything to eat?" His eyes wandered around the boat.

Cautiously Amado got up and began poking about, peering into the wheelhouse. Arvin rose to join him. Rizal looked to the closed end of the harbor, back toward the temple, expecting the little blue truck to come barreling down the road at any moment. He looked to the other boats in the harbor. All looked empty. Some seemed hardly seaworthy: wooden hulls cracked, gunwales splintered, flags faded. The best among them were like Li's, merely rundown, in need of a coat of paint and a few aesthetic repairs; a mix of the venial and the mortal. Amado came out of the wheelhouse frowning, went to the bow to open up the bench seats to see if there was at least some fresh water hidden away. Finding none, he returned to his seat at the stern, Arvin already there.

"Nothing," he said sullenly. "What are we going to do?"

"Maybe the captain went to get us something," said Rizal, shrugging.

"*Chuanzhang!*" Datu roared, widening his eyes and flaring his nostrils in imitation of the captain. The others laughed meekly. The ache in Rizal's stomach radiated to his limbs. He felt his calves cramping for want of water, eyes reddened and dry. The sun blazed down on them. He guessed it was close to noon.

"We could look around" Rizal suggested, nodding to the shops and restaurants rimming the harbor. "Maybe we could find something."

"I don't know about you, *anak*, but I don't have enough money for a half-chewed piece of *chicharrón*," said Datu. "So unless you're buying, I don't see the point in walking all that way."

"A water fountain, then," said Rizal. "A bathroom sink. Anything. And we might as well have a look around the place."

The others looked at each other, silently debating the merits of going into town versus staying put. "Looking like this?" Arvin held up his smelly, soaking shirt.

They stared at one another in silence until finally Rizal grew tired of waiting. "You do what you like," he said, rising. "I'm going." He pulled himself up over the edge of the wall, feet finding the gunwale to push himself up. The concrete burned against his palms and he pulled his hands away quickly, rolling onto his backside before rising shakily to his feet. He began walking and was only a few steps along when he heard the others scrambling to join him. Quick footsteps sounded behind his back and soon they were four astride, heading toward the closed end of the harbor and its temple. The scent of burning incense mingled with that of salt and fish. A metallic buzz of cicadas sounded in the faraway trees on the hillsides, a few vehicles passing by without slowing. Rizal caught a few eyes staring at them from behind lightly tinted windows and windscreens covered in bug splatter. A giant dragonfly buzzed past his ear. The air seemed to be filled with the hum of vein-embossed wings and the endless noise of the greedy seabirds. The others noticed them too, Datu waving an arm and cursing when one flew too close for comfort. They walked past the harbor shops selling fishing gear and the fishermen and women who laid out their catch next to the street, sitting languidly next to baskets and buckets of fish, lounging in aluminum lawn chairs, standing idle with hands clasped behind their backs. Some called out to no one in particular, merchants without a customer, eyes vacant. Their words were weighted by the heat that seemed to draw everything down to the ground and hold it there, a bully tormenting a scrawny, outmatched victim. In their strangled hope, Rizal felt a sense of home. God was here, as he was in Navotas, and yet absent all the same. Like hope itself, God was a mystery, something to be grasped at rather than understood.

It was only a minute before they reached the harbor's narrow closed end, passing the temple, an unfamiliar goddess housed there with hands crossed before her chest, eyes cast out toward the sea. The place of worship was empty now but compelled those who passed to stop and pray, bowing three times before the altar then moving on. The buildings around were bleak and cropped impossibly close together, outsides coated in something black, like mold, that crept up the walls. Many of the ground floors were taken up by small shops. There were a few food stalls. Aged men and women sat in silence at the same low Formica tables Rizal saw around Navotas, rear ends hardening against the backless plastic chairs. Eyes followed the four of them as they walked. Datu raised his arm, a wide exaggerated smile pulling a giggle from mostly silent Arvin. "*Hoy!*" Datu called out, receiving only blank stares in return.

The others shook their heads, laughing quietly. More eyes were on them, work halting in a scooter repair shop as the four of them peered inside on their way by. The scene repeated itself at every open door. Eyes staring at the four dark-skinned strangers from behind noodle carts and fried food stands. They came to what looked like a mom-and-pop general store, the gray and black colors of the marble tile floor muted by a layer of dust. Egg crates were piled beside shelves of liquor and instant noodles and again Rizal thought of home and his mother. The man behind the counter narrowed his eyes in such a way that there was almost a sound to it like the closing of a creaky door. Rizal saw Datu's eyes fall to the fat five-liter bottles of water on the floor.

"Anyone have some money?" Rizal posed the question to them all. Three shaking heads were the reply. He looked back to the narrowed eyes of the man at the counter, the man's brow holding to its furrowed ground. "Then I think we'd better go."

Quietly they filed out of the store, the man behind the counter picking up the phone as Rizal shuffled by last. Once outside they stood on the street, nearly having reached the end of it before it became the divided highway leading from the harbor to central Su'ao. Turning back toward the harbor again, they went to the convenience store near the temple. Amado pointed to the restroom sign, saying, "At least we can get some water from the sink."

They walked by the glass outer wall of the store and found the automatic door. It slid open with a jingle of song. The clerk inside froze at the sight of them, four filth-covered men stretching their arms in the pleasant air-conditioned cool, staring at the neatly ordered shelves and coolers stocked with snacks and drinks. He moved from behind the counter and made his way to a stack of crates full of things yet to be shelved. Rather than putting the items away, he watched the foreigners, wondering where they were from. Seeing they were headed for the bathroom, he followed.

Datu reached the sink outside the bathroom first, turning the faucet to fill his cupped hands with cold water. He drank deeply, "aaaaahing" in satisfaction. He motioned for Rizal to go next. Rizal let the water run over his hands, splashed some over the layer of grit and sweat on his face before taking a drink. His face rose up in the mirror and he saw himself, clothes covered in wet grime. He pulled the I.O.V. tape from his pocket and wiped the droplets of moisture from the case with a paper towel. Then he moved out of the way to let Arvin and Amado have their turns. Arvin let out a rush of air as the water chased away the cocoon of heat that had trapped his body, arms and legs shaking as the bolts of chill jagged down to his toes. Amado crumpled up a paper towel and tossed it at the back of Arvin's head. "*Buset!*" Arvin yelled back over his shoulder, splashing water on his neck, letting it run down his chest and back. Fat splotches covered the countertop and the floor. The sickly smell of powdered soap shavings mingled with that of the urine-spotted floor in the open bathroom to their left. Amado pushed through to the still-running faucet to take his turn when the sound of someone clearing their throat turned them around.

The clerk stood there. Beside him was Captain Li, face narrowed in a deep frown, folds of thin wrinkles closing in on themselves. He stared hard at them, lined up in front of the spewing sink, the sound of running water filling the small alcove. He pointed to the entrance, shouting, "*Huijia!*" Rizal remembered the words as those the captain had used before taking the boat back to port.

They moved quietly past the clerk and the captain. "How did he know?" whispered Amado. Rizal recalled the minder of the general store – how he had picked up the phone, watching them as they left the shop. Li followed them out. The little blue truck was waiting for them. They piled in. This time Li himself took the driver's seat, popping the clutch and putting it in reverse as the last man mounted the tailgate, nearly throwing Arvin off the back as he abruptly backed out.

The truck sped back to Li's boat, tires screeching as it stopped just before the harbor edge. The men jumped down without having to be told, barely breaking stride from the street to the deck of the boat. They turned to see the captain staring down at them from atop the hot concrete slab, white plastic bag in hand. He reached into the bag, pulling out a yellow packet with a smiling cartoon boy in a blue cap on the front. He tossed the packet down to none of them in particular. It landed with a splash in a brown puddle of brine, sending a cloud of rust and whitewash swirling like a mix of blood and curdled cream. Rizal moved to pick the packet up. As he bent down, another landed, splashing the concoction up onto his face. Then another. A two-liter bottle of water narrowly missed his head as he stood up. He wiped a forearm over his face. The captain tossed the empty bag down into the gap between the boat and the harbor wall. It joined a bobbing mass of flotsam there – bits of polystyrene packaging and plastic wrap along with dead and dying fish swimming upside down in circles, mouths circular and gaping their last intake over grayed gills.

"*Chifan!*" Li ordered, miming eating with chopsticks and bowl. The men looked to the three small packets and back to the captain, but he was already on the running board, halfway into the cab of the truck. Arms shot up to protect their faces as the tires squealed again and tiny stones spit out at them. Launched by the balding tires the rocks painted circles in the still water. Rizal handed a packet to Datu and they tore them open. Inside, a sight all too familiar to Rizal. A wavy yellow block of instant noodles and a small silver sleeve of flavor powder. Having searched the boat already, they knew there was nothing to boil water with. Rizal flipped the package over, studying the back. He couldn't read, but numbers he could understand. He looked to his crewmates, holding up the packet.

"These noodles are expired," Rizal said. Datu stared at his open pack, then broke off a piece of the uncooked brick and popped it in his mouth, jaw slowly working to grind the wavy morsel into something that would pass his throat. With some effort he gulped it down dry, tongue searching his palate and gum line for stray bits to swallow. He shrugged.

"Tastes fine to me," said Datu.

Chapter Eight

It was nearly sundown when Li returned, this time bearing buckets of paint to be applied later to the freshly scraped planks. The crew had shared the noodles around, Rizal and Datu splitting one hard, crumbling block, Arvin and Amado the other, eating them uncooked. The third they saved, putting it aside for a shared sense of foreboding each was reluctant to give voice to. Rizal sprinkled the beef flavor powder over his portion. The salty dust sucked the last bits of moisture from his mouth, the two liters of water there was between the four of them not enough to quench anyone's thirst.

They had spent the afternoon lying on the bare wooden benches lining the gunwales, rolling from side to side, arranging themselves awkwardly to avoid falling off the narrow planks, grunting and sighing. The life jackets, if they could not be used for their intended purpose, could at least serve as hard, uncomfortable pillows. The foam mats worked better as covers to keep the harsh afternoon sun off bare arms and faces than they did as mattresses. Out of equal parts desperation and practicality the four men stripped down to their underwear, laying their sweat-, seawater-, and fish-gut-soaked clothing to dry on top of the wheelhouse and over the railing. Many a time Datu swore, shifting the mat from the upper portion of his body to lower when he felt his skin begin to burn. Silently they cursed the sleep that wouldn't come, the approach of night and the return to sea that was inevitable. A familiar thought crept into Rizal's mind, the same one he felt when he watched his daughter carried off by her mother, away from the cemetery and out of his life.

What have I done?

The captain found them lolling on the benches with mats over their eyes when he returned, empty noodle packages crumpled and tossed on the deck. He landed hard with his rubber boots slapping against the planks, rousting them from their half-sleep, a bit of bait slop splashing out of the pail he carried with him. He kicked at one of Amado's empty sneakers, sending it bouncing toward the bow, cursing his way to the wheel. Without word to his crew he fired up the engine. It belched to life below deck, white water boiling between the stern and the harbor wall. Still in their underwear Rizal and Datu scrambled for the spring lines. As he set his eyes on the cleat and the knot he had tied hours before, Rizal searched his memory for the place to pull to see the tangled mess undone. As he stared he felt a rush of air past his head. Amado's sneaker thudded off the wall and fell into the foaming water. Rizal looked back and saw the captain screaming at Amado, pointing to the plastic wrappers on the deck and the water bottle rolling in a half circle as the boat tipped right to left and back again. Though Rizal couldn't understand the captain, he was certain it was the bottle that set him off. Not the bottle itself, but what Rizal and the others had left inside.

Without a private place to relieve themselves the men had decided to take turns with the bottle, taking it into the wheelhouse one by one to drain what little excess moisture their bodies could be rid of. Arvin had been last, the one who was supposed to pitch it over the side. But there it was, full of dull yellow liquid, almost clear. Li screamed and shook, white spittle flying from his mouth. Arvin bobbed his head in contrition, bending down to pick up the bottle. Li stepped back, disgusted, pointing to the stern. Arvin took the bottle and dropped it over the side. It landed with a deep splash then floated there, a bubble of air holding it half-submerged. The captain went back to the wheelhouse, an eye cast quickly back to the spring lines now being pulled in. Looking out to sea again he put hand to throttle and piloted the boat out slowly at first, pushing it harder a few feet from the wall. Amado looked back at his lost sneaker, still floating laces up on the surface of the water. As they moved toward the breakwater the wind raised goose flesh on the crewmen's near-naked bodies. They pulled their dry, stinking clothes back on and listened to the sound of the rumbling engine, breathing in the smell of oily smoke and fish rot.

The push to sea seemed longer their second time out, the boat riding the sluggish and bounding line of the sea farther than the night before. Captain Li remained at the wheel and throttle, crew at the stern, sitting and watching the circling seabirds grow fewer in number then disappear. Night fell and took with it all but the stars and the distant lights of the other boats glowing somewhere out in the thick black soot of sea and sky. The crewmen were too tired to speak, minds too weighted with exhaustion to take notice of much more than the sounds and the unspoken anxiety that kept them from rest. Heads lolled and jerked up again. Muscles ached and cramped, clenched in mid-spasm. Minds attempted transport to places of comfort, failing. Bodies tensed for the hours of pain to come.

Two hours out Li seemed to find that place there in the pitch he was looking for. Abruptly he pulled the throttle to a trawl and stomped out of the wheelhouse. The crewmen rose, bodies calling out their objections. The previous night's tedium and work was begun. Hooks were baited, branches affixed and lights and floats tied. Rizal fought off seasickness, dulled the night previous by the adrenaline coursing through his body, stifling gags and heaves with the back of his hand, slick with fish blood. Across from him Amado did the same. Once in an interminable while Rizal caught the grumbling of Datu to his right, the frustrated toss of a branch line against the deck, one with a hook that just wouldn't set in the soft, rotted flesh of the bait fish. Where the captain had joined in the labor the first night, tonight he stood by, watching and smoking strong, pungent cigarettes. Datu's eyes fixated on the glowing circle of burning ash, watching the smoke rise into the black night, and Rizal knew he wanted a cigarette for himself, mind humming with silent prayer that Datu wasn't fool enough to ask *chuanzhang* for one. Rizal's fingers fumbled as he focused on Datu watching the captain, Li's own eyes on the cousins. Arvin was the slowest, Amado not far behind. Wordlessly Rizal tried to warn

Datu, letting a branch fall against the deck in an effort to get his attention. When that failed he coughed into his hand, cleared his throat. Still Datu took no notice. Rizal clenched as he watched his fellow crewman's chapped lips part.

"Boss," Datu said, forgetting to address Li as they had been told, "cigarette?" He put two fingers to his lips, pushed an imaginary puff of smoke out into the heavy air. Li regarded him quizzically for a moment. His head jerked back, the only sound that of the waves slapping against the side of the boat. Hands stopped setting bait, all eyes on the captain. The smile receded from Datu's face, wilting under his master's stare. Li walked toward him, the lilt of the deck beneath his feet righting itself to suit his stride. Datu's hands found his pockets, eyes holding to the deck. Spray misted up over the gunwale to his back. The hiss of it drew Datu's eyes for an instant. In that split second he was driven backward, spine crunching against the rail. He looked behind to the boiling black water inches from his face, then forward into the crags of the captain's face inches from his own. Li pinned him there. Datu squirmed to free himself, but the old man was strong in spite of his years. The others stood, steadying themselves against the cyclical swaying of the waves. Li screamed at Datu, words firing from his mouth, gusts of wind swallowing them up. Li's hand shot to the front pocket of his shirt, coming out with a pack of smokes. He waved it in front of Datu's frightened eyes.

"*Ni yao ji ge?*" Li yelled, pulling one, then one more, then another, tossing the cigarettes into the sea. Rizal moved toward the two of them slowly. Li whirled round and pointed a finger at Rizal's chest. "*Ni, zoukai!*" he commanded, pointing to the bow. The same finger found Arvin and Amado, ordering them all to the front of the boat. They obeyed, eyes locked on the pair at the rail. Datu's hands found the railing. He tried to get to his feet, but Li was on him again, pushing him back down. "*Ni yao ji ge?*" he questioned again. "*Yi? Er? San?*" With each count he tossed another cigarette into the water. "*Ni yao wo gei ni quanbu, dui bu dui?*" he questioned, waving the remnants of the pack before it also went into the sea. Datu shook his head, soaked with salt spray running down his face.

"Sorry, boss," Datu stuttered, "sorry. No cigarette. Back to work. Back to work, okay?" he pleaded. Li's face softened. His grip on the man's soft shoulders relaxed, then let go. He stepped back from the railing. Then with a stride forward his open palms found Datu's shoulders again and sent him toppling headlong and backward into the black water. Datu disappeared beneath a swell. The crew rushed to the rail, Li staying back, arms folding across his chest. The crew called out to Datu, searching frantically for a sign.

Datu's head broke the surface with a desperate violence, lungs taking in equal measure of breath and water. He choked and sputtered, hands slapping wildly at the uneven surface. "*Tulong!*" he called out, fear and instinct reverting him to his native tongue. His head sunk below the surface, arms pulling him back above only to take in yet more water. He retched into the sea, coughing, struggling to breathe. "Help me!" he cried out before going under a third time. Rizal's eyes whipped around the deck, locking on the white life preserver and rope coiled around a wooden peg on the side of the wheelhouse. He went to retrieve it. Captain Li stepped to block his path.

"*Buxing!*" Li commanded. Rizal froze, eyes moving between the preserver and Datu beyond the rail, struggling for his life. A wave crashed over his head and he was swallowed again, coming up slower this time. Arvin and Amado kept their watch on the sea. The boat was drifting from Datu. The night conspired with the wind and the waves to make a ghost of him, his cries for help the only sign a man was out there at all. The lights of other boats blinked somewhere in the void of black and silent space, distant as satellites. Arvin heard the crackle of the radio in the wheelhouse and considered making a move, but Li beat him to it, striding to the wheelhouse wall, turning around to face them when he reached the life preserver. He patted it fondly, calling out to the man in the water, tired arms still heard slapping in slow motion, clawing at something formless and uncaring.

"*Ni yao zheige ma?*" the captain called out, cupping a hand to his mouth. He patted the preserver again.

"Please!" Datu yelled from somewhere out in the darkness, choking and coughing. Li laughed. He pulled another pack of cigarettes from his pants pocket and took his time lighting up. He exhaled smugly. Then he took up the preserver and walked to the railing. Handing the preserver to Amado, Li pointed to the fallen crewman, arm rising listlessly then falling to his side like a dead thing, then walked away. Rizal moved quickly to help shine one of the lamp lights out into the darkness, finding their lost man. Amado tossed the preserver, leading out the line as Datu flailed toward the float and grabbed on. Together the other three pulled Datu in, the frayed yellow rope dripping as it came aboard. Then Datu was at the hull, his shaky arms reaching for theirs. Straining, they pulled him up. Datu collapsed over the railing with a thud, gasping and vomiting. They all sat there panting under the eyes of the captain. There he was at the wheelhouse wall, enjoying a cigarette pulled from a fresh pack. He blew another cloud of smoke and tossed the butt over the side, orange sparks dying mid-flight. Then he went into the wheelhouse and pushed the throttle. Rizal's head was swimming, dizzy with thirst and hunger as he stumbled across the deck to flop down beside Datu, backs pressed against the gunwale. There they sat in silence for a time until Li came out of the wheelhouse and ordered them back to work, this time using files to sharpen the spare hooks left on the racks. Tired hands worked through the night, sharpening hooks, then bringing the trailing line back aboard, until slim rays of light reached up over the edge of the sea. The journey back to harbor, cast in the pall of a fruitless catch, was serenaded by the squalling of birds, marked by the taste of salt and blood, thick on cracked and quivering lips.

Chapter Nine

A month passed, each day straggling by more or less within the prison of the same routine. Going to sea at sunset. Working through the endless baiting of hooks. Attaching the branch lines. Setting the main line to trail, hauling in the line, tossing back the dead and dying incidental catch, throwing those that held value into the freezer. Since the first night they had not seen another tuna. Li's mood grew ever sinister with each line they brought in that had not hooked his prized catch. Once his crewmen seemed to master their tasks he ceased working with them altogether; he just manned the wheel, taking them out to sea, trawling to set the line, moving them on. He watched his crew and smoked, cursing the men between puffs with the endless chastisements so familiar after thirty days that the men could recite them in a flawless imitation.

Gan ni niang! Kuai yi dian! Kuai yi dian!

Fuck your mother! Faster! Faster!

Each morning they crawled back to the harbor, freezer meagerly stocked, the captain's temper on edge. Then they would unload the catch under the watch of the other captains and crew and vendors and customers at the market. When the unloading of the waterlogged white containers was done, *chuanzhang* would drive them the short distance back to the boat. There they were expected to rest under the blazing sun or pouring rain. Hours after they returned to harbor the captain would come back to the boat, tossing a few packets of instant noodles or potato chips down onto the deck, a bottle or two of water to share between them, a roll of toilet paper. As it was on the first day, the food was often expired and went down with difficulty. Bouts of sickness and intestinal distress took them, the only place to relieve themselves into their own water bottles or over the side of the boat. They dared not leave the boat, not even to go in search of a place where they might get the scrubbing they so sorely needed or to find a proper bathroom. None had money even for a bottle of something to drink or a morsel of food. The crews of the other vessels seemed to keep to themselves, faces darkened by their own set of problems, black rings below the eyes belying a deep soul sadness and cold that seeped into their character and shrunk the senses to those of survival itself. The smell of rot on board the vessel became their own. The men took turns sleeping curled on the wheelhouse floor to block out the elements, the hour or so of rest there the only true sleep they might know from one day to the next.

The remaining hours had in them only the numb frustration of half sleep, a bitter longing for comfort that never came. Hunger stopped any discussion of mutiny short of a few angry words, their weakness staving the instinct for reprisal against the captain's cruelty. Fear of being deported did the rest. Like those back home in the cemetery, Rizal thought, they were being made by some unseen force to endure, and so endure they would.

We are the nameless dead now.

Some nights, though, they did not go out fishing. Instead, the captain would show up with a truckload of barrels, the scent of fuel heavy on them though they were tightly sealed. The crew loaded the barrels onto the boat, backs bent and aching with the cylinders' awkward, shifting bulk. On those nights they would go out farther than they did when fish were their quarry. Rizal, Datu, Arvin, Amado — none of them knew what was happening the first time they transported the mysterious cargo, only that they were passing hour after endless hour in darkness, watching that the barrels, tied together in a squared mass on deck, wouldn't tip whenever a wave swayed the boat far to one side or the other.

Long after sundown, somewhere out on the open sea, the captain would cut the engine, douse the lights, and wait. With a finger to his lips he told his crew to keep their mouths shut. Then they waited, mindful of their breaths lest a thoughtless yawn or cough raise the captain's ire or the alarm of whomever he was trying to avoid. Finally, they would hear it. The sound of a boat rumbling toward them, the chug of the distant engine drawing slowly near. When the sound was such that it seemed the boat must be nearly alongside them, Li whistled, the piercing sound drawing a similar reply. Only then did he flash the lights on again, revealing their counterpart — a larger vessel flying a flag different than their own. The boats drew up broadside and Rizal and the rest of the crew worked to pass the barrels over to crewmen on the other side. Following the mimed orders of the captain, they worked in silence.

When the job was done the captain of the other boat

hastily counted off a few bills that were taken by Li and recounted just as quickly. Then the two men nodded gruffly to one another, no more than a few whispered words passing between them. With that they parted ways. All that remained was the long, slow burn back to port. Though Rizal had little experience with the sea or the outside world, he knew what they had done. He didn't need to say it, nor did anyone else. They weren't just fishermen doing an honest night's work. They were also smugglers.

Mostly Rizal tried not to think. But during the long, hot days, there was little to keep the chatter of his mind quiet. Many times he found himself wondering about his mother and Kidlat, his infant daughter, thinking about what they were doing, how they were getting on without him. He asked himself if there would be any difference in their lives without him there, thirst and hunger asking dark questions a full stomach never would. He pushed the questions aside, speaking of such things only in the most general way as day by day he and the rest of the crew became witness to their own decline.

But they had survived a month. The hours spent writhing on the hard planks, leaning up against the gunwales, languishing in the comparative luxury of the wheelhouse, seemed to go by faster and with less pain than those before. One month of hooks biting through the flesh of their fingertips, of nostrils filled with fish stink and rotting blood and the freezer ice with its sour, burning smell. Black diesel smoke that soaked into their hair and coalesced beneath their fingernails. Thirty days and nights of suffering now erased by the prospect of that first month's pay. Datu in particular was held in money's fever grip. He paced the deck, prodding the others gleefully with questions.

"Will it be cash or a check? *Pakshet*, I can't remember how it feels to find a bit of cash in my pocket. How will we send the money to our families? Do you think we should ask *chuanzhang*? It will probably piss him off. You should ask him, Rizal. You're the captain's little *puta*, after all," he said in jest. The others laughed, hunger and exhaustion cutting even momentary happiness to a fraction of its former worth. They yelled out in unison, "*Gan ni niang! Kuai yi dian! Kuai yi dian*," and laughed harder.

"I don't care how he pays us, so long as that *peste* pays us," said Rizal, Arvin and Amado nodding. They sat upright, opposite Rizal, backs pressed against the gunwale. Their eyes followed Datu as he paced one end of the tub to the other. "*Leche*, Datu, sit down before you wear a hole in the deck and sink us," Rizal chided.

"You're too fat to work on a boat," Amado piled on. "Don't you know the captain hired you for bait?"

Datu waved their jibes away. "Say what you want. I don't care if my belly is big. Just give me a paycheck to match." He stopped beside Rizal and finally sat down, flopping hard onto his buttocks. The boat shifted to his side with a splash, drawing a high-pitched giggle from Arvin, who quickly covered his mouth with a grimy hand. They sat and waited, minds locked in anticipation, for the first time longing for the sun to set and the captain to arrive. Rizal imagined how it would play out. The stack of checks or cash in Li's hand, counting out the bills or passing out the crisp, clean pieces of paper. He stretched and smiled, taking notice they had forgotten their turns in the wheelhouse.

"You *tarantados* are obviously too excited to sleep," Rizal mocked. "You spend all day stroking your *burats*, thinking about money. I'm going to get some sleep."

An empty water bottle found the back of his calf as Rizal made his way into the wheelhouse. He ignored it and lay down, putting his head on the soft toe of a molding sneaker below the wheel. He shut his eyes, straining against the ache of his contorted body and the sweat itch clinging to his skin for a few moments of sleep. Mostly he scratched and twisted and turned, at every motion something digging into a new part of his body. An hour went by before he gave up and went to rejoin the others. The sun was low over the mountains, the sentinel rocks partially obscured by the oncoming darkness. Rizal took up his place beside Datu. None of the others moved to take their own turn in the wheelhouse, its appeal diminishing with the waning sunlight. Soon they heard the high buzz of the blue truck downshifting to a swift stop. The captain emerged from the cab and Rizal saw a third man sliding over toward the passenger door. The man got out and they saw it was Mr. Chen, clad in a crisp white dress shirt tucked into a pair of black dress pants and leather monk straps on his feet. The long late hours of sunlight glinted off a silver wedding band and a bracelet of jade beads, deep green, wrapped around his wrist. A thin gold chain hung from his neck.

The driver then sped off to the opposite end of the harbor, getting out and hopping aboard another boat. Meanwhile the captain pulled four envelopes from the pocket of his overalls and flipped through them, head down as he walked toward the crew. They rose to greet him, Arvin and Amado crossing their hands humbly behind their backs. Li jumped down nimbly to the deck and handed an envelope to each of them. "Money," he said in English, smiling, a word each of them could understand. Li's fingers tore at an invisible seal, prompting the men, and the crew ripped their envelopes open. Chen remained on the road above, watching. Rizal had his envelope open first. Inside he found a stack of red notes. He pulled them out, studying the unknown face, a Chinese man with a receding hairline and light, thin mustache, then the number, one hundred. He counted off the bills, sixteen of them, sliding them crisply from one hand to the other, smiling. He looked to the others. Arvin and Amado too were grinning. Only Datu wore a frown. He held not the notes but a white piece of paper. The last rays of the daylight hours shone through it, and Rizal could see a list of sums on the other side along with some words. Carefully he slid his cash into his pocket and took a white piece of paper from his own envelope, unfolding it to reveal a similar list. He stared at it, only the numbers intelligible to him. The words beside them were written in English. Arvin and Amado stopped smiling and looked at their lists. They stared in silence. Then, one by one, their eyes settled on Chen.

"The cash is your pay for this month," said Chen, "minus expenses, of course." Cautiously he came down onto the deck, bracing a hand on the wall where the elder Li had jumped down. Chen stood beside Rizal, taking his itemized list from him. The rest crowded around.

"You see this number?" he pointed to the first figure on the sheet. It read NT$17,598. "This is your base salary. That is to say your pay for one month. You understand?"

Datu translated for the rest as best he could and the men nodded. Chen went through the rest of the numbers one by one, Datu interpreting.

"This is the amount you pay back each month for the loan from Mr. Benjie. This will be deducted each month until the full amount is repaid."

"This is the room and board fee. You pay each month."

"This is the visa processing fee. One-time payment."

"This is the alien resident certificate processing fee. One-time payment. I keep the certificate for you, with your passport, for safekeeping."

"This is your health-check fee. Also you pay only once."

Health check? thought Rizal.

"This, this is the service fee. Paid to me for the help I provide you. You pay every month."

"This is health insurance. You pay every month in case you visit the doctor."

"This is employment insurance. E.I. You lose job, you get money. You pay this every month."

"This is the fee for your national ID card. One-time fee. I hold cards for you."

Chen stopped. Rizal's head spun. From the shell-shocked expressions of the rest he knew the feeling was mutual. Chen's finger pointed to the last number.

"This is what is left, 1,600 New Taiwan dollars, cash. But don't worry, next month will be more. No more one-time fees. More money for you, okay?"

"Sixteen hundred," Amado said quietly. He asked Datu in Tagalog, "How much in pesos?"

Datu did some quick figuring. "About two thousand."

Their heads sunk. Rizal felt a hand clap him lightly on the shoulder. Chen spoke again.

"Ah, don't feel bad. I know it's not much, but it gets better. Keep working. You're here to work, right? A man works hard, he makes big money. It just takes time. You'll see." With that Chen handed Rizal's pay stub back to him. Rizal took it, a "thank you" emerging from his mouth, though he didn't know why.

The eyes of the rest of the crew remained locked on the figures on their pieces of paper as Chen hoisted himself up onto the top of the wall. He walked toward the blue truck at the opposite end of the harbor, not bothering to say goodbye. Rizal thought about the money in his pocket. Two thousand pesos for a month's work. Less than he could make digging graves and keeping clean his small clutch of apartment tombs in the cemetery. Questions arose.

"Didn't sir Benjie tell us room and board were included? What did he tell you?" he asked them. Arvin shrugged his shoulders.

"The contract was in English. I don't remember what it said."

"He only gave me the last page to sign," said Datu. "He told me not to worry. Just to hurry up and sign or he would give it to someone who wouldn't ask so many questions."

"Did any of you get a health check?" asked Rizal. His question went unanswered.

Amado stood, shaking his head as Li fired up the engine behind them. "My father told me this would happen," he said bitterly.

"Told you what?" asked Datu.

"He told me they would cheat a *migrante* any chance they got."

Chapter Ten

NEXT month, the pay was the same; fees expertly arranged so as to keep the amount owed to the crew down in the dog-scratched dirt. It was the same the month after that. Nobody complained. Nobody said much of anything. The crew's world was a world of quiet. A place of silent survival. Fear. It was always there. Fear of being sent back home. Of having their rations cut. Of what might happen if they did decide to fight back. Fear that if they stood up against the captain, Li would force them to kill him.

"So what?" said Amado when the question arose again whether they should stand against *chuanzang*. "We kill him, we get caught, we go to jail. We'll probably be fed better in there than out here."

Rizal and Arvin nodded.

"They have the death penalty here," said Datu, words deadened by hunger. "What do you think will happen to four brown men who murder a Taiwanese captain?"

Silence fell over the boat. The subject of mutiny was never raised again.

Rizal kept the sixteen one-hundred dollar notes he received each payday in his pants pocket. There the notes soaked and moldered during the night, drying out brittle each day as they baked in the summer heat.

The heat brought with it the storms. Near the end of the second month a typhoon struck. The harbor filled with boats, more than Rizal and the others had ever seen docked at Su'ao. Crews speaking a language Rizal didn't understand worked quickly to lash their watercraft to the wall and to the other vessels side by side. Li too had his men working double time to secure their ship. As he secured lines and drove nails into the hatch door to lock it in place, Rizal remembered the times before a typhoon back home. The night before a storm the only sound heard above the gale force of the approaching winds was that of the concrete seals of the tombs shattering on the ground as they fell loose. When the swirls died down the syncopated gusts might carry with them a truncated portion of the Lord's Prayer. As the howls grew worse the people of Navotas scrambled for what shelter they could find, bunking with a corpse being preferable to chancing the flood brought by the encroaching waves and the endless sheets of rain. A half-remembered part of a prayer was better than no prayer at all when the water foamed, hissed, and smoked over the embankment, bringing the bay inland.

When the typhoons came, Rizal and his mother would venture to the upper level of the mausoleum. There, as a boy, when a tropical storm struck, Rizal would huddle with Mama, up on the cramped second floor, shuttering his eyes tight so he didn't have to see the urns. Only when he felt Mama scoop him up in her arms and take him back down would he open his eyes again. After the storm his mother would go out in spite of his cries, leaving him there alone. When he was older he found out why. The survivors were left to clean up in the hours following the storm's grim wake, collecting the bodies that hadn't been washed away, finding them limp and gray on the tops of the tombs, contorted among the snapped limbs of the tall trees. Whenever a typhoon came there was a part of Rizal that wished it would be his turn. His time to be taken away by the wind and waves.

When the typhoon hit the harbor, Rizal and the rest of the crew squeezed themselves into the wheelhouse, huddled on the floor with knees tucked under their chins. Li had left them with the boat. "Watch," he said as he took off for home, instructing them to keep an eye on things. "Tomorrow," he said, waving at the fast-moving clouds above, "no more."

The storm lasted two days, passing the harbor by then circling back for another pass as though angered by its obstinate will to survive. For endless hours winds rocked Li's boat from side to side, bashing it against the tires lining the wall. The deck filled with water that ran into the wheelhouse and soaked the men to their core, eyes squinting against the stinging rain. Then there was the sound of it. A roar as though all of creation had evolved into a single, terrible beast made to breathe wind and rain down on the small seaside town; a monster that knew only death, destruction, and chaos. Rizal kept his eyes closed as he waited out the storm, taking his turn to move shakily to the deck to bail water over the sides when they were engulfed by a wave passing under the clutch of boats tied together like a chain gang. The other boats were empty, crewmen safe with their families or shut away from the deadly elements in dormitory bunk rooms in town. Only four men – Rizal, Datu, Arvin, and Amado – were left to face the storm outdoors.

When he could bring himself to open his eyes or when his turn came to go out onto the deck, Rizal looked to the mountain forest and saw the trees bend and break, branches whipped up, down, left, right, like the limbs of string puppets pulled by a demented master. Toward the end of the second day the broken branches littered the harbor roads, and in places they were slick with mud. And finally, some hours after sunset on the second day, the typhoon was gone. Rizal and his crewmates emerged together from the wheelhouse to survey the damage. The deck had been chipped by flying debris, hull superficially cracked by its many blows against the tires and the weight pressed against it by the boats behind in the harbor. In absence of their captain, the crew did what they could to straighten up and do some basic repair work. When the captain returned, they knew, they would have their orders.

The blast furnace of heat waned in strength a little with the approach of fall, most days a match of the one before. Rizal felt his mind go numb and welcomed it, hoping his bones and muscles would harden and do the same. Every part of him was sore and tired, body hungry, thirsting. The waist of his pants loosened around his thinning frame, and he took to tying a found piece of fishing line pulled from the harbor water around his hips to save him from having to pull them up every few minutes. He learned what it was to be a man who took orders well and without question; to hear and obey the captain's thundered instructions without so much as a change of expression. To go about life blankly, a page for others to write on or fold in half or throw away. Whatever they wished. He became a man with neither desire nor hope.

His clothes were covered in salt stains, the casing of the I.O.V. tape still in his pocket cracked, damaged during the scuffle when Datu went over the side or sometime during the storm. During the long days he would pull the tape out, freeing the J-card from the casing, looking at the fading pictures within. He daydreamed that he was there at the shows he had never been to, pictured there in the insert in grainy black and white, pretending he was in the crowd, hearing the music. Everything conspired to pull him back to reality, under that blazing sun, back sore against the flat wooden planks, skin and clothes peeling white flecks of paint from their surface.

The days were mostly nameless and numberless to Rizal, Datu, Arvin, and Amado. The only one that held any meaning was payday. The day when, for a few brief moments, they could do something other than bait hooks and tie lines or rip barbs from cartilaginous ring mouths. They did their damnedest not to want or hope for the day; to try as they might to greet it as an unexpected surprise. But they knew, down to the minute, how far they were from seeing their money, paid out as always in cash – in red one hundred New Taiwan dollar bills. Rizal remembered his promise to his mother. How he would return with enough to get them out of the graveyard. He felt the small collection of folded notes in his damp pocket and breathed the stale, diesel-heavy air of the harbor, awaiting the captain's return so they could go out and do it all over again.

As he waited, Rizal tried to figure the number of days

remaining. How many dark journeys out toward the hidden edge of death until three years were up and he would be free? He tried to count in his mind, the haze of hunger sending him back to the start one try after another. He gave up and went back to waiting, trying to blank his mind, swirling with thoughts. He rose, paced, pulled himself up onto the wall's edge and jumped down again. Stretched and patted his fingers against the planks. Ran his hand along the railing. Kicked at plastic bottles and tossed them up into the air to catch them. Curled up in the wheelhouse. Rose again. Climbed on the bow and looked out to sea far beyond the breakwater. He thought of jumping into the water. Letting himself sink down into the cool calmness beneath the garbage floating on the surface. His vision blurred in and out of focus. He looked back toward town, the main street traversed just once before they were escorted back to the one place they were allowed to be. He wished he were anywhere else. A place he could be free from that small, stinking space, their private prison on the gently heaving harbor lined with its ring of familiar trash. A few days after the storm, the boat gleaming in another fresh coat of whitewash, they had rested only an hour or two when the captain returned. The blue truck was replaced by a black sedan, gleaming and spotless, red ribbons running from the hood, up the windshield, down the rear pane and hooked into the trunk. The crew gaped as Li stepped out of the back seat. Dressed in an old, ill-fitting suit, basic black with a white dress shirt, navy blue tie, he held a hand out to someone still in the car. The hand he took was thin, feminine, nails painted bright red. A woman got out. She was stuffed into a white three-quarter dress cinched tight under her armpits. To Rizal's eyes she did not look Taiwanese. Her features, he thought, were closer to his own. Her skin lighter, though, eyes more slender in their taper toward her thin nose. Li helped her out gently. Chen came around the other side of the car, a uniformed driver standing dutifully by his own door, leaving the engine idling. The girl's eyes were downcast. She tittered nervously as the captain spoke words to her that were lost in the noise of the engine. Chen approached the crew, dressed much like the captain in a dark three-piece suit, bright corsage stuck to his breast with a faux-diamond stick pin. In his hands, he carried a red cardboard box with gold lettering across the lid. He reached the harbor ledge, handing the box down to Datu. Datu stared at it, then handed it off to the cousins. They eyed it curiously as Chen explained.

"Wedding cookies," said Chen, pointing to the box. "Today you will have a day off," he smiled broadly, hands in his pants pockets. "The captain is getting married."

The crew studied the woman. She was at least twenty years younger than her husband-to-be, perhaps more. Chen looked at her, clucking his tongue as he turned back to the crew.

"*Chuanzhang* Li paid a big price for this one. Vietnamese bride. Not cheap." He shook his head. "Very beautiful. And they will cook and clean. No complaining. Not like Taiwanese girls," he laughed. Li beamed, fingers clasped tightly around those of his bride-to-be. "*Chaunzhang* Li wanted to show you his new bride. He asked me to tell you to please enjoy a day off. Take a good rest. Tomorrow, back to work. Okay?"

Again Datu acted as translator. The men nodded their understanding.

"Okay...." Chen pulled his hands out of his pockets. He opened his mouth as if to say more. Instead he shrugged and sighed, then turned around, nodding to the captain. Li guided the woman into the back seat and joined her, the driver moving to close the door for them. Chen got in. The driver closed the door for him too. Then the car sped off, leaving the still bewildered crew behind. They looked to the road, watched as Li's car went to the right, past the temple. A column of identical black sedans followed, each with its own red ribbon trailing in the breeze. Rizal looked to the others, scratching his head. He itched constantly now, unsure if he had become infested with lice or if it was merely for lack of washing. He began to speak but was interrupted by a nagging bite at the back of his throat. He coughed into the back of his hand and started again.

"He paid for the woman? Like a *puta*?"

Datu cuffed him on the back of the head, Arvin and Amado laughing. "Watch your words, *anak*," said Datu. "That's your future queen you're talking about."

Rizal smiled out of the corner of his mouth. He rubbed the patchy stubble of his cheek against his knuckles, imagining what Mama would say if she saw him looking so much like the *maganang kumain*. He shook his head. Arvin opened the box of cookies and they studied the small packets before Datu hazarded the first taste, affirming they were edible with a brisk nod. They divided the cookies evenly, eating in silence for a time before Rizal brought up the topic of the captain's bride again.

"I don't understand. If she's not a *puta*, why does he pay for her?"

Datu chuckled. "It's simple, *anak*. He is from Taiwan. She is from Vietnam. He has money. She is poor. He pays her family. They give him a wife. A mother to his children." He sped up as the list went on. "A cook. A cleaner. A servant. A lover. It's the way it works. If you have money, you can buy anything. Everything has its price."

"Even people?" Rizal questioned.

Datu nodded. "Look at us, *anak*. You think we weren't bought and sold, same as her?"

Arvin and Amado nodded. Rizal contemplated Datu's words, thinking of the loan he was repaying, the way the number went down each month but not as much as it should, not all the way, according to what he was paying back. He had not been to school long, but he was not simple. It was something Mr. Chen called "interest" – a concept he still did not fully understand, though he tried. He worked his way through Chen's explanation again in his head before deciding he would rather think about something else.

"So," Rizal shrugged, "a day off. What do you *kupals* want to do?"

Amado's eyes scanned their surroundings. The boat. The harbor. The open sea.

"*Leche*, what is there to do? We're stuck here. You might as well get used to it, *anak*. As long as we're here, all you'll see is the boat and the sea," he pointed. "Like Mr. Chen said, we're here to work. That's all."

Datu raised his chin, looking at the others through narrowed eyes. "I know a place," he said slowly.

"What place?" Arvin shot back.

"A place I heard of before, back home," Datu answered. "A place to have some fun."

Rizal looked around again. "I don't think there's any place like that around here."

"You're right, *anak*. It's not around here."

"Then where?" asked Amado."

Datu reached down into his pocket, pulling out his own stack of hundreds. He flicked through the notes, raising his eyebrows as he looked to the others. He kept a few notes in his hand, returning the rest to where they came from.

"Would you *tarantados* be up for a train ride?"

* * *

"*Ni shuo shenme?*"

The clerk spoke through dented metal slats spotted with rust. Datu tried again.

"Zhong-li," he said slowly. The woman studied her paper chart of destinations, eyes scanning the list of fares and cities and towns, muttering and shaking her head. The blunted end of her pencil moved down the list, stopped and tapped on a name.

"*Taoyuan de Zhongli?*" she asked irritably. Datu nodded, rushing a bite of sweet pineapple cake from his stash of wedding cookies, worried that it had obscured his words beyond understanding. It had been a long walk to the station in the center of town, a mile or more from Nanfang'ao along a winding divided four-lane highway, lined by small square gardens dug into the spare earth next to the road's western edge, nestled against the hillside, and to the east by the sea. It was a walk filled with many misunderstandings once they reached Central Su'ao to the north of the twin harbors, where the four of them tried to find their way, asking for directions as they went. When they came to a bridge passing over a shallow creek with its green grass banks and shallow, rocky bed, a fortyish man in hip waders and a raggedy tank top, cigarette hanging from the corner of his mouth, seemed to understand the words "train" and "station" as Datu spoke them slowly, and pointed past an arcade, down the road past a sign reading "Taiping Mountain," bidding them in that direction. And there, after a few more minutes of walking on tender feet, they found the place they were after. Now at the station the female clerk looked past Datu to the three dark-skinned men standing sheepishly behind, one of them constantly looking down at his feet. She looked too, and saw that he was barefoot. "*Si ge ren?*" she questioned, holding up four fingers, crinkling her nose at the sight of the man's scrunched up toes. The man curled them under as though trying to hide their nakedness. Datu nodded again. She spit the price at him, pushing a calculator up to the pane of glass to show him the amount owed. Datu turned and collected the money from the other three, they pulling loose bills from pockets also stuffed with a few packets of cookies they had taken for the trip, and slid the cash under the pane on a maroon plastic tray. It came back with four tickets and a few silver coins. The clerk pointed to the entrance and the old uniformed guard watching the turnstile. Datu thanked her in English, turning to the others to hand out the tickets. They studied them, eyeing the departure time, then the digital clock mounted above the entrance to the twin platforms, one for trains headed north, the other for southbound.

"Tell me again, where are we going?" Rizal asked, looking blankly at his ticket.

Datu moved toward the ticket officer like he was walking through his own neighborhood LRT station. "I told you, we're going to Zhongli."

The others followed, nodding and smiling to the stern-faced officer as they handed their tickets over to be punched. The officer pointed a crooked finger toward the far platform. They found the stairs to the subterranean walkway beneath the southbound tracks, feet flying all the way down.

Rizal asked, "And what's in Zhongli?"

Datu kept moving. "You'll see, *anak*. Don't worry."

They emerged from the underpass onto the covered northbound platform, a few other passengers sitting on wooden benches or leaning against round concrete pillars. Datu bounded up to a kiosk selling snacks and other odds and ends and bought a stick of deodorant. He looked around, searching for the others, finding them at the end of the slab elevated above the rust-tinged rails. He walked to them, tossing the stick to Arvin, telling him to put some on, staring at the same sets of clothing he had seen them all wear every day for the past three months, scrubbed with seawater earlier that morning and left to dry in the sun.

"We'll see what we can do about the clothes when we get there," Datu said with a cringe.

They stood and waited, shuffling from foot to foot. A straggly cat tiptoed across the tracks, tensing as a rat tail disappeared down a gap in the pilings. More passengers arrived on the platform, sticking to the opposite end. The others pelted Datu with more questions.

"How long will it take to get there?"

"Will we stay overnight?"

"Where will we stay?"

"How will we get back in time for work tomorrow?"

Datu held up a hand, chuckling. "*Leche!* Don't worry," he said, "If what my cousin told me is true, it's not that far. A few hours, maybe. We'll just go and see what happens. As long as we leave early tomorrow morning we'll be back before the captain even knows we're gone."

Rizal, Arvin, and Amado looked to one another, finding little reassurance in the others' shifting eyes and nervous smiles. They paced the platform on tired legs until the nearby wooden bench called. They sat for a few minutes. The blast of a horn pulled them back up. They walked to the yellow-painted edge of the platform, stepping back when the whistle of the station agent sounded a shrill call. A train painted orange and a color like beige lurched into the station, settled, and hissed, doors sliding open. Datu again studied his ticket and pointed a few cars away from the rear. "That one," he said, "number three." He moved off, the others trailing. They followed him to the car's entrance and with some hesitation moved up the tall step to the gangway, then through another hissing automatic door into the car itself. Eyes that weren't shut up in dead man's sleep were on them as they followed Datu down the rows, three seats on either side of the narrow aisle.

Rizal heard Amado whisper to Arvin, "Have you been on a train before?"

"Not on the inside," came the quiet reply.

Datu stopped at a row near the back of the car and pointed to three seats on one side of the aisle, waving at the others to take them. He flopped down with a creak in the seat across the aisle from them. A scowl spread across the face of the old woman behind him as Datu's headrest careened toward her, a box of guavas resting on her lap like a prized pet. Datu raised up his arms and clasped his fingers behind his head.

"Just sit back and enjoy the ride."

Rizal took the window seat. As the train lurched forward he watched the yard pass by, then the brick walls of the houses backing onto the tracks near the station. Having slept much of the way to Su'ao in the back of the van, he was determined to remain awake this time to see the country he had been living in for a quarter of a year yet seen so little of. The lopsided brick flower troughs and walls were soon replaced by a green blur of bamboo, elephant ear ferns, and acacia and paper bark trees. He felt his ears pop as the car seemed to compress around him and then went suddenly dark, dim track lighting running along the slim overhead luggage rack and the aisle at his feet casting the passengers in a dull glow. White lines of lights whizzed past outside the window, and Rizal realized they had entered a long tunnel, passing through a section of crag along the coast. He turned back to see the reactions of the other passengers. Most were asleep, heads lolled back, mouths open. Already a thin, clear line of drool ran down Arvin's cheek from the corner of his mouth. Rizal shook his head and laughed quietly. He stared out the window again as the train shot out of the tunnel, back into the bright, gleaming light of the late summer day that shone off the rippling waves. He watched the trees and the mountains and the sea pass by, until he too was taken by the dead man's sleep.

Chapter Eleven

THEY walked out of Zhongli Station, and were suddenly home. The steps leading up to the station were filled with faces like their own. Men and women laughing, smiling, talking in Tagalog. Rizal and the rest moved among them, stunned. The train had taken them from the remote east of the island, up and around Taiwan's northern coastline, then south along the western plain into the vast urban crush of Taoyuan County. Somehow, it had transported them back to their native land. Datu beamed. His cousin had been right. Here was a place, at least on Sundays, that the Filipino people could call their own. There were others too: Vietnamese, Indonesians, Thais – all milled about in their own groups. Men sipped on tall cans of beer, cups of iced coffee or tea. Women fanned at their faces, beating away the heat. It was late Sunday afternoon, and for a few hours, they were all free.

Taiwanese squeezed through the throngs of foreigners, suddenly a minority in their own town. Rizal looked at the line of yellow taxis in front of the station, drivers leaning back against the passenger doors talking to one another, pointing at this girl or that, saying something that brought a laugh or a nod from the others. None seemed in much of a hurry to find the next fare, and none showed worry that the foreigners might understand what was being said about them. As for the ones far from home, no one seemed in much of a hurry to do anything other than stand and sip and get out as many words in their own language as they could; words bottled up over the past days, weeks, and months. Only a few were stunned enough to be speechless. Rizal, Arvin, and Amado were among them. Datu, though, was back in his finest pool hall element. He slapped a hand against unfamiliar backs, pumping the crowd for information.

"Hey, *kabigan*, where's a friendly place to get a beer around here?"

A man pointed to an underpass leading below the tracks to the backstreets behind the station. Datu crooked his head in that direction and the men followed him to the tunnel. Once inside, the underground echo chamber hummed with energy. It beamed with the brightness of wide eyes and the flashing of smiles. Rizal's native tongue was almost foreign to him after hearing the same few words blasting from the same mouth the past few months. Throughout the tunnel, people rested their backs against the concave sides, leaning and talking, feet splayed along the walkway. Stairs led up to the street on the other side and the men emerged to a line of bars, restaurants, and shops, with signs in Tagalog, Bahasa, Thai, Vietnamese.... Datu pointed at a clothing shop and sauntered across the street. The narrow sidewalk was all but blocked by carousels of T-shirts, shorts, and pants that found space among the lines of scooters and bicycles. Datu began flipping through a rack. The others joined him.

"It's about time we updated our look, eh?" Datu said, pulling out a knock-off Polo shirt and holding it up to his shrunken belly. His lips curled into a contemplative frown. "What do you think?" he asked Rizal.

Rizal looked up from the counterfeit Levis he was eyeing. The cardboard sign atop the carousel read two for three hundred. "*Guwapo*," he told Datu, giving him a thumbs up. Datu put the shirt over his forearm and continued browsing. Arvin already had two shirts and a pair of khakis over his arm. Amado had nothing.

"Hey," Datu jutted his chin at him, "you're not going to walk into the bar wearing those rags. You at least need some shoes."

Amado shrugged. "More money for beer," he said, stepping out from under the overhang into the sunlight, raising his face to meet the sky. Datu shook his head, looking for something in the stubborn man's size.

The others made their buys and changed behind the sheets hung from the shop ceiling like shower curtains. Rizal wished he could shower. For the time being a change of clothes and some deodorant under his arms was enough to make him feel like a new man. He walked out with a new set of clothing on, another in a plastic bag. Arvin and Datu did the same. Amado chose to remain just as he was, Datu barely managing to convince him to put on the cheap pair of cloth size sevens he bought for him, the sense of shame he felt at the train station evaporating now that he was back among his own people. They walked on, Datu's eyes searching the overhead signs leaning out over the road. Sausages sizzled on BBQ carts. Clay ovens on wheels were filled with baking sweet potatoes. The heady mix of aromas had the men salivating, bellies aching for a bite of food – real food. They came to an intersection and turned right. Datu's finger pointed to a sign, reading the name for them.

"Here we are, *batang lalaki.* Manila North."

The shop window was lit up with an outline of red, green, and clear Christmas lights, and rimmed with a strand of gold garland. A chalkboard outside the door listed the beer and drink specials. Rizal didn't need to know how to read to recognize the Red Horse beer logo. Instinctively his mouth began to water. Though money was always tight back home he could usually scrounge enough plastic, metal, and glass from the nearby *estero* running from the city into the bay to sell to a junk shop for some beer money – cash his mother didn't know about and thus couldn't scrutinize the way he chose to spend it. Datu pushed open the door, and the jingling bell above signaled their arrival in the darkened interior. Pinoy pop blared over a karaoke system, a teetering middle-aged man warbling through a Regine Velasquez ballad. A waitress greeted them, her forehead beaded with sweat, black hair pulled back in a ponytail. She smiled as she said "Four of you?" grabbing four menus as she asked, then leading them to a corner table near the kitchen. Through the swinging doors they could hear the hiss of fire and steam, the shouts of pinoy cooks calling out orders before the doors swung closed again. Datu's eyes widened as he sat and took up a menu. He read it out for the rest.

"*Lumpia ... pancit palabok ... pork adobo ... chicharrón ... pork sisig ... bibingka....*"

"*Halo-halo?*" asked Amado. Datu nodded. Amado looked to the other tables and saw the plastic crates on the floor filled with empty bottles of Red Horse. "To hell with the *halo-halo*," he said, licking his lips, "let's get some beer."

Datu motioned for the waitress. She came over. Forgetting the beer, if only for a moment, he ordered food first, drawing out the name of each dish, reveling in the sound of old favorites that were as much a part of home as the eighteen-wheelers that shook the Zabarte Road shanty where he was born and raised. The waitress took his selections down, face a blank sheet. As she moved away Datu reached out and touched her elbow. She stopped and looked back with vague annoyance.

"And, miss," said Datu, pointing at a nearby crate of empties, "six large bottles of Red Horse, please."

Rizal raised his eyebrows. Arvin and Amado smiled. Datu's face was a light shining over their dark corner table. "I'm going to enjoy this," he said, rubbing his hands together. The yellow crate of beer arrived first. The waitress popped the caps off at once and left them to pass the bottles around themselves. Datu did the honors, handing one off to each of the others with glee. Hastily he tipped back his own and drained a large portion of its contents, exhaling in satisfaction. He looked at the label like the face of his one true love. Rizal took a small, self-conscious sip. Amado took in even more than Datu in his first pull, Arvin just slightly less. They set their bottles down and enjoyed the warmth emanating from their empty guts.

Datu surveyed the room, fuller now than when they had walked in just a few minutes before.

"Every Sunday," he said, still looking around, locking eyes on another Filipina waitress, "my cousin said it's like this every week. People get their day off and come here, or they go to Taipei Railway Station. He told me I had to come see for myself."

"Your cousin worked in Taiwan?" asked Rizal, forgetting the brief mention of it Datu made their first long day on the boat.

"Years ago," Datu scratched his head, trying to remember if he had said so before or not. "He's back home now."

"What did he say?" asked Amadao. "About how it was for him here, I mean."

"Not much. Mostly he talked about Sundays. He hardly said anything about the work. He said it was ... work. There wasn't much else to say. 'It's *leche* to talk about work,' he would tell me. He was much older. I was the little *anak* annoying him with questions all the time. No wonder he didn't say much."

"He was the one who told you to come here?" Rizal asked.

Datu took another long pull of his beer. It was almost gone. "Not exactly. I mean, he didn't encourage me, but he didn't tell me not to go either. He said I could try, if I wanted. He said no place is paradise. But to get a job, some of us have to leave. It's just the way it is. Unless you know somebody, or somebody who knows somebody."

He drained the last of his beer, grabbing another. He belched audibly and exhaled the fumes over the table. Their waitress came and set down the first dish, sizzling pork *sisig*. Datu rubbed his hands together and passed around the sets of cutlery. They dug in, pulling greedily from the plate and stuffing the small pieces of minced meat into their mouths several at a time, savoring the juices and relishing the chewy texture. Hands darted over and under the others. In a matter of minutes the plate was picked clean, a few lines of grease the only indication any food had been there at all. Amado finished his beer and grabbed for another, his hand wrapping around the wet, cool neck. Arvin was nearly done with his. Rizal still had three-quarters remaining. They eyed him.

"Not much of a drinker, *anak*?" asked Arvin. Like the rest, his face was flushed, cheeks burning red. His eyes were glassy, a smile parting his lips. The others leaned back and regarded the youngest crewman. Rizal looked down the neck of his beer, peering at the white foam spilling toward him. He put the bottle to his lips and tipped his head back. His throat ached as he chugged down the rest of the 8 percent beer, stomach burning. With a cringe he put the bottle down, eyes slamming shut. He had always nursed his beer, savored it, not knowing when he might be able to buy another. He wasn't used to chugging it down. But when he opened his eyes there was another bottle in front of him, to be shared between him and Amado it seemed, and three smiling faces. Amado nodded his approval. In the span of a few songs blared from the karaoke machine their first crate was full of dead soldiers. Datu called for another six bottles, the waitress taking their order with the same look of indifference. When she was gone, Datu leaned over the table.

"So, what do you think of her, eh?"

"Who?" asked Rizal.

Datu pointed with a jut of his round chin. "The waitress, of course. *Putang ina*, I've been away from my wife three months. If I don't have a woman soon my balls will catch fire."

The others raised their eyebrows.

"You're married?" Amado's tone suggested a level of disbelief bordering on complete.

"Is it so hard to believe?"

Silence for a time. Arvin asked him how long.

"Ten years, *gago*," Datu sighed as their second order of beers arrived. He grabbed a bottle and took another long pull, staring down at the neck as he finished. "Ten *long* years." He drew out the 'long' until he had to take another breath to finish the sentence.

"Kids?" asked Rizal, thankful the conversation had drawn attention away from his slow intake. His head was already swimming.

"Three," Datu answered wistfully. "Two girls," he paused, "and a boy."

They nodded. Datu asked if the others had any children, directing the question toward Arvin and Amado. They shook their heads. Out of mischief more so than manners he said to Rizal, "And you, *anak*? Have you any little *anak* of your own?" Rizal laughed, face turned toward the floor. He shook his head no, the smile quickly disappearing from his face as he thought of his daughter and the shame that kept him from telling the others about her. The spark of light in Datu's eyes that usually appeared only when he was joking had now taken up a spot of permanence. Arvin and Amado struggled to keep up as Datu finished his second beer, reaching immediately for another. Rizal held his bottle below the table edge. His worries shifted to how much the meal was going to cost them; if they would have enough to pay the bill if they kept sucking down beers like this. He kept the thought to himself.

"You didn't answer the question," Datu turned to Rizal again. "What do you think of that little *ganda*?"

Rizal looked around to find her, spying her at the bar, piling a tray with drinks. She was pretty. Eyes tired, but there was a kindness there not even exhaustion could hide. Her long black hair was tied in a practical ponytail like most of the other waitresses, swept back from a face with high cheekbones and a narrow nose leading to lips fuller than her otherwise gaunt facial features might have suggested. He looked down to her legs, three-quarters revealed below a short black skirt. Rizal tilted his head from side to side, feigning careful consideration.

"Not bad," his voice lilted upward. "You've got your eye on her, *tiyo*?"

Datu pretended to inspect his bottle. "Ah, that's over for me. 'Leave chasing the girls to the young,' my old man always said." Datu scoffed at the memory. "'You'll live longer,' the bastard used to say." He shook his head. "He was one to talk, the old dog. But no. My day has come and gone. You, you go for it, *anak*."

Arvin and Amado nodded. Rizal felt a cold sensation shrinking his stomach. He looked for the waitress again and found her at the far end of the room, placing the last of her tray of drinks on a table littered with empties. She stacked the empty bottles and glasses on the tray and made for the bar again, weaving through tables and guests wobbling, laughing, slapping one another on the back. Rizal leaned in close to the table.

"What do I do?"

The others chuckled, their laughter lost in the white noise of the room. Datu cleared his throat.

"It's easy," he said. "We're almost out of beer. What I'll do is call her over to order more. When she comes, she'll pick up the empty bottles to take them back to the bar. Before she has a chance to collect them, you spring up like the *galante anak* you are and offer to carry them for her. Don't take no for an answer. Then she'll follow you, and when you get to the bar, you talk to her."

"What do I say?" Rizal peeled the label from his bottle, dropping bits of torn paper onto the table.

"*Huwag mo akong inisin!* Do I have to think of everything?" Datu waved his hands above his head in mock exasperation. "Tell her she's beautiful. Tell her you want to go back to her hometown and meet her parents. Tell her you can't live without her and if she won't agree to bear you seven sons here and now you'll break one of these bottles on the edge of the bar and slit your wrists."

Rizal stared at him, eyes wide and blinking. Datu's held their gaze. "Really?" Rizal finally managed. Datu's eruption of laughter was such that it drew attention from the surrounding tables and beyond, belly rumbling with all its former glory. While the galumphing emanations still shook Datu's cheeks he raised a hand and called for the girl. "Miss?" he called through his own laughter. The waitress made her way over, empty tray in hand, puzzling at the man's impish grin. When she arrived she looked at Datu coolly, waiting, saying a silent prayer he wasn't one of those old fools with wayward hands she would have to slap away from her backside. Rizal felt his throat closing tighter with each passing second she was there, standing beside Datu in silence. Datu remained quiet, then shrugged his shoulders in feigned embarrassment as though he had just that second remembered why he summoned her.

"Oh, my apologies, miss. Six more beers, please." Less than discreetly he nodded toward Rizal. "Rizal..." Datu prompted, coughing into his fist. "Was there something you wanted to do for the lady?"

At that Rizal bolted from his chair. Clumsily he began picking bottles from the table, knocking one over as he went for the neck. He filled the plastic crate and picked it up, brushing past the waitress, headed for the bar. With raised eyebrows she turned to watch him pass. He set the crate on the bar, a similar look of confusion lighting up the face of the bartender, then beelined for his seat again, sitting back down.

"Okay, sir," said the waitress to Datu, slipping her pen behind her ear, tucking her empty tray under her arm. "I'll be right back with your beers." Hardly had she turned round before Datu, Arvin, and Amado roared with laughter, drawing yet more smiles and stares from those around them. Even Rizal couldn't help but laugh at himself.

"Not bad, *anak*, not bad," Datu said between snorts. "But you might have forgotten something," he erupted again, louder than before. The fit was contagious. Before long Arvin and Amado were incapacitated, eyes tearing, gasping for breath. They slapped each other on the shoulders and leaned into one another. Rizal shook his head at his own failure. He got up, the long laughter of the others devolving into shorter, breathy chortles, hands wiping tears from the corners of their eyes. They watched as he made for the bar again. There she stood, back to their table as the bartender filled up their crate for the third time. Rizal stood beside her, waiting for her to notice him. When she didn't, he tapped her on the shoulder. She turned to face him, eyes tired, half closed.

"Yes?" she asked. "Did you want something else?"

Again he froze. His mouth opened to speak but all he heard was a magnified croak sounding from his clenched throat. He swallowed, putting the back of his hand to his mouth, holding up a finger to ask for a moment to regroup. She looked at him, raising an eyebrow as she had back at the table. The bartender placed the last bottle in the crate, but she ignored it, instead keeping her eyes on the skinny boy struggling to gain composure. A slow, noiseless laugh pushed up her shoulders and her hands reached out for the crate. A hand on her forearm stopped her. She looked at the boy again, then at the hand lingering there on her arm, uninvited. Her tired eyes went wide.

"Maybe in whatever jungle village you come from you can touch girls without asking," she scolded, "but where I'm from you keep your hands to yourself or you lose them. Got it?"

Rizal's hand shook. He took it back. "I'm sorry," he said, eyeing the door. Any means of escape. He felt his bowels loosen and for a moment the ultimate embarrassment seemed a possibility. He swallowed hard. "I just wanted to talk to you."

She took her hands off the crate and considered him. "About what?" she shot back. "About how beautiful I am? About how you want to meet my parents? About how if I don't agree to give you seven sons right here and now you'll slit your wrists?"

Rizal turned back to the table and saw three fools,

heads rearing backward with laughter, bodies taken whole by involuntary spasms of hilarity. He shook his head, cursing Datu for his booming voice. His eyes found the floor. "Something like that," he mumbled. He started to slink back when a hand found his arm. He looked down to see her fingers on his forearm.

"You can start by helping me with these," she handed him the full crate. "I'm going on break," she said, pulling her apron up over her head. "If you want to talk to me, come and find me out back." She cast a sinister glare at Datu and the others, still howling. "But leave your little friends here, okay?"

Rizal swallowed a lump again, stultified by her half-closed eyes. "Okay," he managed. The waitress put her apron down on the bar and disappeared through the swinging doors to the kitchen. Rizal looked to his crew, finding their laughing fit finally ended. Datu held up his hands in question. Rizal shrugged his shoulders and smiled. He brought the beers back to their table, setting the crate down without sitting himself. Then he turned and made for the front door, three dumbstruck faces following his every step as he went out. With quickened pace he blurred past the shop window and disappeared around the corner. There was a narrow alley there, a small concrete culvert for diverting rainwater between the buildings. A stray cat waddled ahead of Rizal as he contemplated finding another way around the back of the building. The cat howled at something unseen around the corner, haunches rising. Rizal decided to follow. His ragged shoes traversed the expanse of the shallow dip, avoiding the concoction of water, mud, and garbage. Sideways he crept through to the back of the building and went around the corner, startling the waitress there. She paused whatever she had been doing, the sole of one foot pressed flat against the dimpled gray concrete of the foundation. He found himself looking at her legs again, unaware he was staring or for how long his eyes lingered. She lowered her eyes to meet his and shook her head at him, laughing.

"You could have just come through the kitchen," she said. "No one would bat an eye at another brown face back there."

Rizal raised his eyes up and felt his face flush with color. There was hardly any space in the back alley, what little there was made all the smaller by the presence of the first woman he had seen up close, other than the captain's bride, in three months. She looked unsure, as though it just now occurred to her that it may have been a mistake to invite him, harmless as he appeared. The wall of the neighboring building to the rear was just a few feet from the restaurant. Rizal stepped over to that wall, fingering the holes in his pants pockets. Then he turned around and raised the sole of his foot and placed it against the opposite wall, standing just as she was. She laughed again. He soaked in the sound of it, lowered his chin, trying to think of something, anything, to keep her there as long as he could. He started by asking her name.

"You want to know my name?"

Even Rizal could see she was toying with him, awash in his ineptitude with the opposite sex as much as he was in the sound of her voice.

"Yes," Rizal said shyly.

"Yes what?"

"I want to know your name."

She smiled, breathing in the same way a person might if they were savoring the taste of a cigarette. She let him dangle there a while before she answered.

"Jasmine."

Rizal looked up, swallowing a beer belch that puffed his cheeks. She laughed at him again, making him feel triumph and defeat in the same fleeting instant. "Jasmine," he repeated. She nodded, head tilted at a sideways angle. She took her foot off the wall, switching it for the other. Rizal did the same.

"*Leche*," she drew out the word, "you're like an annoying little brother, copying whatever you see."

The words stung, though Rizal told himself it wasn't her intention. He put his foot down, trying to think of something else to say. He settled on his name.

"What?" she asked. "Do you always speak so quietly?"

He felt that sting again, cringed at it. "Rizal," he repeated. "It's my name, if you want to know."

She shrugged her shoulders, then said, "Well, I know now whether I want to or not, don't I?"

Rizal was lost. He considered slinking back the way he had come, not stopping until he was back at the station. Then he could catch the train to Su'ao and in a matter of hours be back on the boat, curled up on the wheelhouse floor. Though he was taller than Jasmine he felt her looming above him, towering there just a few steps away yet entirely unreachable. He couldn't move, and once again couldn't speak. She looked at him and asked a question in a tone that said, in the absence of better company, they might as well talk about something.

"What are you doing here, Rizal?"

"What am I doing here?"

"I mean what do you do? You know, for work?"

"I'm a fisherman," Rizal answered, hopeful. She quickly shrunk him back down to size.

"Everyone in there is a fisherman," she cocked her head back toward the restaurant. "A fisherman, a factory worker, a nurse, a caregiver. What else can we do here?"

She caught the look of confusion in Rizal's eyes. "Never mind," she said. "So you're a fisherman. How long?"

"Three months," Rizal answered quickly. She scoffed, face darkening. A cloud passed over the small patch of sky, the thin rectangular strip above their heads turning from blue to gray.

"Three months...." she looked away then back at Rizal again. "You like it?"

"Like it?" Rizal thought. With everything that had happened until then he hadn't had time to think about it. Nights of numb labor bled into days of tossing and turning that washed like the tide back out into more work. One day after the next those tides moved in and out. There was as little point in thinking about the tides of their days and nights as there was in contemplating the many other pieces of life over which they held no power.

"Hello?" Jasmine called Rizal back. "I said, 'Do you like it?'"

"It's okay," Rizal answered. "It's a job. That's enough."

Jasmine shoved her hands in her pockets. Rizal watched the pink nails of her thumbs disappear beneath the faded black strips of her belt loops. He crooked his chin toward her.

"What brought you here?"

"Me?" she pointed a finger at her chest, drawing his eyes there then quickly away. "I used to be a caregiver." She paused. "But I didn't like it. My boss was not a good man. He hired me to look after his mother. Her mind was already gone. Every day I had to tell her who I was, what I was doing there. I don't think she could understand a word I said. She fought me no matter what I did. If I gave her medicine, she knocked it to the ground or spit it out. Said I was trying to poison her. When I took a towel to wipe her mouth, she hit my hand away. Every day I had to feed her, bathe her, even change her diaper." She shook her head, cringing. "When I wasn't looking after her, my boss would send me to his brother's house in Hsinchu. His driver would take me there and I would clean their whole house, all four floors. If his house didn't need cleaning he would send me to his office to clean there, or to his wife's clothing store to work as her shop assistant. At their home when I wasn't looking after *ama*, I cooked. I cleaned. They even had me pulling weeds in the garden behind the house. I stayed for eight months without one day off. Working around the clock, morning till night, night until morning. If I was able to sneak in an hour of sleep here and there I was lucky. And the pay," she rolled her eyes. "I barely saw anything. Everything went to paying back the loan I took to get here, the broker's fees. Even room and board. Can you believe that? They told me I would have free room and board. Then I get here and find out it's taken out of my pay."

She was angry now. She looked as though she wanted to spit on the ground. She sighed, swallowed, closing her eyes, looking up toward the gray cloud which had yet to pass. Rizal did the same.

"He was not a good man, my boss," Jasmine said again, trailing off once more. Her eyes glazed over. Rizal caught them sidelong as she looked away, down to the alley's opposite end. "So I left," she said. "I ran away. I called my broker to tell him what happened, but he said I was a runaway. The police were looking for me. He said I had to tell him where I was. He would come and get me, take me to the police station. Then I would be sent back home, back to the Philippines, never allowed to return here. But I can't go back. I owe so much money. And there are no jobs. What was I supposed to do? I was on the street for days before I found this place. The boss here is Filipina. Young, like me. Not even thirty, but she has so much. She is married to a Taiwanese man from a rich family. She said I could work here, get paid under the table. She said she wouldn't tell anybody, the same as she did for the others working here, and I believed her. I've been here four months. Even if I did decide to go home I couldn't. My broker has my passport. And if I go to the police about it I'll get thrown out of the country. So I guess I'm stuck." She sighed again. "I don't know why I'm telling you all this. I don't even know you."

Rizal looked away, down toward his end of the alley. The cat he had seen before was there now, licking a paw, dragging it over the top of its head.

"I'm sorry," he said. The words came out weak. He almost wished he hadn't said them at all. Jasmine shrugged.

"Why?" she asked. "You haven't done anything wrong." A gust of wind cooed through the alleyway, picking up bits of plastic and paper, flinging them off the walls and depositing them down in the sludge of the culvert. Jasmine slapped an arm against her thigh. "Well, now you know my sad story, Rizal the fisherman." Her eyes widened and she stepped toward him. Rizal felt his heart race. He pressed his palms back against the wall. She was in front of him now, lips not more than a foot from his face. He gulped hard and tried not to look so afraid. She pursed her lips. "The question is, can I trust you won't tell my sad story to anyone else?"

Rizal felt sweat form on his forehead, dripping under his arms. It flowed from his palms and in an instant he was soaked with it. His skin felt tight, a hot film pulled over his bones. An itch seized him and he scratched at the back of his head, feeling his hair greasy and matted. Jasmine raised an eyebrow at him for the third time.

"Yes," he croaked, feeling his voice break.

"Yes what?" a smile found its way through the seriousness of Jasmine's expression.

"Yes," Rizal's voice croaked yet worse, "you can trust me."

Chapter Twelve

RIZAL's eyelids availed themselves of his eyes slowly. He had a splitting headache, and when he swallowed he tasted vomit. Next to him was the bag from the clothing shop, filled with his old filthy clothes and the second set of new. Beside the bag was Datu, asleep on the train station bench. Rizal bolted upright, a rush of blood and pain sending a hand to his forehead. The bench was beside the station's front steps, shaded from the sun. Around them people walked up the steps, willfully avoiding the four foreigners. Rizal looked around. The day before the station had been filled with Filipinos, Thais, Indonesians, and Vietnamese. Today theirs were the only foreign faces to be found. A sick feeling gripped his stomach. It was Monday. They had to return to Su'ao in time for the night's work. He pushed at Datu's backside. Arvin and Amado occupied another bench beside theirs, one resting his head on the flank of the other.

"Wake up," Rizal pleaded with Datu. Datu waved a hand back at Rizal and nuzzled his head deeper into the crook of his arm. Rizal pushed harder and finally Datu's eyes shot open. He cringed at the light and sat up, hand finding his forehead.

"Where are we?" he watched the people passing them by. "Ask that woman where we are, *anak*. I don't...."

"We're at the train station!" There was panic in Rizal's voice. "Turn around, *kuya.* See?" Datu turned his head, nodding slowly. He lowered his face into his palms, groaning.

"How did we get here?"

"I don't know." Rizal felt something jab into his leg. He reached into his pocket, pulling out a knife and fork, realizing he must have taken them from the restaurant. His stomach sank and rebelled. He forced himself to stand. He said, "We need to get back to Su'ao. The captain will be angry if we're late." Then he put the cutlery back into his pocket and went to wake up Arvin and Amado. They arose with pain and confusion, Arvin wiping spit from the corner of his mouth.

Arvin broke into a wide, dumb grin as he waved good morning at a pretty young woman while she hurried by. Rizal realized the man was still quite drunk. Amado seemed to be the least affected of them all. He stood and stretched, bending down to touch his toes then rising to arch his back. In a momentary panic Rizal reached into his other pocket and was relieved to find some money still there. Enough at least to get him back to Su'ao. He told the others to hurry, and they made their way slowly up the steps to the ticket counter.

"Su'ao," Rizal said slowly to the man behind the glass, holding up four fingers. The man punched at his keyboard and he held a calculator up to the window. Rizal elbowed Datu who looked at the numbers and nodded, shuttering his eyes up again with a grimace. Rizal collected money from everyone and paid, taking the four tickets. He looked at the time printed on them and then at the clock, finding it was still another forty-five minutes until their train would leave. It was nearly noon. He swore under his breath. Amado wandered off to find a water fountain. Datu and Arvin were already stretched out in two of the blue plastic seats in the small waiting area. Rizal joined them in the same row and a minute later Amado flopped down beside him. Datu's breaths came slow and deliberate, words much the same.

"I guess we had a good time last night?" He laughed then cringed and groaned all at once. Rizal tried to remember. The night was a rush of half-recalled scenes that may never have happened and words that could have been spoken or not. Datu arched an eyebrow and asked Rizal about the girl, Jasmine. "Did it go anywhere, *anak*?" Arvin and Amado leaned forward to listen. Rizal thought back. He closed his eyes and tried to remember, searching for anything that might have happened between them. An image flashed in his mind. A pen held by a slender hand with pink fingernails, scribbling on a piece of paper. The paper was a strange color. A light red turned darker by the dim lighting of the bar. The paper slid across the table and Rizal saw his own hand reach out for it, taking it and tucking the folded slip away in his pocket. His eyes shot open and his hand went back to the pocket containing his money, pulling out the few hundred-dollar notes he had left. They were folded in half and he rifled through them as fast as his beer-soaked brain would allow. Finally he found it, the bill marked with blue ink. He studied the markings for a time, then passed it to Datu.

"What does it say, *kuya*?"

Datu took the note and looked at it, widening his eyes then squinting, trying to bring the words into focus.

He laughed and slammed his eyes shut at the pain the laughter brought. He passed the note back and tented his fingers over his gut, smiling at Rizal.

"What?" Rizal asked, agitated. "Tell me what it says."

Datu held to his exaggerated smile until the exertion caused him more pain than it was worth. "It's an address and phone number, *anak*," he explained. "I guess she wants you to write to her, or call."

Rizal's heart soared and quickly sank as he reminded himself he had no address and no phone. He looked longingly to Datu. "You could help me, *kuya*?" he asked. "You could help me write something to her?"

Datu laughed, reaching to pat him on the knee. "Sure, *anak*," he said, "I will help you."

They sat with their necks bent backward over the curved seat backs, staring up at the ceiling or sitting with eyes closed until the call of the station agent wrested them from their uncomfortable repose. Their train was arriving. It was late, if only by a few minutes. But it was now nearly one o'clock. Rizal tried to remember how long it had taken them to get there. He thought of asking Datu. The older man was consumed by his hangover. Rizal decided not to bother him. They boarded the train, finding their seats among faces that were not like theirs and eyes that followed them until the moment they sat down. They were two and two, across the aisle from each other. They stretched their backs against the seats as they had at the station. The doors hissed and closed. The beige-orange train lurched forward, rust-tinged wheels clacking slowly along the tracks. Rizal closed his eyes and tried to will sleep down from a high shelf in his mind, surges of alcohol sugars casting the shelf in a halo of bright light. Looking to his left he reached over the sleeping passenger beside him and pulled the window shade down. It filtered the light rather than blocking it out, but it kept the sun off his eyelids, quieting the impulse to wakefulness.

Gradually Rizal's mind calmed and his blood pumped at a more restful torpor. Through half-closed eyes he watched as the others fell asleep. Amado snored, much to the agitation of the Taiwanese woman at his side, her fingers clacking noisily away on a laptop. A thought sent Rizal's hand back to his money. He pulled it out and separated Jasmine's note from the rest, moving it to the right pocket. He thought of her face, wondering if he was remembering it as it really was. His thoughts came in fitful spurts like a child choking the flow of a garden hose by bending it in half then straightening it out again. He eventually drifted off to sleep, hands clasped peacefully over his stomach. In dreams he would forget seconds after waking he found her, standing in the alley where they had first talked, leaning against the wall. Him watching her. She watching him. And in that dream he would forget he wished something – that he could go back. That life could be made of him just standing there and looking at her. If life could be nothing more than that, his fleeting thoughts said, it would not be wasted.

A touch on his shoulder awakened Rizal some hours later. He opened his eyes and all those pleasant thoughts rushed out and dissipated in the air-conditioned atmosphere of the passenger car. He looked up into the face of Datu, his eyes still as bloodshot as they were that morning. The train was slowing, the clicking of the wheels coming at intervals further and further apart. Rizal turned to look out the window and found the sun was already close to the horizon. A panic gripped him. He wheeled back to Datu.

"We're late!" he yelled, voice dry and gravelly. Datu remained calm.

"Easy, *anak*. There's nothing we can do about it. The train was delayed. We were stopped at one of the stations for more than half an hour. You slept right through it."

Though spoken calmly, the words did little to ease Rizal's mind. He looked to Arvin and Amado. They stood in the aisle side by side, leaning on the backs of the seats ahead of them. Looking back through the car Rizal found it mostly empty. He too got up as though the act of rising might see the train stopped sooner and they on their way back to the harbor. God willing, he thought, they would beat the captain there and all would be well.

The train finally came to halt and Rizal led the rush, others stumbling down the step behind him from the creaky gangway to the platform. They ran from the concourse through the underground passageway to the station hall. An elderly uniformed agent threw words at Rizal he did not understand, holding them up at the turnstile until Datu explained the man was asking for their tickets. Datu pulled his from his pocket, Rizal and the rest searching their own for the wayward scraps of paper. Rizal was the last to find his, hidden within the folds of Jasmine's bill. He handed the ticket over hastily to the agent and passed through. They flew down the station steps, past the lone taxi driver leaned up against the passenger door of his car and turned right down the road leading toward the harbor, Rizal leading the way, struggling to remember the directions. In a panic Rizal broke into a sprint that the others, especially Datu, found difficult to match. He heard Datu calling somewhere behind him, but he pressed on. Rizal's heart boomed in his ears and his lungs burned as the minutes passed by; and still he ran, but he ignored the pain as he went by the larger port at the end of the highway, then the temple of their own harbor and rounded the corner leading to the narrow road that went to the harbor's open end.

He was within sight of Li's mooring when he stopped, the pain in his chest magnified by the sight of the familiar blue truck and a pair of figures standing in front of it. Even in the looming darkness he could see Li's face burning in anger. Mr. Chen was beside him, arms folded across his chest, his mouth a thin line of contempt. The others caught up to Rizal a half minute later and bent double, wheezing, fighting off waves of nausea brought on by the bout of exercise and the booze-heavy blood pumping through them. They stopped behind Rizal and one by one rose from their crouch to the realization they were in trouble. A swirling kaleidoscope of red and blue lit up the faces of Chen and Li and the crewmen whirled around to see a pair of police scooters headed their way. The officers stopped, one dousing the four of them with the bright of his flashlight as he dismounted. Both officers advanced, one hand on their holsters. The crewmen stood still, watching the officers approach, hearing the footsteps of Chen and Li from behind. It was Chen who spoke first.

"*Chuanzang* Li is very disappointed in you," he said.

"He gave you a day off, and you made him look foolish by running away. He lost face because of you."

The officers stopped. The others looked to Datu for translation. He stayed quiet. One of the policemen spoke words they didn't understand, a hand still on his holster, the other held out in an appeal for calm, flashlight now tucked away in a belt loop. The crew turned their backs on the captain and Chen. The cops were but a pace away now, two to their four. An instinct sounded in Rizal's mind. The impulse to flee. Back home, people who went away with the police had a habit of not coming back. If they did return they did so with heads wrapped in duct tape and black trash bags leaking black blood. "Salvage victims," they were called – one of many new terms for the users, the dealers, and the innocent bystanders who wound up dead at the hands of the police and the contract killers, born of Duterte's savage war on drugs and the poor who turned to them for escape. Rizal's pupils skittered from one end of the lot to the other, then settled on the officer's gun. It shone metallic under the harbor lights casting a yellow pall over the road littered with small stones and sand and bits of broken glass. Rizal breathed in the fish gut and salt scent. In the span of a breath the officers took him down. He felt a foot behind his own take away his legs; he twisted and fell to the concrete, feeling it hot through his clothing. Amado was next, then Arvin. Datu went down on his own, dropping to his knees with his hands in the air. Rizal and Amado had their hands secured with cuffs, Datu and Arvin with zip ties. They lay there belly down, looking up at the pant legs of the uniforms standing over them. Li and Chen moved to join the officers. The crew strained to look up at Chen as he spoke, but he was too close. They could only stare at the well-shined toes of his shoes.

"*Chuanzhuang* Li came and found you were not here. So, he must call the police to report you as runaways." Chen paused, allowing Datu time to translate, prompting him with a soft kick to the ribs. "To run away is a very serious thing. The police waste their time to come here. They put themselves in danger. You could all go to jail." Again Chen stopped. Datu did his best to turn a language he had a basic command of to their own. Their eyes widened, stomachs clenching at the mention of jail. Chen saw this and raised his hands for calm, a shoe crunching on a small, brittle stone. "However, I have negotiated with the police for you. They are very angry, but they agree you will not go to jail tonight. Instead, you will pay a fine. Ten thousand each. And you must promise you will not run away again. Okay?" Datu translated. When he finished four heads gave shallow nods, chins almost tapping against the concrete. Li nodded to the officers and they moved to take the restraints off the crewmen. Rizal felt the steel slide from his wrists. He sat up but remained on the ground, the others doing the same. They looked up at the four men above them.

"Now," said Chen, "you must apologize to *chuanzhang*."

Datu spoke the words in Tagalog. Chen's finger found Rizal. He stared up at it, swallowing the knot in his throat. He wrapped his arms around his knees and looked down. Datu elbowed him. Out of the corner of his eye Rizal looked at him. Datu mouthed the word "sorry." Rizal raised his head and spoke it softly. Li cupped his ear as though he hadn't heard and Rizal said it again, louder. Li nodded, scowling. He looked to Datu and Chen's finger moved, going down the line until all had said the word Li wanted to hear. Li looked to Chen and nodded again. Chen said something to the officers. The cops tipped their caps to the captain, turned and walked back to the scooters, lights still twirling. They got in and drove the short distance to the station, there on the far side of the harbor. Li and Chen watched the officers park and amble back into the station, then turned their attention back to the crew.

"Get up," said Chen. They did. Li's anger had boiled quietly in the presence of the officers. Now that they were gone, it overflowed. Li looked to Rizal and in his eyes he found fear. He stepped to the man, cowering like a boy, putting his hands on the collar of Rizal's shirt, screaming. Li pushed him and Rizal stumbled, looking to the others for help. They stood still. Li was on Rizal, pushing him closer to the harbor wall edge. He kicked at the bag left on the ground – the one that held Rizal's old clothes and the other set of new. Li pulled at the new shirt Rizal had on, gripping the fabric between his fingers. Though Rizal could not understand the captain's words he seemed to be asking about the clothing itself. Its newness only seemed to magnify their crime of leaving without permission. Li bent and picked up the bag, looking inside.

"*Shi bu shi ni de?*" he screamed. Rizal reasoned the captain was asking if the bag was his. He nodded rapidly. Li said something else, again pointing an accusing finger at his new clothing. Then he reared back and threw the bag into the harbor. It landed on top of the water and sat there a moment before the still water came in through a hole in the plastic and it began to sink. Rizal turned. His heart fell at the thought of the I.O.V. tape, still there in the pocket of his old pair of pants, bound for the harbor bottom. He turned back to Li and found him seething, head flicking between he and the other three. The captain pointed to Rizal, then the others, then to the boat, speaking sharply.

"Now," said Chen, translating, "*chuanzhang* says it is time for work."

Chapter Thirteen

Dear Jasmine,

I'm sorry it took so long for me to write to you. I'm ashamed to tell you (or did I tell you the night we met?), but the truth is, I don't know how to read or write. I never got to go to school. Not for very long, anyway. I guess that's how I ended up here, doing what I'm doing now. Datu is helping me write this. It's a little embarrassing, but it's the only way. The paper and pen we had to beg from the members of another crew — a group of Pinoys, just like us. We saw them just once, when their boat came into harbor near our own. Thankfully they had what we needed, and were willing to share. I haven't seen them again since. They said they take long trips out to sea, months at a time. One of their crew was already drowned, they said. The captain made no effort to retrieve the body, just left it out there at sea. I hope to see them at least once more so I can thank them properly, give them something in return. Right now I have nothing to give. I hope whatever happens they all are safe and don't suffer the same fate as the man who drowned and won't even have a funeral.

It's been two months since I saw you. Since we met I've thought about you every day. I hope you don't mind me saying, but thinking of you helps me get through the days here in Su'ao. Every day is the same. We sit on the boat all day waiting to go out. In the summer it was always so hot. We just sat and sweated and tried to sleep. Then when it started to get dark the captain came and we would go out on the sea all night catching fish. The captain yells at us all the time. The only words I've learned in his language are the bad ones. Sometimes the captain puts his hands on us. He even pushed one of us into the sea once. He could have died. I never really thought about it before, but he could have drowned. Now whenever we go out I have this feeling one of us might not come back. We'll be one fewer, and we won't be able to say anything. Our broker, Mr. Chen, even told us so. If one of us dies, the captain can just throw the body into the sea. It's in our contracts, he says. There's nothing we can do about it. We'll just do what we do every day, coming back one less, and one less, until none of us are left.

Now it is fall. At least that means there will be no more storms, I hope. A typhoon hit Su'ao a couple months back. We were left alone on the boat. I'd never been so frightened in my life. For two days and nights we huddled against the wind and the rain. With every gust I thought, "This is it. This is the moment I'm going to die." But it was strange. In those times I felt death nearest, those were the moments I was least afraid.

It's starting to get cold now, even during the day. We have no blankets so we just try to cover ourselves with our sleeping mats. In the summer, we used them to block out the sun. Now we use them to fight off the cold. We wash ourselves with sea water, but the water in the harbor is dirty. The captain's new wife brings us our food now, but it's the same as it was before, just some instant noodles we can't cook and a bit of water. It's not enough for four men. I feel dizzy when I get up too quickly. I've lost so much weight. I was always skinny, but now I'm really just skin and bones. My mother would have a heart attack if she saw me. And my stomach always aches and grumbles. But we can't go into town for anything. We went once and it felt like everyone was watching us. Once in a while I notice a police car driving slowly by or a pair of officers riding their scooters past our boat. I can't help thinking they're keeping an eye on us. The day we came back — the day after I met you — two policemen were waiting for us with the captain and Mr. Chen. They put us in handcuffs and said we had to pay a fine for running away. It was so much money that last month we actually owed more than we earned. I'm tired of working for nothing. Five months and I have only a few dollars in my pocket that I have to hide from the captain. I'm afraid he'll snatch it out of my hand and throw it into the harbor if he sees it. Money I can't even spend. I feel trapped here. We all do. But there is no way out. So I try not to think about it.

Two and a half more years, Datu says. Then we'll be free. I want to believe him. Even now as he writes this for me, he tells me to have faith. I don't know. It seems foolish to hope for anything. It's like being in prison. Back where I come from, I knew a lot of people who had been to jail. They say when you're inside, you don't hope. You just do your time and let the routine take you from one day to the next and the one after that. So that's what I'm doing now. Doing my time. Every day that goes by is one day closer to being free. When my time is up, I'll go home. Back to my mother in Navotas. I'll look back on my time here as a kind of sentence, I think. Maybe I'll even tell people that's what happened. I got sent away. It sounds so much better to say I was sent to prison than what actually happened. I feel so stupid sometimes. How could I fall for this? I should have known it was too good to be true. I should have known people like me never get a chance.

But enough of my complaining. I want to know more about you. You've done well for yourself here. Better than me, anyway. I think you must be very strong. You had problems but you overcame them. You got yourself away from the bad situation and found something better. If I had half your courage I would do the same. Instead I just sit here on the boat, day after day, daydreaming rather than doing. In a way it's like I never left home. There I would be doing exactly the same thing. Wishing for something better. The only difference is now I have the captain to yell at me instead of Mama.

There I go talking about myself again. I'm telling Datu to cross this part out but he says to leave it all there. He's the one writing it for me so I don't have much choice. So please, tell me how you've been these two months. Tell me what you've been doing. I know hearing about you and your life will make me feel better. It will give me strength to get through these long, long days. I hope to hear from you soon. I'm going to give you the address of the convenience store in town. Datu tells me you can mail letters through the stores here. His cousin told him so, he says. I will sneak away to mail this to you, and once in a while I will sneak back to see if you have written to me. Don't worry about me. Navotas people are strong. We live with the dead and the tombs are our homes and playgrounds. I hope you are well.

Rizal

P.S. This is the first letter I've ever written, by the way. I hope I don't sound strange to you.

Chapter Fourteen

THIS *is a temporary place of rest, Rizal. The families of the dead rent the tombs for five years. When five years pass, if they can find the money, they buy a permanent burial site elsewhere, beyond these walls. But when the time runs out, if they can't pay, someone like Datu pulls the bodies out. The lucky ones get put in bone box, those small compartments hardly bigger than a shoe box at the front of the rows of apartment tombs. Most of the bones, they get put into a rice sack. The family name is written in black marker on the outside. The sack gets tossed in that broken-down shack at the rear of the grounds, the one I tell you never to look inside. Now you know why, Rizal. There are piles of bags in there, falling over and down one another. Skulls and leg bones and things with names I'll never know pouring out, cascading like a waterfall of reminders that this ... this is what becomes of us all. I know the day will come when you will go against what I tell you. You will look inside sooner or later. It's just the way people are. The things we're told not to do or that we can't have are the things we want most of all. But never disrespect the dead, Rizal. Let the other children play their games, tossing a skull back and forth like a game of "hot potato." But not you, Rizal. You may be different. But that doesn't have to be a bad thing. It can be the greatest thing about you.*

Such were Rizal's dreams of late. Memories of his mother, the cemetery, home. The times she tried her best to guide him and those when he resisted her advice with all he had. Now he wanted nothing more than to be back there in the place he knew. He would listen now. He would respect the dead and the living and all those who had tried their best to guide him and put him on a path that would not see his bones tied up in a rice sack, the name his father gave him – the only thing his father had given him – written on the outside for wayward sons of the future to find.

He kept the letter hidden in his pocket, afraid of what might happen if he snuck away to mail it. He thought of trying to slip the folded piece of paper to the captain's wife, then thought better of it. She might not understand what he wanted her to do, he reasoned. He rarely heard her speak. She dropped off their food in the afternoons, sometimes under Li's watchful eyes. When she did, she hardly so much as looked up. While everyone looked at her – she was quite pretty – she seemed to look only at her husband. Li, meanwhile, watched her and everyone, glaring at one whose eyes might linger too long on his new bride.

Three days after Datu had helped Rizal write the letter, Rizal found himself daydreaming, recalling his dream of the night before, really – his mother's warning of the shack at the rear of the cemetery grounds and its waterfall of bones. He stood on the deck of his new home, feeling as though not only the boat but he himself was floating; thinking of those bodies intermingled, a rib from a man here, laid lengthwise across a collar bone, perhaps from a woman – two beings who had never known each other in life, now destined to be together in death in that way without reason that could make the living lose sleep or stare off into space for hours. *Where will my bones be laid to rest?* Rizal wondered. *And does it even matter if they wind up sitting in a rice sack a hundred feet from where I lived most of my life, or if they are cast down to the bottom of the sea, a thousand miles from any place I've ever known?* He stood there, thinking these thoughts, eyes staring at nothing, not knowing he was actually staring at the captain's wife, there with the daily food delivery. He felt an elbow dig into his side and came back from the world within to the world in which his eyes were locked on the captain's wife, gawking without seeing. Beside the captain's wife was the captain himself, staring back at Rizal. Quickly Rizal lowered his eyes. He saw the others – Datu, Arvin, and Amado – sitting, he the only one still standing. They were opening their packs of noodles along the far gunwale. Rizal looked back to the captain, nodded his apology to Li, then again to his wife, whose name he had never been told. *I am fisherman*, he thought. *She is wife.* Li gave a look that said he neither accepted nor rejected the gesture, only that he would remember it. Li's wife, her face told that she too thought often of other places and perhaps was thinking of them now – locations she had spent time in her younger years, where words of elders went in through one ear and out the other. Those words she heard repeated now, their meaning tragically revealed in a place too far removed from one in which they might make her a bit of difference.

On the evening of the third day they went out to sea once again. The captain was quieter than usual. His stream of epithets, usually aimed at the crew, the instruments in his wheelhouse, the sea itself, was missing. He stayed at the wheel, staring at the horizon. Rizal was against the gunwale, arms outstretched along the rail. Li barely seemed to blink. It was as though he were alone, surrounded by an invisible shell separating him from the outside world. The sky went from a jaundiced orange to black in a matter of minutes, with the sea turning to a mass of thick, swelling crude. Li just pointed to the lines and hooks and the crew got to work, the setting of hooks, the tying of lines, all done by muscle memory. They blanked their minds in the face of the hours of dumb repetition to come and all those on the nights to follow. Theirs was now a world without sound or smell. Even the thick cloud of stench billowing from the chum buckets could probe deep into their nostrils and register nothing but the sigh of a beaten man.

The crew felt the captain's eyes on them as they worked. He stood there, back against the outer wheelhouse wall, chain smoking his way through his usual two packs of cigarettes. He flicked orange embers into the soft breeze coming from the east. Rizal's fingers worked without feeling, passing over the soft, quivering flesh of bait fish. Barbs dug at the calloused tips of his fingers and were turned back by the hardened masses of dead skin. Lines being set to soak ran over his coarse palms to his mind's ignorance. He watched the main line stream off into the nebulous dark, blurring and fading as the floodlights lost their hold, surrendered to the sea until they were brought back in.

They set the last of the branches, and the speed of their trawl was increased, the boat rumbling further out to sea. The crew took up seats at the rear, sitting in silence. Tonight there was no task given by the captain to sharpen hooks or pull up and replace planks or tinker with the craft's sputtering engine of which they knew little. With nothing to do, their heads nodded with the rise and fall of the craft, heavy eyelids following the sea's primordial rhythms. Rizal felt his head dip and his eyes snapped open, a bolt of fear sending a shake through his aching legs. He looked across and saw Arvin fighting off sleep. It had already taken Datu. Amado soon followed. Rizal thought to make a noise to wake them, fearful of what the captain might do if he were to turn and find them dozing. There was no sleeping at sea. Even on the run back toward the lines, when there was little to do but wait, by the captain's command they could rest only with their eyes open. Still, they took whatever sleep they could, growing bolder with every minute gone by that the captain did not take notice.

The boat's old engine choked and sputtered, jolting them all back to alertness. They heard the first words from the captain's mouth since they had gone to sea, his usual foul language returning. He swore and cut the engine. The sputtering ceased with a rattle and the gentle waves held them in near silence. Li stomped from the wheelhouse and made for the hatch at the stern. He lifted it up and smoke poured from the engine hold. He swore again, waving the mass away from his face like a cloud of black flies, frowning. He looked back toward the crew, eyeing one then the other as though searching for a culprit. A man to take the blame.

Rizal all but held his breath. His was the seat closest to the hatch. The captain looked at him, pupils wide in the light cast from the bright white bulbs hung from the wheelhouse. The breeze picked up, swinging the lights and sending their shadows crawling over the captain's face like fat leeches looking for a place to suckle. One of the lights swung and bounced against the aged wood, the crack of metal against the wheelhouse the firing of the starter's pistol. At the sound Li let the hatch drop. It bounced and was closed, the force of it ushering away the last wisps of smoke. He pushed through the dying smoke and was on Rizal in an instant. Rizal raised his arms in defense as a hand shot out to hoist him up by the collar. Words flew from the captain's mouth, a mix of his own tongue and shards of broken English. Rizal stumbled back against the rail, felt it press against the small of his back. The deck tilted and the sound of water filled his ears, momentarily drowning the captain's tirade. When the boat tilted back Rizal saw the frightened eyes of the others. The captain's words flew by him. One seemed to snap Datu from his stupor. Shakily he stepped toward the grappling pair and spoke quickly to the captain. Li swung out blindly at him, the back of his hand glancing off Datu's shoulder and jaw. Rizal heard Datu shouting.

"His wife!" Datu yelled. "He's angry about his wife!"

Rizal's mind shot back to the afternoon. He thought of how he watched her without watching, far away in his dream. Then he thought of the captain, watching him. About how quiet he had been on the way out until the failing engine caused him to snap. His wide eyes shifted from Datu to Li's frothing mouth and betel-stained teeth. He blurted an apology but the words were swallowed by the sound of rushing water and a consuming darkness. A void opened before him and he felt suddenly cold. His limbs flailed in slow motion and he realized he was in the roiling water, staring down into endless abyss. His throat felt like it was stuffed with rocks and he clawed for the surface, breaking just as a wave tumbled over his head. He retched seawater as he broke the cusp again and gasped for breath, looking up to the looming hull and the rail just out of reach. Li stood there, hands planted firm, screaming like a madman. The others pleaded with the captain. The words came to Rizal's ears in broken strands as the rolling waves boiled around his ears. Already he felt his arms tiring as he slapped at the amorphous surface. Salt water invaded his nose and mouth, choking his fevered apologies. The captain strained to listen between rantings, cocking a hand to his ear.

"*Ni shuo shenme?*" he called out, craning over the railing. Rizal watched as the stern turned toward him. The boat was drifting away. He made to swim for it but the captain pointed a finger at him, shouting. "No!" he yelled in English.

Rizal tread water, heaving for breath, tasting salt at the back of his throat. A wave caught him flush in the face and he threw up clear, warm liquid again. Chills began to shake him. A false feeling of warmth emanated from just below his skin; his limbs slowed, and the bobs beneath the cold water's surface came more frequently. He alternated between the surface world and the slow descent into the murk below. He looked down into the fathomless nothing and there saw his escape. He came up once more and looked to the boat. His three countrymen stood beside the captain – the man bent on letting him drown. The crew stood by, powerless in their fear. When Rizal slipped below again, he let himself go, exhaling, feeling the energy flow out of him. His muscles relaxed themselves, and in his mind the conscious thought of survival slipped away, bubbling up toward the shrinking light of the surface with his last willful breath. He closed his eyes and felt himself falling into the miasma, arms floating above his head. From his empty lungs the ache transformed into a calming full-body warmth. *I am the nameless dead now*, his thoughts spoke. *The arms of the angel of death are around me.* He had only to let those arms take him and he would be free. *Now I lay me down to sleep....* The Lord's Prayer. The words that came before the storms.

He drifted until consciousness had almost deserted him. Down and down until he felt himself suspended within a cocoon of darkness and warmth, neither descending nor rising. Then, something pulling him upward. An unseen hand guiding him back from where he had come, arms and legs limp and wavering.

The arms of the angel of death are around me, guiding me to the gates of....

Rizal broke the surface and felt the breeze on his soaked skin. His eyes fluttered open, and his body expelled the seawater choking his lungs and stomach as he was hauled up and over the railing by two sets of hands, another manning the crook used to bring him up from the world below. Then he was on his back on the deck, coughing and sputtering.

Three sets of worried eyes watched Rizal before the captain's face filled his world. Li grabbed Rizal, fingers squeezing his mouth hard, pushing the flesh of his cheeks between his slack jaw. Rizal choked and struggled. The captain spoke through clenched teeth, saying things Rizal could hear no more than he could understand. Li shook Rizal's head then released him with a hard slap across the cheek. Then Li walked back to the wheelhouse, pulling a cigarette from his pack and lighting it on the way. He said something to Datu and he and the others helped Rizal to the planks along the hull and he sat there, head down. Slowly his mind came to grips with how easily his mind and body had resigned themselves to the end. Hot tears fell from his eyes. Datu took up a seat beside him, Arvin and Amado standing. Rizal felt the engine roar back to life more than he heard it. Above him he heard Amado mumble something about it overheating, how it just needed some time to cool. The boat turned around. There were still lines to take in, catch to sort. Work that needed to be done, whether by four sets of hands or by three. Rizal's head sunk further. His mind released. Unconsciousness took him. He would not wake until sunlight touched his face and he found himself in a world where death had come to visit him; a world in which death no longer held sway.

Chapter Fifteen

RIZAL sat shivering in the wheelhouse, knees tucked under his chin. At his feet was the letter Datu had helped him write to Jasmine. The ink bled in waves toward the bottom of the page, words transformed into meaningless blobs of faded color. Beside the letter lay what little money Rizal had left — the few hundred-dollar notes remaining after their ill-fated trip north and his plunge into the sea the night before. He had smoothed them out, pushing his fingers along their length, pressing them into the planks to dry them. Now, outside the wheelhouse, the sky was gray, a thin drizzle blown in sheets by a blustering wind. The others took pity on Rizal, letting him have the shelter of the wheelhouse to himself. He sat there, breathing the greasy air, thinking thoughts that should have brought forth some sort of feeling. But there was nothing. No anger or sadness or even pain. Only the impulse to leave. To go back to the one place he had been happy since his arrival in this new world, if only for a night.

Rizal stood in his soaking wet clothes, then bent down again to gather up his money. He left the letter where it was. The others rose with worried eyes, looking at Rizal as though he might keel over at any moment. It was late in the morning, still a few more hours until

Li's wife came with her afternoon delivery. They were used to the hunger now, as much as one could become accustomed to the way the feeling stripped away the soul. They stood around Rizal. He looked to all of them, their eyes meeting his, cold and resigned.

"I'm leaving," Rizal said flatly. There was little else to say; a statement as superfluous as it would be to say he would continue breathing. It was a courtesy. A gesture of friendship. He extended them another. "You can come with me, if you want." The others stared at him for a time, blinking away their shock.

Amado asked, "Where will you go?"

"Zhongli."

Then Arvin, "What will you do?"

"Whatever I can."

"Where will you stay?" asked Datu.

"Anywhere, so long as it's not a *paking* boat."

The others chuckled softly. There was a sadness in their laughter. It told Rizal they would not go with him.

"The captain will report you," Datu said, worry in his voice. "The police, they'll come looking for you."

"I know."

"They'll throw you in jail," Amado said, "then they'll kick you out of the country. You won't be able to come back."

"I know."

"Why don't you try to talk to Mr. Chen?" Datu pleaded. "Maybe he can do something about this. He could get us transferred to a better boat, or get us another job. We could tell him how Li mistreats us and all that's happened...." He glanced out to sea and the expanse of gray clouds. Rizal looked past him to the land — the fold of it that rose up from the sea and jutted abruptly up to the mountains, now shrouded in a thin, whispering mist that seemed to fill the world with white silence. *Anywhere*, spoke his thoughts. *Even up the mountain and into the empty valleys on the other side. Anywhere*, the word repeated, *is better than here.*

"When will you leave?" Arvin asked.

"Today."

"You'll take the train?" Datu's words lost some of their worry, gaining the edge of more practical matters. Rizal nodded.

"Keep your head down, *anak*," Amado said.

"My other set of clothes is dry," Datu pointed to the compartments beneath the benches at the bow. "I hid them away. You should take them."

Rizal nodded his gratitude, embarrassed that he had nothing to offer in return. Then he remembered the cutlery he had taken from Jasmine's bar. He went to the wheelhouse to retrieve the knife and fork, stashed there in one of Li's old discarded rubber boots. He brought the set back, holding it out to Datu.

"A trade," he said, "for your clothes."

Datu bellowed with laughter. It was the laugh Rizal remembered from the day they first met, back at the airport in Manila. The laugh of a different man. Rizal looked at the man now, his body bled of excess, leaving behind only loose skin and a withered, sagging face. Datu took the cutlery and went to get the clothes for Rizal. Rizal changed in the wheelhouse, tying the piece of fishing line around the loose pair of pants, Datu's large shirt hanging well past his waist. The dry fabric (well, nearly dry) felt strange against his skin. He touched it with his fingers as though caressing a memory brought to life. Emerging from the wheelhouse, he looked to the other three again.

"You're sure you won't come, *mga kapatid*?" Rizal asked.

They looked to one another, alternately shrugging their shoulders. Datu answered for them.

"Sorry, *anak*," his voice lilted downward, along with his gaze. His eyes rose up then to meet Rizal's. "We wish you luck," he paused, "but it's too dangerous. You'll be on the run."

Rizal shrugged. "I know."

"You can accept the risk?"

"No more risk than if I stay here."

The others nodded. Rizal gave it one last try. "You should come with me," he said. "It might not be safe out there, but it's better than staying here with him."

Amado sighed. "Two and a half more years," he said, not looking at any of them. "Two and a half more years and we're free." He sighed again. "It's not so bad."

They stood apart. Rizal reached out a hand and shook each of theirs in turn. They nodded to him. Then he lifted himself up onto the top of the wall, head swimming at the effort. He turned to look at them one last time, new clothes already growing damp. They stood there with wide, wet eyes and sopping clothes and skin, drizzle beading on dark and peeling foreheads. Rizal nodded a final time, turned and walked down the road. They watched him go until he made the turn right toward the temple. Going past the temple and then the convenience store, he was then beyond sight of the small world of Nanfang'ao Harbor, a world beyond the world, a place where death visited in secret and left without word for the lives taken or nearly claimed. Rizal was gone, and to a man the others wondered if they would ever see the boy again.

Once more Rizal walked down the rain-slick highway to the train station, past the gardens and then the bridge over the shallow creek, the drops letting up enough on the way that he was not completely soaked. He had nothing with him but Datu's clothing and the few hundred dollars he had left. When he got to the station he was met by pair of stray dogs lounging on the steps, coats a ruddy mix of tan and black, a ridge of coarse hair standing up along the length of vertebrae exposed by hunger. Rizal raised a hand to feel his own protruding ribs and one of the animals lifted up its head laconically then lay its chin back down on the stone, blinking at the near-empty traffic circle. A lone taxi was parked alongside the front step. The driver was inside with the seat back, bare feet up on the dashboard, mouth wide open, snoring. Rizal looked around. The station was all but deserted, the town that had grown around it shut up behind steel doors. The old fishermen were at home with their wives and their old, lazy dogs. The shopkeepers were inside, out of the rain, listening to their radios in the dark, chewing betel nut and sipping on cold beers or drinking hot, thin tea. The young were gone, leaving the town for the city. Soon Rizal would be gone too. Already his thoughts floated back to the boat, the boys sitting in the rain. Taking their turns in the wheelhouse. Waiting for their food to be tossed down to them like feeding time for a flock of mangy goats. He thought of going back. Trying one more time to change their minds. But he knew they wouldn't come.

He went to the agent and bought his ticket, then to a nearby convenience store for a small can of Coke and a pack of peanuts to take the sway out of his steps. Returning to the station he took a seat on one of the hard plastic molds where a handful of other passengers were waiting, no one paying him much mind. He sipped his cold drink and savored the taste of food that didn't go down like chunks of plastic. He thought of what he would do when he got to where he was going, wondering if Jasmine would be there. She might be angry with him, he thought. Mad that he hadn't written to her like he said he would. He would have to explain. He hoped he would have the chance, knowing all the while it was just as likely he would arrive there and she would be gone. Maybe she was like him. She might have her own reason to run away. Or perhaps she had been found, sent home already. Back to the Philippines with little more than she had shown up with in the first place.

The other passengers seemed to ignore him and everyone else, sitting with arms folded, eyes straight ahead. The station smelled of grit and disinfectant, one odor lying clumsily on top of the other. They mixed with the smell of engine oil beat down low to the ground by the mist coming off the still warm tracks and the diesel from the trains; the pleasant industrial musk of the tar on the railroad ties. The air was thick, and Rizal felt it filling up his head, clogging his nose and mouth. He took long, deep breaths and found himself sweating. The sound of a bell ringing over the speakers lodged among thick cobwebs in the corners of the ceiling nearly had him out of his skin. The attendant sitting beside the turnstiles called out, and Rizal heard the wheels of a train slowing to a standstill. He pushed himself up, checking the numbers on his ticket against those on the board to ensure he was getting on the right train. Then he went through, out to the same northbound platform he had stood on before, walked the length of the cars until he found the one with the number matching that on his ticket, and boarded.

Much like the station, the train was mostly empty. Rizal found his seat and collapsed into it – a row to himself. He took the seat by the window. As the train lurched away from Su'ao he felt his breaths return to normal, heartbeat slowing as the click of the wheels along the tracks picked up its pace. He watched the gray world pass by through the double panes, a lens of fog building up between them. For an instant he saw a flash of the harbor; the boats, the discarded lines on the roadside, the old yellowed buoys left in piles, the twin humps of rock beyond the breakwater. Then they were gone. The train entered its first tunnel and the world went black. On reaching the other side Rizal tried to look back. But there was nothing to look back to. Only the immovable mountain and the rain turning its bare black outcrops amid the foliage slick like blood on a butcher's floor. Rizal turned to face the headrest in front of him. He could think of no reason to stay awake. So he closed his eyes and slept, falling in and out of awareness until he heard the name he waited for crackle over the speakers. He heard the sound within the jumble of words he did not understand – a sliver of meaning among the meaningless. It wasn't much, but it was enough to bring him up and out of his seat and power his legs down the aisle to the gangway. For a moment he stood there in the doorway, perched on the top step, wondering if he should get off or just go back and sit down, let the train take him all the way around Taiwan and back up to Su'ao again. Then he could take his beating or whatever punishment the captain had in store and go about serving the two-and-a-half years left on his bid. A bell rung out in the station and he knew it was time to decide. Go back to the hell he knew or take a chance on the unknown in Zhongli.

When he got off the train Rizal found Zhongli much as he had left Su'ao, overcast and dark. The line of taxis was there, drivers lifting their heads out of their newspapers to look over the straggle of potential fares coming out of the station. None called to him. He walked on by and tried to remember where to go. He remembered it was the other way, behind the station. He ducked into the tunnel running beneath the tracks to the other side, pausing at the bottom of the wet steps. The rain ran in shallow gutters along the walk, clotted with cigarette butts. At the far end of the tunnel a young woman made her way toward him, head wrapped in a shawl. Rizal began walking toward her – no, an old woman, he realized as he got closer and she came into focus. *All that time under the sun*, he thought. It had done something to his eyes. The world had been clear before. Now it was blurred, uneven.

The woman moved past him, eyes finding an excuse to study the tile mural running the length of the tube. Rizal ignored her too. He walked slowly up the steps at the opposite end, emerging on the back street Datu had led him down before. He saw the lines of bars and restaurants, clothing shops. The places for food and drink were open. Many of the shops were shuttered. It was nearly evening and the weather was bad. Rizal walked down the street, looking into the mostly empty establishments, sliding doors opening like eyeless sockets. Some still had chairs stacked on top of the tables, legs sticking up into the air. Men and women were taking them down, working slow but steady. Rizal found something familiar in their pace. The tired movements. The resigned expressions. He looked for the lights. The bright bulbs that in a few weeks' time would be back in season. He remembered the name, though he wouldn't recognize it. Manila North. The window with the garland lining.

The light rain soaked his head and shoulders as he moved from beneath the awning to the street, weaving among the scooters and motorcycles parked haphazardly, some straight, others at angles that forced all those after to follow their crooked line. His toe caught a kickstand and he cursed the pain down to a dull throb. As he swore, he caught sight of something familiar. The bulbs. The garland. This was the place. Limping slightly he pushed open the door and walked in. It was dark inside, like he remembered. Quieter than it had been before. The staff were on afternoon break, the restaurant closed up for a couple of hours between the midday and the evening rush. The workers were lounging at a rear table near the kitchen. Waiters and waitresses, cooks and busboys and dishwashers. All faces like his, some resting on forearms or the stained cedar of the table itself. Those who were awake looked to him, and he strained his eyes, looking for a familiar face. A woman stood and spoke to him in his own language, asking if she could help him. The words too were blurred to him as he looked past the woman, trying to see if Jasmine was there. Then he heard his name. It was said in the form of a question at first, then a statement. He saw her rise and step out from behind the other woman. There was Jasmine in front of him, and all he could do was stare. A distant thought returned to him. Something about life being made of nothing but standing and looking at her beautiful face. She regarded him with worry and he almost felt like apologizing. The other woman asked Jasmine if she knew him and if it was all right. Jasmine said she did and it was. The other woman went back to the table. Jasmine took Rizal by the arm and led him to another table along the wall, away from her workmates. Clumsily he slid into a seat across from her and the whole thing felt like some strange dream. He wondered if it was real. If he was really still back on the boat in Su'ao, daydreaming in the wheelhouse, rain soaking into his brain, short-circuiting his thoughts. He wondered if he had finally lost his mind and a wave of sadness hit him broadside. It was all he could do to keep from crying. Jasmine reached out across the table and he felt her warm fingers around his.

"You look thin," she told him. He thanked her and she laughed and the sadness was chased from his mind. She paused, studying him for so long that he felt embarrassed. He looked every which way but at her. She cornered him with her darting gaze until he had no choice but to meet it. "Why are you here?" she asked, voice weighted with concern. "You never wrote me back."

"I left," said Rizal.

He felt her fingers tighten their grip.

"You ran away?"

Rizal nodded, lowering his head. Her grip loosened and she leaned back.

"What happened?"

Rizal poured out his story to her. Everything he had said in the letter and how it had been destroyed when he was thrown into the sea. She listened, nodding, taking his hands in hers once more. He kept his eyes down as he spoke, the ache of sadness in his chest beating against his ribs. When it was done, he shook his head and finally found the courage to look at her face. Her eyes were wet, lashes fused together from blinking back tears. She stroked the back of his hand and he felt heat in the paths traced by her fingers.

"What will you do now?"

He sighed and thought.

"I don't know."

She leaned back, his hand slipping from between hers. She looked beyond him, to the table by the kitchen doors. The men and women there did their best to seem indifferent, like they hadn't been listening in. Jasmine tapped a finger against her cheek and shot up. She went to the table, and Rizal heard her whispering rapid fire to the woman who had first greeted him. The exchange lasted a minute, then she was back, sliding into the chair across from him, smiling. He raised an eyebrow, clasping his hands in front of him on the table.

"You start tonight," said Jasmine.

Rizal watched her smile, without a notion to ask what it was he was about to begin.

Chapter Sixteen

"RIZAL, table six."

Rizal looked at Rosie.

"That one!" she pointed.

"Yes, boss."

Rizal scrambled for the gray bucket tray, moved clumsily among the tables and patrons, just missing a man's head with his elbow. He cleared the plates, scraping off the leftover food, gathering up the cutlery and glasses. Then he picked up the tray again. It weighed heavy on his thin arms, like the water pail back home. He had been busing tables for an hour and already his shirt was soaked through. Rosie had made him shower first, before letting him anywhere near the customers. He was grateful for the chance to properly wash himself for the first time in months, and to get a fresh change of clothes – a shirt from the restaurant's lost and found, a pair of pants loaned from one of the cooks. For now, a cheap pair of plastic blue flip flops would have to do for shoes. He brought the tray back to Rosie and stared at her. She cocked an eyebrow and pointed with her thumb to the kitchen. He nodded sheepishly, made for the double doors and stepped into the super-heated space filled with the hiss of gas burners and steam. The cooks chattered with one another, laughing and swearing as flames licked at the bottoms of pots and woks. Rizal caught himself staring as one of the cooks flipped a pan filled with sautéed vegetables and caught every one. He turned and nearly ran into a waitress. Apologizing with a shallow nod he took the tray to the dishwasher, who was an older Taiwanese man, around sixty. The names Rizal had been told were a blur. He remembered Rosie, the boss, of course. Jasmine gave him the rundown on her. She was from Manila. A former caregiver who married her ward's son. Now she ran the restaurant, catering to the Filipinos who came in for a taste of home. Rosie was kind, Jasmine said. Tough, but with a good heart.

"Work fast and you won't have a problem with her."

And so Rizal tried to work quickly. He set the tray down with a clatter, the dishwasher shaking his head and using words Rizal had heard out of Captain Li's mouth many hundreds of times. The old man even wore hip waders, just as the *chuanzhang* had. Rizal caught himself staring and the old man pointed to an empty tray then back out the double doors. Snapping from his stupor, Rizal took up the clean tray and went back out, moving among the tables, looking for empty plates and glasses. He caught Jasmine watching him from the bar and shot her a quick smile. She returned it before pointing out an empty beer bottle on a nearby table. He snatched it up then went to the place near the kitchen doors Rosie had told him to stand where he could look around the room and see what needed doing without being in the way. There was a busing station there with clean glasses, mugs, plates, and silverware. He set the half-full tray down. A man called for a new knife and he brought one to him, taking away one that had fallen on the floor. When he got back to the station Rosie was there.

"You learn fast," she nodded. "Quick on your feet too."

"Thank you, miss."

"Keep it up and you'll have no problem here," she said, then turning a touch stern. "I pay minimum wage, cash in hand at the end of the night. There's a small office in the back with a cot. You can sleep there until you get some money together and sort out a place to stay." She turned to face him head on now, eyes glowering. "But remember, if I even think you're stealing from me – I mean if I find a fork missing, a napkin, anything – you're done. Back on the street. Once you cross Ms. Rosie, there's no going back. Got it?"

Rizal gulped, feeling the lump he swallowed go down cold. "Yes, miss."

"Good," she brightened. "Sorry, *anak*, I don't mean to scare you. But you know how it is. Sometimes you give a man an inch of kindness and the moment you turn your back he strangles you with it. Do you know what I mean?"

Rizal stood frozen, unsure of the right way to respond. She laughed, putting a hand softly on his arm.

"Relax, *bata*," she looked into his eyes. "I look at you and I don't see that kind of man."

Rosie walked away to speak to a waitress. Rizal took a deep breath of smoke-filled air. Most of the men seated at their tables were smoking cigarettes. The overhead ventilation fans struggled to keep up. Rizal didn't mind, glad to smell anything other than the smothering stink of fish guts. When a woman raised an empty coffee mug,

Rizal grabbed a fresh pot from the station and carried it over. Nervously he took the woman's cup and filled it, setting it down lightly in front of her. With slow, careful strides he took the pot back to the station. Then he went back to moving about the room, gathering plates, scraping the discarded bones and scraps into a hefty black garbage bag at the busing station. The bag filled quickly and he took it out back to the disposal bin, swinging it twice to heave it over the side. It landed with a thud, and again he smiled at the simple pleasure of a job well done.

At around ten that night the last customers pushed themselves slowly up from their seats and paid their bills. The doors closed, and Rizal helped clean the tables and the bar, and he stacked up the chairs on the table tops. He took out the garbage then helped the kitchen crew hose down the kitchen. He even helped the dishwasher with the last load of dishes, scrubbing plates in the deep stainless steel sink. It was nearly midnight by the time they were done. The waitstaff had all gone home. The cooks followed, the dishwasher close behind. Rizal emerged into the empty restaurant and found even Jasmine was gone. A part of him felt sad she hadn't stuck around. He was exhausted, but the anticipation of his first true rest in months swelled his chest with a feeling of contentment. He breathed deep of the nicotine-infused walls and could almost feel the place alive and breathing with him. He heard footsteps behind and turned to see Rosie there, the skin beneath her eyes swollen and dark. A lit cigarette hung between her fingers and she raised it up to take a long drag.

"Come on," she nodded to a door beyond the bar,

exhaling smoke in a thick cloud. "Let's go get you set up in the office."

He followed her back through the door, hearing it swing shut behind him. It led to a short, dark hall that in turn led to another door at the rear of the building. Rosie opened it and switched on the light. There was little inside the office save a small desk along with a gray filing cabinet, drawers locked with the key left in the keyhole of the upper compartment. Rosie pulled out the key and pointed to the cot folded up in the corner. Rizal pulled it out and unfolded it. The cot creaked at the joints, with the frame showing signs of rust in the dense humidity. The thin mattress was held in place with springs; and when it was unfolded he tested it, pushing down with both hands. Rosie laughed, expelling smoke up toward the chain dangling from the overhead light.

"It'll hold a skinny little *daga* like you, don't worry," she smiled. She reached atop a bookshelf filled mostly with binders and pulled down a ratty blanket, tossing it onto the cot. "In case you get cold," she said, looking around the room to see if there was anything else he might need. She put out her cigarette in the ashtray on the desk and it sat there smoldering. Rizal took a seat on the cot, bouncing up and down a couple of times, stopping when he felt her glowering down at him.

"You know where the bathrooms are," she said. "Feel free to use the shower again if you want to wash up. There aren't any clean towels left so you'll have to get creative when you dry off. You know where the staff fridge is?" Rizal nodded, remembering where Jasmine had pointed it out in the small break room off the kitchen. "I had one of the cooks fix you a plate. It's on the top shelf," said Rosie. "Help yourself. Grab a drink too if you want. But don't go grabbing anything else, *naunawaan*? Remember what I said about people who steal from me."

Rizal nodded nervously. Rosie couldn't help but laugh again.

"Good boy," Rosie reached down, patting him on the cheek. "Unfortunately you'll be stuck here until I come back in the morning. If there's some kind of emergency you go out the exit in the back. But if you go out and the door closes behind you, you'll be trapped outside. Got it? I'm not about to leave you with a set of keys just yet."

Rizal nodded again.

"Okay," said Rosie, looking around again. She tapped a short rhythm on the desk then stuck her thumbs into her pants pockets, rocking slowly back and forth on her flats. "I guess you're all set. Turn out the lights before you go to sleep. And try not to burn the place down."

Rizal lowered his head, smiling down at the floor. "I won't, miss."

"Goodnight, Rizal."

"Goodnight, boss."

Rosie walked out, leaving Rizal alone in the office. He looked around the room and felt the chill in the air now that the place was empty and he had stopped moving for the first time in hours. Though his stomach screamed for a bite of food, he decided to wash up first. He found the shower again and stripped down, leaving his clothes to hang on the hook inside the door. Earlier in the day, before his shift began, he had had to rush. Now, he could take his time. The tile floor was cold, and he stood on the balls of his feet before the water warmed then became almost scalding hot. He settled down flatfooted and gasped as the water took him in. He let it run over his body, turning around in a full circle, breathing in the thick steam. A basket with small containers of shampoo and conditioner and a sliver of soap hung from a silver metal hook attached to the wall by a clear-plastic suction cup. By luck he grabbed the bottle of shampoo first and squirted a few globs onto his palms and ran them through his hair. He felt the knots gradually slacken and release their stubborn grip until he could run his fingers through and the tangles gave way. The scent of flowers rose up with the clouds of steam and he let it fill his nostrils, breathing deep. Then he took the bar soap and worked it to a lather that he rubbed over every inch of skin his hands could reach. He looked down toward the water swirling into the drain, watching it wash away. He stood there for as long as he could, until the water began to run cold, turning the tap as far left as it would go to try and coax more heat. When it would give no more he finally closed the taps and stood there in the whirling clouds of vapor.

When he opened the door, the cold air rushed in and he remembered what Rosie had said about the towels. He looked around frantically for something to dry off with, eyes locking on a roll of paper towels. Gingerly he padded across the freezing tiles to the roll and snatched off a few sheets, patting himself down with them until they were soaked through. He grabbed a few more, folding one sheet on top of another and repeated until he was reasonably dry. Then he put his clothes back on, shivering. He was damp but clean. He walked over to the fridge and opened it up, peering inside. There as Rosie had promised was a plate, a sheet of plastic wrap with beads of condensation hanging off the inside covering the mound of food underneath. Rizal sighed. He picked up the plate and peeled back the layer of plastic. He pulled it up to his nose and breathed in. Pork *sisig* with a fried egg on top. He grabbed a can of Coke and shut the door. Then he took his food back to the office, shutting off the lights along the way. He sat in the office alone, savoring the food, avoiding the temptation to shovel huge clumps of it into his mouth until the frenzy overtook him. The plate was clean in a matter of minutes. He took in a gulp of his drink and exhaled long and full. He set the plate on the desk and shivered in part at the rush of sugar and caffeine in his blood but also at the chill of the room. He pulled the blanket up over his shoulders and drank slow. As he did his thoughts again drifted to Su'ao. To Datu, Arvin, and Amado. They would be out on the water now. Tying lines. Fixing bait. Setting the lines to soak. Hauling them in again. Working to pay off the debts they had taken for the right to work.

As he thought of them Rizal could feel the room rocking as the boat had beneath his feet. The cot seemed to sway, dipping its corners down toward the floor then up again. He felt his stomach turn the way it had all those nights working under Li's scornful watch, and for a moment he thought he would be sick. He stood, putting a hand over his suddenly swollen stomach. He put the drink down and belched, holding the air in his cheeks before blowing it out. The feeling subsided and he paced the small room, taking in his new surroundings again. He pulled his forearm to his nose and breathed in the pleasant scent of soap, pulled the blanket, still on his shoulders, tighter around his body. The quiet in the empty building was almost total, the settling of the foundation, the occasional clattering of the pipes the only sounds to be heard. He was tired. He sat on the cot again and laid himself down, resting his head against the thin pillow. Sleep held itself at a distance, though. Something in his thoughts was restless. His mind bounded from Jasmine to Rosie, Zhongli to Su'ao and across the sea to Manila, Navotas, his mother, his daughter. He pictured his mother then, alone in the cemetery. Now things were different. He thought he might try to write to her. At least tell her what was happening. He would leave some pieces of his story out, of course. No need to worry her with Li throwing him into the sea, beating him, feeding him expired food, leaving him to rot day after day in the sun and the rain and the storms and the funereal fog that enveloped the harbor in the cool early mornings. She could have someone read the letter to her – perhaps Mrs. Pilapil could do it – and hear a version of his truth. One not quite so sad and dismal as it really was.

Rizal rose up again and took his evening's pay out of his pocket, counting out the crinkled bills. After a few weeks, he thought, he could finally send some money home as he had promised. Even if his mother couldn't read the letter she would be happy to receive the money and know her son was doing well. Doing something right for the first time in his life. Maybe, he thought, she would even be proud of him. He sighed and went to the office door, walked down the hall to the dining room with the tables all stacked with chairs, then into the kitchen where the dishes were piled up, clean and gleaming. He remembered his own plate back in the office and went to fetch it, brought it back to the kitchen and scrubbed it clean and placed it atop one of the towering piles of white ceramic. Then he went to the dining room again and stood there awhile, the exit sign casting things in an artificial ember glow. The red color seemed to fill him with warmth. He realized the blanket was still draped over his shoulders. He pulled it up once more, hands holding the corners over his chest. In a few hours Rosie would be back, Jasmine too. He turned and went down the hall and into the office. He lay down on the cot and was asleep in seconds, his weary head reeling with a thousand thoughts and dreams and feelings compacted into a single mold, the overhead security camera watching as a boy – a scruffy-haired young man – finally slept with a smile on his face.

Chapter Seventeen

THE next morning Rizal awoke to Rosie coming through the door. Shyly he pulled up the blanket over his bare shoulders and she paid him the dignity of turning around while he dressed. As his shirt came over his head he found she had brought him breakfast: some *pandesal* and *champorado.*

"I made it myself," she told him as she set it on the desk, inviting him to sit and eat. Rizal wolfed down the food while she watched. Glibly she began a remark about the last time Rizal had a proper breakfast but stopped partway through. Rizal pretended he didn't hear, tipping the bowl back to get the last few bits of porridge into his mouth. He asked her the time and she told him it was nearly ten. The kitchen crew would be reporting shortly for prep work, the waitstaff later at eleven o'clock to get ready for the lunch rush. She asked Rizal how he had slept. He had slipped so quickly into unconsciousness that he had to think about it before answering that he had never slept better. Without her asking he gathered up the bowl and plate and took them back into the kitchen to scrub them clean. She followed him there with a look of bemusement, watching as he moved clumsily under her gaze.

"Relax, Rizal," she said, drawing an embarrassed smile

out of the boy. “Take your time. You’re not on the clock yet.”

Rizal slowed down, drying the dishes methodically before putting them away. Rosie said she had some work to do in the office, sending him scrambling ahead of her down the hall to fold up the cot and stash it away in the corner. Eyeing the desk he quickly snatched up a wayward speck of food and tucked it away in his pocket, hoping Rosie hadn’t noticed. She shook her head at him, pushing her palms down toward the floor, wordlessly telling him to calm down. His face flushed with color, his hollow cheeks taking on a fullness brought by the sudden rush of blood. Rosie reached into her black leather purse and produced a magazine, handing it over to him. Rizal took it, staring at the cover – a pair of bright-eyed women looking back at him with wide, red mouths. He looked to Rosie, throat suddenly dry.

“You’ve got some time before your shift,” said Rosie, tapping the magazine cover with a gel-capped fingernail, light blue. She was dressed in pastels, makeup and accessories to match. “Something for you to kill some time.”

Rizal felt heat rising from his collar. Shakily he handed the magazine back to Rosie, meekly offering, “I can’t, miss.”

She pushed it back to him. “Of course you can. I’m only lending it to you. I haven’t had time to read it yet. You can have a look first. Leave it on my desk when you start your shift. Okay?”

Rizal took the magazine back, looking down again at the cover. “Thank you, miss.”

Rosie went around the desk and sat down while Rizal stood there, opening the pages to look at the pictures, moving his lips silently. Her voice interrupted the charade.

"We'll figure something better out eventually, but for now sleeping here will have to do. The police might be looking for you, you understand? On account of you leaving your job."

Rizal nodded.

"You're welcome to work here as long as you want, so long as you stay out of sight. Once in a while the NIA pops their head in, but my husband has some *guanxi* with a man on the city council. He lets my husband know ahead of time when the cops are planning an immigration sweep. Actually, my husband is preparing to run for a seat himself in the next election. If he wins it will be even better for us. But anyway, if immigration is going to come in, we'll keep you out of sight while they sniff around." She stopped. "You know what I mean when I say *guanxi*?"

Rizal shook his head.

"It's like favors," she explained. "I do for you, you do for me. That sort of thing. The whole country runs on it," she laughed. "Well, maybe that's an exaggeration, but it's kind of like how ours runs on bribes."

Rizal smiled bashfully.

"But if you want to get out of here, go to a shelter or something, you just tell *Tiya* Rosie, all right? I know what it's like to be alone in a strange place."

Rizal nodded and sighed, warmth rising in his chest. He looked at Rosie as she sat studying an open binder he hadn't noticed her take. His eyes lingered on her face. Before he could embarrass himself by staring too long he turned and left the office, forgetting to close the door at first. Turning back, he stayed close to the wall, trying to hide behind the open door. Quietly he pushed it shut, cringing at the click of the plunger. Then he padded down the hallway and went to the table where the staff had been taking their break the day before. The chairs were still piled on top, legs jutting up in the air. Rizal took down a chair and sat, opening the magazine again. He sat there a while, flipping through the pages, looking at the pictures of beautiful women and handsome men. Some were faces he recognized. Movie stars from the VHS tapes he and his friends had watched in Mr. Bongalos' arcade during a time when he had a beat-up VCR that jammed and ate more tapes than it spat out unharmed before the old man finally sent it to the junk shop. Rizal flipped through to the back of the magazine, then looked up at the clock mounted on the wall, wondering when Jasmine might come in. The steel security door was up. Sunlight streamed through the front window, flickering on the strands of garland and the green and red lights. Rizal's thoughts turned to Christmas – the one time of year he might have got something new. A gift from his mother. Not new, exactly. Something he didn't have before. As simple as a box of candy, maybe a shirt or a pair of shorts from the goodwill box at the nearby parish. He made a promise to himself that he would save enough to send his mother a gift this year. Something *she* could open on Christmas morning. He would get a present for his daughter too. He would hold on to it, take it back to Manila when he finally returned. Find her and give it to her in person. And when he went back, he and his mother would move to a real neighborhood. One with a church he could take her to for midnight mass on Christmas Eve, where the other parishioners wouldn't stare and judge. They would sit in the pews like regular people and hear mass, and she would be proud of her boy. Her boy who traveled across the ocean to make a better life for his family. Then they would go back to their home – a real home on an upper floor, where dust couldn't float in through the open door and the spring and summer floods couldn't reach them.

His thoughts were interrupted by the opening of the front door. Through the haze of light he saw some of the kitchen staff wandering in together, laughing and chatting. He smiled at them as they walked by, some nodding to him, others wrapped up in their own conversations. They walked into the kitchen. Once inside their voices and laughter echoed off the tiles and Rosie emerged from her office, poking her head through the kitchen doors to lend her voice to the chorus, yelling out what needed to be done. The voices fell to a hush then silenced altogether as she told them to make sure their stations were clean before they started chopping vegetables, peeling potatoes, and making soup stock. As Rizal listened with his head tilted back toward the open door, he felt a tap on his shoulder. He turned and there was Jasmine, standing over him with her hair pulled back, still slick from her morning shower. Her face was made up, light lipstick today instead of the dark shade she had worn the day before. Her skin was bright, new, like she had left yesterday and come back a different person. Rizal tried not to stare and again fought the rush of blood to his cheeks in vain. She put a hand on her hip in mock annoyance.

"Aren't you going to say good morning?"

"*Magandang umaga*," Rizal said shyly. He looked up to see her turn an ear toward him, pointing to it as though she hadn't heard. He said it again, louder than before.

"*Anak ng kamote!* I'll bet you were the kind of child who would have starved rather than cry for your mama's milk," she teased, sliding into the chair across from him. Other members of the waitstaff were coming in, some heading into the kitchen to add to the din and help the crew with their preparations. Others took up seats near the kitchen door or went to the bar to chop lemons and limes or stock the shelves with racks of clean glasses, cups, and mugs. Rizal tried to think of something to say to Jasmine, thinking of how easy it had been with Rosie. Why was it more difficult with her? He could see Jasmine looking around as though trying to find some excuse to get up and he scrambled, spewing out the first thing that popped into his mind.

"Where did you sleep last night?"

He began kicking himself immediately, rushing to recover. "I mean *how* did you sleep last night?" It hardly sounded better. Jasmine laughed it off.

"How did I sleep? The same as anyone. On my back, in my bed. Sometimes on my side. How did you sleep? Or should I say where?"

Rizal sighed, rolling his heavy head around, aghast at his own awkwardness. "I slept in the office." Jasmine raised an eyebrow.

"Rosie's office?"

"Yes."

"Alone?"

"Ai-ya!" Rizal exclaimed. "Of course alone. Who else would be with me?" He pulled at his shirt collar.

"Then you slept well?"

"Best sleep I've had in months," said Rizal. "It was nice to be on a bed instead of the floor or a bench with the waves rolling me over or rain falling on my head." He saw Jasmine's face turn serious, and he felt sorry for chasing away her smile. He tried to lighten the mood. "Is it nice out there? In the city, I mean. I can't go outside because...." He looked down. Speaking to his sandaled feet, voice lower than before, he said, "Rosie says it's not safe."

Jasmine leaned forward, letting her purse slide from her shoulder. She set it on the seat beside her. "She's right. You're a runaway now. Until you file a complaint you're just another *migrante* who left his job. Your captain will report you missing, and that means they'll pull your work visa and you're in the country illegally. And if they catch you they'll ship you back home. It's best you stay here until you file your case."

Rizal raised his head again, looking at Jasmine. She watched his brow furrow. His eyes then darted to the door as he heard the bell above the frame chime. A Taiwanese man wearing a smart, crisp suit walked in and Rizal's lungs seized momentarily before Jasmine's calm demeanor convinced him there was nothing to worry about.

"Rosie's husband," said Jasmine. "He's a good man. Comes in sometimes in the morning to bring Rosie a coffee, but I think he just wants to see her before he goes to the office. He's very busy. She is too, obviously. I don't think they get to spend much time together."

Rizal watched as the man walked through the restaurant, then into the hall leading to Rosie's office, a pair of paper coffee cups in a cardboard tray in his hand. He tried to remember what Jasmine had been telling him. Something about..., "My case?"

"Your complaint," Jasmine explained. "Lots of people here have filed already. There's a phone number you call. They take your name, hear your story, do an investigation. If they find out your boss mistreated you or did something against the law, they help you. The problem is, the case might take a while. A few weeks. A couple months. For me it's been even longer. It's hard to say. And while the case is open you're not allowed to work. Lucky for us Rosie knows people who run the shelters for *migrantes* who have had a hard time here. If we need to make some money they send us here, or someplace like this, under the radar. I'm at a shelter while I wait for my case to finish. When it's done I'll try to get another job. A legal one."

Rizal took it all in, nodding.

"You think I should call the number?"

Jasmine looked around the restaurant. "You want to be stuck here the rest of your life busing tables? Sleeping on Rosie's cot? Looking over your shoulder for the immigration cops?"

Rizal shook his head, clasping his hands on the table.

"Then call the number." She softened a little, seeing the worry on Rizal's face. "I can help you, if you want. We can call later, during the afternoon break. What do you think?"

Rizal nodded.

Jasmine's smile returned. She stood up, patting the

back of his hand. "Good. Now I'm going to help the bar staff get ready. Find me after the lunch rush. We'll make the call together."

With that she was up and gone, moving with a flourish behind the bar. Rizal's head swum with thoughts of her and Rosie and what would happen when they made the call. The world peeled back and disappeared as he faded into his thoughts. Some time passed before a blur of color brought him back. As his eyes returned to focus, he realized there was a man in a red-and-white T-shirt sitting across the table. He recognized him as one of the kitchen staff but didn't know his name. The man cocked his chin at him and sat back coolly, squinting in a way that reminded Rizal of Kidlat and his bag of gasoline.

"Your name's Rizal?"

Rizal studied the man before answering. The man was older, thirty-five or so. Short hair parted at the side, slick and thinning on top. His face was a tangle of lines and wrinkles, features drawn in by some unseen pull, calling them all toward center. His eyes were glassy, dark. Serious. He took a drag on a cigarette held loose between his fingers, letting the ash fall to the floor. Most of the kitchen staff smoked, Rizal had noticed, often while cooking over the big gas burners, relighting sweat and spit-soaked butts on the open flames. A faded tattoo, a mash of blotted black dots that might have been a tiger, bled into the dark skin of the man's forearm. The man raised his eyebrows and Rizal realized he'd been staring. He remembered the man had asked after his name and nodded.

"My name's Isko," said the man. "I hope you don't

mind but I heard you talking to Jasmine and thought I should say hello."

Rizal fixated on the man's tattoo again before realizing he was being rude.

"Hello," he nodded to Isko, still unsure of the man.

"She was telling you about the number we *migrantes* can call when we get in trouble, ah?" asked Isko, not waiting for an answer. "*Amputa*, a waste of time. You know, I called that number three months ago, and what do you think they told me?" Rizal shook his head. "They say, 'Oh, you just like to complain. What does it matter if you have no days off? Day off means no pay, ah. You're here to work, so work.' *Putang ina!* I slammed the phone down so hard it almost broke in two, and that was the end of it. They didn't say anything about an investigation. Nothing about helping me find another job. You know they even had the nerve to tell me to go back to my boss? And this was another *migrante* I spoke to! The *hudas* told me I should apologize to that *bastardo* boss of mine so I could go back to work. That *puta* who stole my pay and kept me locked up in a shed at night after I worked sixteen hours a day in his fields. I should apologize to him?"

Rizal pulled back from the table. Isko's voice shook. His fists trembled, flexing and clenching on the table. He took a deep breath, closing his eyes slowly, opening them again. Rizal felt he should say something but froze, unable to speak.

"It makes me angry, *anak*," Isko said, voice softer now, a touch of resignation manifesting in an apathetic shrug of his narrow shoulders. "But what can we do? It's like back home. If you know someone, somebody high up, everything will be okay." He looked around the room, waving an arm at the others. "But who do we know here? Only other *migrantes* like you and me." He pushed himself up out of the chair, wincing at some unseen pain. A hand shot to his lower back. He hissed through his front teeth. "That's what sixteen hours a day for eight months straight and a concrete floor to sleep on at night does to you, *anak*. And when you ask somebody for help, what do they say? That you're making trouble. They say you like to complain." He paused, stretching his spine, turning slowly from side to side with his hands pressed against the small of his back. "They tell you to shut up and get back to work." He shrugged again. "Call the number if you want, Rizal. I just wanted to tell you what to expect ... in case you were getting your hopes up."

He walked away, patting Rizal on the shoulder as he passed by. Rizal cringed at the man's touch, suddenly tired of all the patting. All the downward looks from people standing above him. He crossed his arms over his chest, wishing there was somewhere he could go. Outside, away from the restaurant. Away from people. Someplace he could just be alone. Remembering the place where he had first spoken to Jasmine in private he stood up and strode back through the kitchen to the rear exit, propping the door open with a crate. He turned to the left and paced the narrow alley, stopping after a couple of turns to press his back against the bare concrete. He looked up at the sky, dotted with high-ranging puffs of white cloud, blinking against the bright light shining down into the narrow crack between the buildings. He stood there until a voice called to him. He turned and saw Rosie leaning partway out the door.

“Rizal,” she said, beckoning him inside with a wave of her arm, “time to get to work.”

Chapter Eighteen

THE child looked at him with all the bright-eyed wonder of a mind not yet saddled by the worries of age. Rizal looked back. Somewhere within the limpid iris he saw his daughter, Liezel. Her name was a world, one he had let pain and shame, fear and doubt separate himself from for too long. Into that world he sunk now, and as he did he felt the clutching strands of regret reach for his heart and take hold. He set down his bus tray, arms weighted by fatigue and guilt. How long since Liezel had last crossed his mind? And why now? Why only when he looked into the eyes of an unfamiliar child did he think of her, the girl of his own flesh and blood? He stood there watching the child. She faced him, peeking over the rail of one of the booths along the far wall. Her bob-cut hair fell and covered an eye. Her mother reached to sweep it away, holding a hand against the child's cheek to pinch the flushed skin. The little girl cringed and smiled at once, pulling her head away. The swath of hair fell over her eye once more. Her gaze was pulled to Rizal. He smiled from the corner of his mouth, the sheepish expression a cheap cover for the daggers of depression bleeding him slowly from the inside.

He looked down to the mess of bones and half-chewed food and mingled remnants of drinks sloshing in the bottom of his tray, detritus of the dinner hour, picked up the tray and walked to the kitchen, backing in through the swinging doors. He turned and saw Isko slowly stirring a pot of *arroz caldo* and the man nodded to him. Rizal nodded back and turned away, scraping excess food into the garbage can beside the dish pit, then adding the plates and cups to the pile separating the washer from the rest of humanity. Rizal noticed the garbage can was nearly full. He tied the bag in a knot, then hefted it up with a grunt. He placed the bag on a dolly and wheeled it toward the rear exit and backed through, leaving the dolly to prop open the door. He lifted up the heavy bag again with some effort. As he turned to heave it up and over the edge of the bin, he froze. Four men were there, dark uniforms bleeding into the blackness of the night. Copper badges glinted in the moonlight. Rizal felt the bag fall from his grip and his hands dropped dead at his side. One of the men put a finger to his lips and Rizal remembered his last encounter with the police. Hands fell on his shoulders, turning Rizal around. He was pushed back through the doorway, the column of four following behind. He heard the click of the dolly wheels on the tiles, the hydraulic door hissing shut. The kitchen crew took no notice of their presence until Rizal and the four policemen were clear of the rear hall and its stacks of boxes. A voice rang out behind Rizal and suddenly every head turned, eyes reddened by smoke and steam.

"Nobody move!" yelled one of the officers. They fanned out through the kitchen, herding the crew away from the still-bubbling pots and flame-licked pans and woks toward the dish pit. Before long all were assembled there. Rizal stood in the middle, breathing in sweat and fear.

Two officers remained while the others walked into the dining room, returning a short time later with the wait and bar staff, then going to turn off the burners on the stoves, the kitchen already filling with the smell of burnt food. Outside Rizal could hear the clatter of dishes and the shifting of chairs as the customers filed out amid a din of hushed conversation. Rizal found Jasmine as the waitstaff joined the huddled mass, her faced warped with fear and the rapid aging of a moment presided over by the hand of immovable fate. Rosie barged through the kitchen doors last, bouncing them off the wall, cursing the officers in a mix of English, Mandarin, and her native tongue.

"What's going on?" she yelled, "Why do you have to shut down my business and harass my staff? *Walang hiya ka! Ni you shenme wenti?*"

The tirade seemed only to bemuse the officers. They stood back in a line, smirking. The staff lowered their faces. Rosie stood between them and the officers, arms folded across her chest. When she spoke she leaned forward at the waist, throwing the entire force of her being into seeing off the invaders with a primal display of motherly protection. The officers took Rosie's abuse with glazed expressions until one raised a hand and said something that stopped her mid-sentence, words dying on a breath resigned to the laws of an indifferent world. The man addressed them in English.

"We are with the National Immigration Agency."

Rizal listened, though this time there was no one to translate for him. The words strafed his mind with the menace of the unfamiliar. He looked around to gauge the seriousness of the situation by the expressions of the others, finding it was grim. The officer spoke flatly, in the way one talks of a foregone conclusion.

"We have received a complaint of foreigners working illegally at this restaurant. We will check everyone's documents. Those who have the proper working papers and identification will be released. Those without papers on hand or without papers at all will be brought to our offices in Taoyuan City for interviews and processing. Please be patient. We will call on you one by one to produce your papers, and we will take down your information. It may take some time. Miss," he looked to Rosie, still fuming, "please translate what I have said for those who do not speak English."

Rosie turned to face them, stating curtly, "They are going to check your working papers and IDs. I'm sorry." The bluster and anger of her voice was dead, fire gone from her eyes. She moved to comfort a young waitress who broke down crying. Throughout the group frightened eyes found each other and in them saw their sense of doubt avowed. The murk of fear shrouded them as they were called to speak in hushed tones with an officer at the far end of the kitchen, voices sounding a mix of hisses and whispers. One by one each was sent back to a separate huddle opposite those yet to be summoned. Soon Rizal saw he was next. His legs felt as though they belonged to someone else. A hand steadied him by the shoulder and he saw that Isko had been by his side the entire time. Numbly Rizal walked a shuffling path from the universe of the huddle to the one occupied by the officer and joined it. The man spoke a few words in English, none of which Rizal understood. From the corner of his lowered gaze, he saw the officer beckon someone. He heard Rosie's heels clicking quickly across the tiles. The pointed toes of her shoes soon mingled with Rizal's view of his own ratty sneakers and the officer's black uniform boots. The officer spoke again. Rosie translated.

"He's asking if this is your legal place of employment."

Rizal shook his head. The officer spoke again.

"He's asking where you were working before you came here."

Rizal spoke the name of the place that had been little more than the few square feet of deck space to him: *Su'ao.* Rosie said the name to the officer. He looked confused for a moment, lifting his pen from a small notebook to his lower lip. He said the name in different ways, changing up the tones until finally he settled on a combination that seemed to stoke something in his memory. "*Oh, Yilan de Su'ao,*" he said, writing it down. He said the next word in English, one Rizal did recognize.

"Fisherman?"

Rizal nodded. Another question came. This one Rosie answered for him.

"Two days."

The officer nodded, neither satisfied nor disappointed, occupying that deadened middle plane populated by those with their task laid out before them and little choice but to see it done. Without looking up he waved Rizal away to the larger group, only a few remaining in the smaller one yet to be called forward. They stood in silence, watched over by the other three officers. From beneath the brims of their caps the officers' eyes moved over the waiters, waitresses, cooks, bartenders, and busboys, darting from one to the next. Rizal saw that one had his hand held precipitously over the handle of his baton. He drummed his fingers on it, tapping out a marching beat in time with the rhythm of the hands of the clock mounted on the wall. The clicking of the second hand was the only sound save that of the last set of shuffling footsteps as a waitress became the final addition to their quivering mass. The Taiwanese dishwasher, disinterested as he casually smoked a cigarette, and Rosie stood together, off to the side. Rosie was called back by the officer who had asked the questions. She walked toward him, head down, arms folded low across her stomach. Again the officer spoke to her, she to the group.

"I'm sorry, everyone. They are going take you to the National Immigration Agency office in Taoyuan City. They'll take down your names and the details of your cases. If they think you have been taken advantage of or treated unfairly, you might be allowed to stay. If not ... it's likely you'll be deported for running away."

A murmured panic spread through them as heads whipped one way then the other, searching for an answer, a way out. Finding neither they quickly learned that there was nothing for them to do except to wait like children for further instruction. They stood detached from bodily sensations except the tingle of fear creeping along their spines. When they were told to move they did so not because they recognized the command but because to them all sound *was* command. Rizal followed the group with leaden steps as they moved through the deserted dining room, funneling out the front door to the street. As he went through the door he saw a tall black-and-white bus with tinted windows. Two more officers stood on either side of the front passenger door, waving the workers through. He walked up the steps into the darkened interior, a count of the bodies passing by sounding off as each new man or woman boarded. He flopped into the first seat he saw and looked around for Jasmine. Before he could find her someone fell into the seat beside him. It was Rosie. He found a heat growing inside him. An anger he couldn't place until he remembered her words of her husband's connections. His *guanxi*, she called it. How they would be warned before anyone would come poking their nose around *her* restaurant. He could feel Rosie's eyes on him. His remained straight forward as the last were herded on board. Once the last of them took their seats the engine rumbled to life and the bus pulled out onto the road. Rizal watched the city, cloaked in darkness, passing through the square lens of the large front windshield. Traffic flowed around them, scooters speeding to pass then pulling up in front at the frequent stoplights bathing the inside of the bus in sanguine tones. From behind him Rizal could hear the sniffles and muffled cries of the others. He stared out the window beside him, watching the flashing bulbs of the brightly colored signage of the betel nut stands, where women sat on high stools. He began tuning it all out, wanting to forget every part of this place. The sights. The smells. Every word spoken. Every person he had met. He wanted to travel back in time, to when he and Kidlat sat staring out at Manila Bay, talking about the future. A time when there was only them in the world and no one else. This time he would listen to his friend's warning. He would stay where he was, where he belonged. Again he felt Rosie's eyes on him, then the slight touch of her hand on his knee. The touch drew his eyes to her, and he saw the silver trails of tears traced down her cheek, the shadows of raindrops on the window alighting on her face.

"You hate me, don't you?" Rosie said, chin falling to her chest. To this Rizal said nothing. Her hand pulled away from his knee. He let the hand fall away. From her last reserves of courage Rosie summoned the energy to tilt her head to look at him again, studying his blank expression in the window's reflection. He spoke to his reflection, hearing his own disembodied voice.

"I don't hate you."

She sighed, unconvinced. "Yes, you do." She shifted her body away from his, brushing his leg with her own as she crossed one over the other. Leaning an elbow on the outer armrest she spoke into the aisle. "I would hate me ... if I were you. Everything I said about it being safe. My husband's connections. You probably think it was all a lie. And maybe you're right. Maybe he was lying to me. Maybe I was lying to myself. I knew the risk when he said he was thinking of running for office. How it would make us a target for his opponents. He asked me if I knew what it meant, and I told him I did. I was blinded by it, Rizal. All I could see was the future. My husband and I, the power couple. He the councilman, me the businesswoman. I only thought of myself, of how far I've come since I came to this country. Now everyone is paying for my selfishness. Everyone knows. If someone let happen to me what I've let happen to all of you, I would hate me. I'm sure there isn't a person on this bus who doesn't wish I would throw myself under the wheels."

Rizal expelled hot breath against the window pane, fogging the glass. He turned to her and saw that she was looking away. There was something he wanted to tell her. A burn in the back of his throat trying to escape.

"I stole from you." Rosie turned, blinking back disbelief.

"You what?"

"From the restaurant. The first time I came to eat here, I took a knife and fork from you and brought them back to Su'ao. I gave them to my friend, just before I came back to start working for you. I don't remember taking them. I was drunk. But I did," he said softly. "I took them."

He raised his head and their eyes met. Rosie shook her head.

"Why are you telling me this?"

Rizal spoke truthfully, "I don't know."

They turned then to face forward. The bus fell into silence, the sniffling and moaning leveling to quiet contemplation of the worst-case scenario. Shadows cast by the street lamps wavered over them, moving them through bands of darkness and light. Some time passed before Rosie spoke again, speaking as another of the shadows crossed her face.

"I'm sorry."

The shadows crossed Rizal's face a few more times before he responded.

"Me too."

A short time later the bus slowed to a stop outside the NIA office in Taoyuan City. The door hissed open and the officers guided the men and women off the bus and hustled them through the front doors. Inside they were made to sit grouped in the waiting area, officers stationed to the sides of the rows of seats and at their backs. A new version of the process that had played out in the restaurant kitchen began. One by one the workers were called into one of four interview rooms, some entering and leaving quickly, others remaining within for an hour or more. Some emerged crying, barely able to walk, others wearing expressions stolid and blank. Rizal watched them all go then return to their seats. Rosie was not seated with them. She remained standing to their right. An hour went by before she was joined by her husband. The heat Rizal had felt rising in him when Rosie first sat beside him on the bus welled up again. Before it could reach its peak he was conscious of a shadow growing across his lap. He looked to its source and found a bored-looking officer standing over him.

"Come," said the officer, holding out an arm, guiding him to the first of the small interview rooms. Rizal rose and walked calmly there, anxious to get it over with. He strode through the open door, taking the seat opposite a woman who did not look up when he entered. She was not dressed in an officer's uniform but in a plain dark pantsuit, her hair neatly tied atop her head. Rizal sat and waited, hands clasped in his lap. His eyes peered over the top of the woman's clipboard as her pen scratched at a form until she felt his gaze. His eyes darted away, hers back to the form. Her pen continued its mysteries until finally she spoke, addressing him in English.

"My name is Lin," she said, voice tired and hoarse. "I work for the Ministry of Labor. Do you understand?"

Rizal smiled nervously. He understood that her name was Lin. The rest he tried in vain to piece together. The woman rolled her tired eyes, stood and went to the door. She opened it and called out to someone unseen.

A conversation ensued in the lobby between yet more voices until the words ceased and heels clicked across the floor. Rizal looked to the doorway and saw Rosie walk in. Lin spoke to her in Mandarin. She translated in Tagalog for Rizal.

"This woman is from the Ministry of Labor," she said, adding, "it's the part of the government that deals with foreign workers."

Rizal nodded. Lin spoke again to Rosie, Rosie to Rizal.

"She is asking if you have your passport or your alien resident certificate?"

Rizal shook his head. The conversation continued in its circular manner.

"Any form of ID at all?"

Rizal explained that his passport and alien resident certificate were being held by Mr. Chen, his broker. Rosie told Lin and she wrote something on one of the form's blank lines. She asked Rizal if he knew Chen's full name. Through Rosie he said that he did not. Lin shifted her chair, cringing at the squeaking of the legs against the floor, the sound echoing sharply in the close confines of the room. She resettled herself and continued with her questions, not bothering to look up as she did.

"She needs your full name and date of birth, and your nationality," said Rosie.

Rizal gave them.

"Now she is asking why you ran away from your job."

Rizal took a deep breath, pausing long enough for Lin to stop her scribbling and raise her eyes to him. She tapped the end of her pen against the clipboard, holding her stare. Rizal looked to Rosie. Rosie nodded at him. Rizal inhaled deeply again and began recounting his story. As the words came, he felt the inborn heat he had experienced while on the bus and when Rosie's husband had entered the building flow outward with them, leaving him cold and numb. This entropy continued until it was as though his temperature and that of the room around him were one, and he could fade into it, becoming the same as the walls, the table. In his mind he became the same as the furniture. Another object, like the chair, something that gained name only by someone sitting on it; deciding its purpose. His name was Fisherman. Or had been. And now? What would they decide for him? What new name would he be known by?

He told of Captain Li's tyranny on the boat. Of how they were made to spend most every minute of their lives on the decrepit tub, forbidden even from entering town. He heard the story of being tossed into the sea pass his lips as though he were speaking of someone else. Someone he didn't know. The man called Fisherman. He told Lin about the near starvation. Being forced to eat expired food. Weeks and months spent in the daze of hunger and dehydration. As he spoke Rosie repeated his words, an unintelligible hum in the periphery of Rizal's consciousness. As he came to the end of his story his voice gained volume in his own ears, the temperature gradually returning to his body. And as he finished he felt himself rejoin the world of humanity. The room was silent then; the only sound the scratching of Lin's pen struggling to transcribe the last of his words. She flipped the page and began writing on its blank back. When she finished, she pushed the page across the table, speaking to Rosie again.

"She says you have to sign your name." Rosie stepped

beside him and pointed to the space. Nervously Rizal took the pen from Lin's outstretched hand. Methodically he wrote out the letters one by one. The sheet hissed back across the table. Lin studied it, flipping it over then back again, nodding. Rizal watched her. The room seemed to breathe in and out with him, unsure of whether or not to expel him back into the world of the living. Some time passed before Lin put the form down on the table, studying it for a while, though her eyes were blank, like her mind was elsewhere, perhaps inhabiting the place Rizal had just described, ensconced in the terrible world he had brought into her small corner of existence. She set her hands neatly in her lap, then stared at Rizal and said something to him. Once more Rosie translated.

"She says you will likely be placed in a shelter," said Rosie, pausing. "She also says she is very sorry."

Chapter Nineteen

"YOU will sleep here."

Rizal looked around the small room, which had three walls taken up by bunk beds. Above and below men lounged on thin mattresses, eyeing him from positions of repose. There was one empty space in the lower bunk against the far wall. The lolling men nodded to Rizal as the Taiwanese man at his side guided him to the bunk, a hand placed gently between his shoulder blades. Rizal struggled to remember the man's name. He replayed in his mind the journey to the shelter in Taoyuan County. He and the rest of the workers rounded up at the restaurant had spent two days at the NIA office in the city. Some were kept in holding cells, waiting to be deported back to the Philippines. Others, like Rizal, were relatively free, though not so much that they could leave the bounds of the cavernous lobby, except to go to the bathroom. On the morning of the third day they were told to gather their things, if they had any, and brought outside. There a series of vans were waiting, headed for shelters scattered around the country. Rizal was rustled aboard one of the vans with another man, one of the kitchen staff he had not formally met.

In the hustle and confusion, Rizal had forgotten to look for Jasmine. But there was no point searching for

Rosie. After the first day at the station neither she nor her husband had returned. Her former staff were fed three times a day, brought rice boxes, portions of rice, meat, and vegetables like the meal Rizal had in the van on the way Su'ao when he first arrived, by yet more new faces – kindly looking folks, the women in long skirts, men neatly dressed without flair in khakis and plain collared shirts. It was explained to those like Rizal who could not understand that those people were from a Christian organization that helped *migrantes*. Rizal and the others took their rations with quiet humility, shame burning in the marrow of their bones. But they ate all the same, wry smiles slowly showing on tired faces. Gradually the usual din made its return to the lobby, to the point where grim officers reminded them to keep their voices down, drawing laughter and tittering that expanded upon itself until the cacophony's life cycle started anew.

The shelter, though, was quiet. The other men observed as Rizal looked at the bed, made up with its sheets tucked under the mattress, corners crisp and clean. He was alone, the man from the kitchen who had come with him dropped at a different shelter on the way. Rizal looked down at the fluffed pillow with its starched fabric, freshly laundered, just beginning to sag in the rain-swollen air. He put his hands on the blanket, appointed with what looked to be children's cartoon characters. Then he turned and sat down. The Taiwanese man stood over Rizal, smiling. He was around forty, Rizal guessed, round pustules giving his cheekbones a pointed look. Wrinkles were permanently etched on his forehead, which boasted a high line of short, wiry hair.

Thick-framed glasses gave his eyes a wide, exaggerated kindness. The sleeves of his track jacket were pulled up on his forearms. A Filipina woman came to join him, placing a hand where the arms of the jacket were pulled taught against a ropy bulge of muscle. She whispered something in his ear, a hand covering her mouth. Rizal expected the man to say something to him then, but it was the woman who broke the silence.

"Hello, Rizal," she said in Tagalog, her accent placing her from the south, "my name is Tala. This is my husband, Paul." The man raised his hand in greeting, smiling. "We run the shelter together. I was just telling my husband you don't speak much English, so it might be better if I explain how things work here."

Rizal found himself staring. He shook himself from the momentary stupor brought on by the sweetness of her voice and Paul's kindly features. He nodded, feeling his cheeks grow hot. Tala smiled down at him and continued.

"This shelter is for people like you who have had … *difficulties* in Taiwan. We can give you a place to stay, something to eat. Help you with your case and to find another job, if you wish. If you want to go back home, we can assist with those arrangements too. Whatever happens next is up to you. But no matter what you decide, just know that we are here to help. We don't work for or with the government. We do get some funding from them, but we are on the side of the *migrantes*, always."

Her husband nodded his agreement, seeming to follow her words in Tagalog with some understanding, to Rizal's surprise.

"Actually, we fuck the government," said Paul. "We

fight those bastards every chance we get." Tala shot him a reproachful look, soon chased away by a smile, and went on.

"We usually have anywhere from fifteen to twenty *migrantes* staying here," Tala went on. "This room is for the men. The one beside is for the women. Not all shelters have men and women staying under one roof, but we do. It's important for you to know that you cannot go into the women's room unless you're invited. And even then, only during the day. Understand?"

Rizal nodded quickly.

"Good," said Tala. "You should also know that everyone who stays here pitches in. Outside on the living room wall you'll see a white board with a list of jobs and names beside them. Every week we change responsibilities. One week you might be on cleaning duty. The next you might help in the kitchen. Everyone does their part. *Naunawaan?*"

Rizal nodded again. The simple exertion sent his head swimming. He put a hand to his forehead. Concern clouded Tala and Paul's features. Paul spoke to his wife in English, she then to Rizal in their language.

"My husband says you must be tired after all that's happened in the past few days. You should probably take it easy today. Take some time to settle in. It's nearly lunchtime. Today the women are cooking. Tomorrow it will be the men. We'll leave you to rest a while. You can get to know your roommates, then meet the women over lunch. How does that sound?"

Rizal felt a weighty emotion welling up, compressing his throat. He shrugged his shoulders and said, "*Mabuti po naman.*" Paul and Tala smiled at him once more and left him there, closing the door behind. Rizal leaned back against the wall, feeling its coolness against his skin. A pair of bare legs swung over the edge of the bunk above. A man lowered himself down and turned to face him. He was exceptionally short. Even standing, his head barely cleared that of the seated Rizal. His temples were flecked with gray, eyes dappled with the same. He studied Rizal, looking him over. Seeming satisfied, he extended a hand.

"Rizal, eh?" he asked. "Your parents were patriots or something?" The man chuckled softly. "Never mind. My name is Makisig, but you can call me Mak. That's Fermin; and that one over there is Nimuel," he pointed to the others, men closer in age to Rizal but still a few years older. They nodded curtly as they were introduced. Each was dressed in a tank top and shorts in spite of the chill permeating the room's cement walls, covered in a thin layer of faux barn board paneling. Rizal resisted the urge to pull the blanket up over his shoulders. Mak pursed his lips and looked around the room. "So," he drew out the word, sending it to join the long, shuffling march of silence pulsing from the boy before him, "what was it before you came here? Factory, farm, or fish?"

"Fish," Rizal said quietly.

Mak nodded, framing his jaw with his thumb and forefinger, scratching at a thin layer of stubble. "Fish is tough," he frowned, "I fished for a while. The first time around." He pointed to Fermin and said, "He did it on his second go." He looked then to Nimuel, furrowing his brow. "Nim has been a factory man from the start, yes?" Nimuel gave a nod. "No *migrante* stays fishing for long, if he can help it. Even if you fish back home they don't tell you what it's going to be like over here, do they?"

Again Rizal shook his head, the dizziness returning.

Mak paced between the bunks. "They don't tell you much of anything. Just put you on a plane and say, 'Here you go. Figure it out for yourself.'" He laughed bitterly. "Some do. Some don't. When it's all done we're lucky to go home with a couple of pesos. But then what do we do?" Again a chill fluttered in his laughter. "We sign ourselves up again and go back for more. Right back into the shit. The same story with the same ending. But what am I saying? There is no end. Just a beginning and a middle. Over and over. Tell me, *anak*, how many times for you?" Fermin and Nimuel leaned forward in their bunks to listen.

Rizal held back his answer, unsure of how it would be received. Then, with a swallow of cold, stale air, he gave it. "One, *kuya Mak*," Rizal said, noting the chill seeping up from the floor, through the thin foam sandals he had been given to wear at the front door. They were blue, he noticed, like the sea. "It's my first time."

Mak's eyes brightened. He looked in disbelief to the others. "Look, boys. A rookie!" Rizal caught the smiles on the other men's faces. "Bad luck you caught fishing on your first time, *bata*," said Mak. "At least you know better now. Depending on your case, they might be able to help you change your work category. If you can get it switched, you can get yourself a factory job. Not easy, but it can be done," he looked again to the others, all nodding in unison. "The trouble is the factory owners can be even bigger *bastardos* than the boat captains. But at least they're *bastardos* on land. Some of those captains, they...." Seeing the heavy look in Rizal's eyes Mak let his words end there. "Well, you know how they are. If you didn't you wouldn't be here, would you?"

Rizal wondered if it was a question he was supposed to answer. Before he could decide, a knock sounded at the door, Paul's muffled voice from the other side telling them it was time for lunch. Mak strode hurriedly to the door and opened it, Fermin and Nimuel close behind. Tentatively Rizal raised himself up and followed, peering around the edge of the doorway to spy a team of seven women placing dishes on a table laden with steaming plates of food. One woman put down a bowl of bananas, another a plate heaped with chopped pineapple. Yet another woman emerged from the kitchen holding a steamer of white rice, her hands covered by oven mitts. She set the steamer down and saw Rizal peeking around the corner like a shy child.

"Come," she said, smiling. "Sit. Eat with us."

Rizal stumbled out, catching his toe on the door frame. The sound drew momentary stares and the others lowered their faces to hide mischievous smiles. Rizal shuffled to the table, waiting for the others to take their seats. The woman who had called him to the table motioned to a brass-framed chair with a green polyester cushion beside her. The chairs were a mishmash of donations and findings, no two a match. Everyone sat, the table cramped with bodies and food, the men already helping themselves in silence, the women commenting on how good the food looked and how hungry they were. Tala and Paul sat too, each taking a helping of rice first in a small porcelain bowl. When they finished Rizal did the same, eyeing the pair of chopsticks beside his plate. The woman next to him caught him staring.

"We can get you a fork, if you like," she smiled. She looked to be around Mak's age. The other women were younger. As Rizal braved his first tenuous glances around the table he saw that two of them couldn't be much older than he. As they filled their bowls and plates Tala cleared her throat and the din quieted, the women stopping their actions, the men slowing theirs.

"Everyone," said Tala, "today we have a new guest. His name is Rizal. So he doesn't have to tell the tale a thousand times, I'll tell it for him. He was working on a fishing boat at Su'ao before he joined us. His story is much like the ones we've heard from many of the fisherman who have come to our shelter. Rizal's captain treated his crew terribly, and I'll leave at that. If he wants to say more about it, that's his choice. But as always, please don't bother him about it. We all know what it's like to go through hard times. Sometimes you want to talk about it. Sometimes you don't. Luckily Rizal managed to get away and the Lord led him to us. I would just like to say welcome, Rizal. I know things haven't been easy for you. But believe me, this is the first step toward things getting better."

Rizal felt himself blushing. He raised his head with a crooked smile then lowered it again to continue pushing rice around in his bowl to form it into a clump he could lift to his mouth. A nudge from the woman to his left brought his eyes up again, and she held her own sticks in her hand, showing him the proper way. He positioned his hands as hers were slowly, checking the placement of each finger, then set about the task of eating again. It was easier now. Grains still fell back into the bowl and into his lap, but more made it in his mouth than escaped. In the span of a few minutes he was eating without much trouble. He could see the woman's lips part in a motherly smile of approval and the chill he had felt before began to fade slowly away.

After the meal the women cleared the table, and the sound of running water and dishes clinking against one another in the sink echoed into the living room. There the men sat, breaths drawn out by full stomachs. Paul and Tala took their seats at a pair of desktop computers, each set up in a small cubicle in a nook off the living room. They began typing away, faces cast in the blue glow emanating from the screens, pausing only to sigh or stretch their backs. At the front of the living room, sliding screen doors led to a small balcony. There Mak and Fermin were leaning on the low wall overlooking the street. The street ran along the upper edge of a shallow valley dotted with gardens and farms centered by white-tile homes made gray by the smoke of the nearby factories. Mak and Fermin smoked their cigarettes in silence, exhalations of smoke punctuated by short, satisfied belches. Rizal remained at the table until a pang of guilt got him to his feet and guided his hands to the plates and pans and cutlery on the table. He gathered up some dishes and took them to the kitchen, the women quickly shooing him out, playfully admonishing him, telling him his turn to clean would come. He tried to remember their names from the hasty introductions all jumbled together during the meal. When he returned to the table, the chairs were pushed in, the couch and seats in the living room around a small wicker coffee table taken up by sprawling bodies. He decided to join Mak and Fermin on the balcony.

They turned when they heard the screen door screech along the track, then returned their stares back to the valley haze. Rizal leaned his forearms on the top of the wall next to Mak.

"So this is what you do every day?" Rizal asked nervously. Mak smiled, taking another drag and blowing out smoke with ceremony.

"Not much else to do, *anak*," he shrugged. "If your case is still open, you can't look for work, unless you're looking for something under the table. Those two," he crooked his head back toward the cubicles, "they don't encourage that kind of thing. But they understand a man can only be idle for so long." He paused. "Even if your case is closed and they say you can change your employer, it's like there's a black mark on you. You didn't finish your contract and the next man wants to know why. They think we're troublemakers. Runaways. They actually think we're out to cheat them, if you can believe it. Us cheating them," he scoffed. "Not all of them. But enough."

"And they talk to each other," Fermin chimed in. "The brokers talk to the bosses too. They say, 'Watch out for this guy. He left his last job. Ran away for no reason,' even if there was a reason. A damn good reason. They fuck us, *anak*. Once you've run away they just want you to go away for good. Plenty of fresh meat. One thing we've never had a problem with in the Philippines is making babies, am I right? The next batch of *migrantes* can't wait to come over, straight out of the womb. They'd swim here if they thought they could make it."

"They don't know how it really is," Mak shook his head. "So who can blame them? But like I said, what can we do? I need work; and if the pay actually came through like we were promised, I would make a pretty good living here. As it is I still owe my broker for my first broken contract. And I'll owe him another eighty thousand pesos plus interest when I sign on for the next job, even if he doesn't lift a finger for me except to type a few words on that *ugok* computer of his."

"There's no way around it," Fermin shrugged. "Paul and Tala, they're trying to change things. They tell us how they're trying to get our governments to get rid of the brokers, the fees that fuck us in the ass. Unions will come, they say. We just have to be patient and keep fighting the good fight. They're good people. They fight with us and when we bleed they bleed too. It's just that they're fighting a few bad ones, and those bad ones have old connections and deep pockets." Fermin stopped then and turned out his pockets, cigarette dangling between his lips.

"And our pockets have nothing but holes, *anak*."

Chapter Twenty

Two weeks at the shelter. On alternate days Rizal's wakeful hours revolved around the kitchen, preparing the daily meals. Mak showed Rizal how to do the prep work, chopping vegetables, cutting meat, keeping watch on the sizzling pans and boiling pots while the others took their cigarette breaks. Rizal liked the work. Something to pull his mind from the fog that seemed to hover around the apartment in the idle hours. It hung over the men and women there, seeping into their minds, blanking their expressions. It was a look Rizal knew well, one he had lived with all his life back in Navotas. Each day one or more of the *migrantes* would leave with Tala and Paul. Court hearings, appointments at the Ministry of Labor, arbitration meetings with former employers. Those who stayed back at the shelter wished those heading out luck, eyes straying from a hand of cards or the television screen or the computer monitor for the briefest of moments. Thoughts of what might happen later, at those meetings and hearings, such notions were best lost to the distraction of something else, even if it was the tenth round of *pekwa* or a TV show they didn't understand.

Rizal preferred the days in the kitchen to those he was on cleaning duty, emptying the garbage cans as he had when he was ever so briefly a busboy, sweeping and mopping the floor, dusting the furniture. He put himself into the work where some of the others went through the motions. The work occupied his thoughts and took his focus off the uncertainties in his mind. Here and there spats flared between the others. But for Rizal there was only the work and the slow passage of time down its long, hollow tunnel. Each day he felt himself moving down it toward something unknown and unnamed.

Names were repeated to Rizal over and again, most failing to take root for reasons he could not explain. He remembered the names of the men in his room. Those of the women would stay for a time before fading away, snatched by a subconscious hand poking its fingers into his mind. Mostly it was a time of confusion. A time of gratitude for the bed he slept in at night, the three hot meals he enjoyed during the day, and yet a time consumed by a sadness he could not place. The tasks were his savior. Short conversations and laughter, however forced, were his momentary escape. During the dark times between, he waited for news. Once every few days Tala came to him, telling him he had to be patient. His was a clear case of mistreatment, she said. Once the decision came down he would be free to look for another job or go home. Rizal's thoughts turned to what he would do if the decision went in his favor. To stay or to return home, as poor as he was when he had left. Poorer, actually. Indebted to *Tiyo* Benjie for the loan he had taken. Back to Mama and the cemetery and Navotas with a debt hanging over his head. A return to those walls cordoning off his world into the walkways between the tombs and mausoleums where the future lay somewhere between the cold gray eyes of Datu Death and the sightless black sockets of the dead.

Tala had offered to try and get word to his mother about what had happened to him. Rizal said no. As far as *Mama* knew he was working. Perhaps prospering. Even if they could reach her, there was no point in adding to her worries. Better to say nothing, he thought. Still he hoped that when he did return it would be with something to show for it. Something to make her proud. And in that thought he knew that he would stay and try again. He would look for work. Not on a fishing boat. Never again, if he could help it. Remembering Mak's advice he asked Tala about changing his designation to factory worker. Again the answer was to wait. Nothing to be done until his case was resolved.

And so Rizal waited, forgoing the trips Paul and Tala organized from time to time to parks or other places around the city. The others said there were meetings happening now. Gatherings in Taipei, Taoyuan City, Zhongli. *Migrantes* getting together. Organizing. Forming advocacy groups and empowerment organizations. In Yilan, said Mak, the fishermen had even formed a union – in Nanfang'ao, no less. The others talked about going to Taipei. A rally, they said, for migrant worker rights, right there on the checkerboard floor of the Main Hall of Taipei Railway Station. They would go. They would march and chant and dance and sing. People would see. They would have to see because there would be nowhere else to look but at them, the *migrantes* who cooked their meals, cared for their old and sick. The ones who did the dirty and the dangerous jobs no one else wanted. There was excitement in the shelter. For the first time since Rizal arrived there was something in the air. A sense of hope, maybe. A weight lifted off all their shoulders. All but one. Something still pulled at Rizal, dragging him down. The others smiled and made their plans. Rizal smiled with them, the brightness in his eyes fading the moment they turned their backs. He was a shadow there, and he would be the same at any rally, any march, any demonstration. Anywhere people believed change was possible, he would be the morning mist that rose up the mountain slopes and formed dark clouds that dropped buckets of rain in the afternoon. He said he would go with them, but in his heart he knew it wasn't true.

Sitting on the edge of the group silently when the Mandarin tutor came once a week, Rizal picked up a few basic words and phrases. As it was with the names, there was something in the way. The friendly smiles or words of small talk that greeted his presence in the first few days faded to perfunctory nods and glances when he entered a room. The rest waited for him to speak. Rizal waited for a moment when he might have something worth saying.

Nights passed by with little sleep, Rizal turning over from side to back to side, eyes staring wide at the walls and the ceiling. The bedroom door called to him to rise and walk out. To go down the stairs and take to the road and just move. Go anywhere for the act of movement itself. He hated the stillness. The sitting and waiting. An entire life – *his* entire life – had passed him by like this. The resentment was worst during the quiet hours of the night.

In the darkness Rizal seethed and wondered how the others could sleep. How, he wondered, could they will their minds to rest so easily? Was it strength, or was it weakness? A flaw or some mystic attribute; a stillness of soul they somehow possessed; one he somehow lacked? As the others in his room slept he came to resent them too for their ability to shut it all away for the night and refresh themselves with the sunrise. The feeling grew around and within him until it was all he had left. The bitterness and pain took him away from the boy he used to be. Something had to happen, and soon, he knew, before there could be no way back to a core shunted away to a place called Nowhere, lost in an ever-shifting maze.

At the end of the second week Tala came to Rizal. She found him sitting in the living room, flipping absently through the pages of a magazine. He let her stand there awhile, knowing she was waiting for him to turn, to acknowledge her presence. He enjoyed the fleeting moment of control. The moment lasted a few seconds before he broke and turned to her. She knelt, pulling a piece of paper from an envelope torn across the top edge. She removed a letter and unfolded it, smiling at him. Rizal waited, sucking at his teeth with a nervous impatience. He watched her eyes scan the lines quickly, words visible but backward to Rizal in the light shining through the page from behind. Tala lowered the paper and smiled at him again.

"It's good news, Rizal," she said. "Based on interviews with your former crewmates and your sworn statement, the ministry has found yours to be a case of abuse. You're free from your contract. That means you can take another job, if you want. Or you can go back to Manila. It's up to you. But you're free. You have nothing more to worry about."

Her smile faded as she watched Rizal's blank expression go unchanged. He turned away from her, staring out through the glass doors leading to the balcony until his vision blurred and he blinked the world back into focus. He felt the warm touch of Tala's hand on his forearm and turned to her again. He saw the worry on her face and still was unmoved.

"Isn't this what you wanted, Rizal?" asked Tala. "It's what we've hoped for. And so quickly. It can take months to resolve a case. I thought you would be happy."

The others around them had stopped what they were doing, all eyes on Tala and Rizal. Mak had gone with Paul to see about a placement at a factory in Hsinchu, a half hour by car to the south. Some of the men were on the balcony, smoking and staring out at the valley. The women were either in their room, speaking with family back home, or sitting at the kitchen table, too soon yet to start with the dinner preparations. Rizal had taken in their stories passively during the past two weeks. Rubylyn, four times sexually assaulted by her ward's son before she managed to get away. Mira, raped by the patriarch of a wealthy Kaohsiung family. At night the others heard Mira's mournful cries, Tala checking once every few hours to make sure she hadn't done anything rash. Many of the women at the shelter carried with them stories of gross violation. Of being treated as little more than prostitutes hired for the gratification of decrepit old men not yet dispossessed of an inborn tick of perversion.

When Rizal could bring himself to look into their eyes he wondered how they went on. A mystery greater still, how they could bring themselves to stay. To look for work again after being groped and touched, watched, viewed in their most private moments by carefully concealed electronic eyes planted in bed and bathrooms. Rather than grant Rizal strength, their will only sank him deeper into depression's fathoms. The question now in his mind was not how they went on, and whether it was noble or strong, but why were they made to, and how it broke his heart to know that there was no reason. None they could ever know in this lifetime.

Rizal's tired eyes looked to Tala's. "Will I have to go back out to sea again?" he asked slowly, anything to delay a response that would come terrible in any form. "Will I still have to be a fisherman?"

Tala sighed. She tapped at his arm with the edge of the envelope and smiled mutely. "No," she said, voice calm and cool. "No more fishing if you don't want to. They've approved your request for reclassification. You can work in a factory if you wish."

Rizal sighed. A weight fell from his shoulders. As it left his head fell into his chest and of a sudden he felt a wave of fatigue run through every cell.

"What about my friends?" Rizal asked.

Tala sighed. "They are free as well," she said. "And none too soon. When the captain was interviewed, he said one of the men – Datu, I think was his name – pulled a knife on him while they were at sea. A knife and fork, actually," she laughed. "It was just too absurd. From what your crewmates said, they hadn't seen knife or a fork since they left home. And nothing like that was found aboard."

Rizal shook his head, recalling the trade for Datu's dry clothes, though he could not smile, not even at the thought of a mutiny mounted with a set of stolen cutlery.

"The ministry asked the captain why the man would pull a knife on him," Tala went on. "He denied knowing, at first. But eventually he admitted that he might have given the man a smack upside the head. For working too slowly, he said. For being lazy. They asked him if this was the first time he struck one of his crew. Again he denied. After a time, though, he said he did it whenever he had to. He said he struck his crewmen because it was necessary. 'Because when a dog disobeys, you have to hit him.' Those were his exact words." Tala blinked back tears. "I'm sorry," she said.

Rizal didn't hear her, didn't have to ask himself whether she was apologizing for her tears or for all he and the others had been through. The next sensation he knew was Tala's hand stroking the back of his head.

"It will be all right, Rizal," she soothed. "It's going to be all right."

Chapter Twenty-One

THE van hummed down the four-lane freeway, weaving between the eyes of taillights, rumbling over the warning strips on the right, menacing the concrete barrier between north and southbound lanes on the left. Rizal had not seen such traffic since leaving Manila. On the east coast of Taiwan's main island the flow had been light, the road at times empty until the oncoming bend of the coastal strip revealed the next traveler. Here on the highway through Taiwan's western floodplain the lanes were like the marshaling yard of some intergalactic hub, where gleaming metal transports of the cosmos glided into position among one another at pace. Rizal gripped the hold above the passenger side window to his right. Mak laughed in the seat beside him.

"What's the matter, Navotas?" he jibed, "First time in a car?"

From the front passenger seat Tala turned and smiled. At the wheel Paul cursed and laid on the horn, glaring at a silver sedan crawling along in the fast lane as they blew by. The van lilted to the right. Rizal gritted his teeth, certain they were about to tip over and be spilled along the roadway like the contents of a tin of meat. Mak whooped. Paul cursed again; and Tala put a healing hand on his elbow, the touch of her fingertips drawing from him an elongated breath and a lighter foot on the gas pedal. They slowed, and when space allowed Paul pulled the van to the far-right lane, where cars slowed for an exit ramp headed west. When they hit the ramp Paul pointed to a passing sign.

"Zhubei," he said, repeating it again for Rizal and Mak. Rizal mouthed the word silently. Mak drew it out like a chant, "*Zhuuuuuuuuuubeiiiiiiiiiiii, Zhuuuuuuuuubeiiiiiiiiiiii.*" Rizal thought of Datu, Arvin, and Amado, hoping they were all right and saying a prayer for the well-being of his friends before new sights stole his attention. The van puttered down the exit ramp among a steady procession of cars, trucks, and scooters, side mirrors glinting in the late-afternoon sun.

The exit ramp led to the two-lane boulevard running straight into Zhubei. Palms lined the median, green fronds hanging their browned tips low over the passing traffic. The van slowed, dragging the surrounding land and cityscape into focus. From first glance Rizal could tell this was not like Taoyuan or Su'ao. It was something in between. High-rise apartment buildings missing the black mildew of age rose over rice paddies, green shoots in stagnant, sediment-rich ponds of clear lacquer and brown. Two- and three-story houses stood in the middle of small orchards and fields, guavas covered by white plastic bags that flew like the flags of a new harvest. As they passed a river Rizal thought to ask the name of the shallow, muddy current running in rifts of foam and froth over rounded beige stones tumbled down from the distant mountains, the question dying in his throat. A water buffalo drawing a cart driven by a man wearing nothing but a pair of gray clam diggers rolled up above his bare feet swayed its head obstinately as it pulled its burden down the side of the road.

Next to the road were restaurants with low, round stools set across the sidewalk at small tables, pedestrians ambling between them. Students in uniform made their way somewhere, laughing and joking with one another, a small boy chasing a larger group ahead. Rizal looked at them through the dark tint of the window and smiled. Beside him Mak kept up his chant, adding a long whistle as his darting eyes caught sight of a young woman in a short black skirt. Paul laughed knowingly, Tala striking him playfully on the arm. He turned the van onto another wide boulevard lined with rolling steel gates guarding large industrial complexes, their names spelled out in English and Mandarin. One would be the factory that had agreed to hire Mak and Rizal. Rizal watched the factory gates go by, a knot compounding in size in the dwindling pit of his stomach, wondering which it would be and what lay beyond those gray-and-white-spackled walls and their heavy red doors manned by uniformed security guards.

Still the sight of the uniform put pace to Rizal's heart as he remembered being wrestled to the ground by the police under watch of an indifferent sky and the gentle heave of Su'ao Harbor. His heartbeat quickened as the van slowed and Paul waved to a guard, who in turn motioned them through a factory gate. Paul eased the van into a parking space in a small lot across from a building fronted by a series of glass doors under a brutalist rectangular overhang. The engine cut and Rizal sat rooted to his seat, feeling an ache in his fingertips until he realized his nails were dug into the armrests.

He stretched his fingers loose and turned to see Tala standing at the side door, pulling it open for him. He exited into the bright afternoon sun, the city lost behind the compound's walls and the admin building looming before them. For a moment he thought about the places he had been. How everywhere *migrantes* went in this country they were cut off from everyone else, hidden behind some barrier natural or man-made. Paul held out an arm toward the glass doors and Rizal, Mak, and Tala followed him there. Before they reached the doors one of the clear panes was pushed open and a woman emerged. Rizal stopped and regarded her black leggings rising to a black blouse and a top held closed nearly to her narrow chin by round buttons that looked like smooth puffs of cotton pulled toward her sternum by loops of white string. She was thin, eyes sunken and tired. Wordlessly she held open the door for them to walk in. Paul led the way, Mak following with Rizal at his back, Tala coming in behind.

A blast of cool air struck Rizal as they entered the building. Everything within had a look of newness about it. An appearance of things that were to be passed by, seen but not touched. In the corner sat a polished wooden figure of a round-bellied Buddha draped in beads. Beside that a small fountain, a marble ball rolling in the shallow upper pool, moved by the water's mechanized current. The woman pointed at the sculpture and the fountain, speaking without stopping. Tala said something to Rizal about wind and water he only half heard. They continued to a hallway lined with white doors affixed with golden nameplates, the woman taking them to the door nearest the end. Reaching out a hand to run his fingers along the walls, Rizal found they felt thin to the touch, as though he had but to lean on them and he would fall through into the unknown on the other side. As the woman unlocked the door to her office she caught sight of Rizal's fingers tapering away from the pristine whiteness of the wall and his hand shot back to his side, down into his pocket. She walked into the room, the rest following.

The office was as sparsely furnished as the lobby. There was a plain black wooden desk, on top a monitor and keyboard along with a small reading lamp with a pull chain. Curtly the woman yanked the chain down and switched on the monitor. Tala took one of the silver-framed chairs across the desk from her, Paul motioning for Rizal or Mak to take the other. Mak slid in with a smile, settling in like a bear scratching its back against the trunk of a stout tree. The woman began typing, lips pursed. Paul cleared his throat and spoke something that sounded to Rizal like a question, the woman grunting out a response. Tala translated for Mak and Rizal.

"This is Miss Liao, the woman responsible for hiring you both."

Rizal thought to thank her. Before he could the woman resumed speaking. A printer on a shelf behind her desk buzzed to life, spitting out sheets of paper. She turned and collected two of them, passing one to Mak, one to Tala to hand to Rizal behind her. Rizal looked at its sea of Mandarin characters, eyes rising to Miss Liao. Once again her eyes were glued to the glow of her monitor, eyes pinpricks of caffeinated focus. A silver thermos sat to her right, her hand brushing the screw-in lid dotted with beads of brown liquid as she sought it out blindly and brought it to her lips then set it back down. A short time later she was finished inputting whatever information the machine required. She stopped, clasping her hands before her on the desk, speaking quickly, Tala doing her best to keep up.

"She says these are standard contracts.... Standard salary for *migrante* factory workers in Taiwan.... Everyone is paid the same.... You'll have health insurance.... Room and board is subtracted from your pay. You'll be staying in employee dorms on the factory grounds.... Days are nine-to-five, plus overtime, Monday through Saturday.... Sundays technically off, but shifts are available if you want to make some extra pay to send home.... Service fees and all standard deductions levied by your brokers apply...."

The woman continued speaking. Tala sat, listening and nodding for a time. As Miss Liao spoke Rizal remembered how Tala had explained to him that he was still bound by contract to Mr. Chen, just as he was to *Tiyo* Benjie. How it hadn't been possible to prove any wrongdoing on their end, and so their agreement was still valid, the debts he owed to both withstanding. As he was lost in that jumble of thoughts, Miss Liao finished speaking. Tala turned to face Mak and Rizal, saying, "That's about it. Any questions?"

Mak's eyes were glazed. He looked down at his fingernails, shaking his head at no one in particular. All eyes moved to Rizal. He felt his temperature rise. Time was taken away by their stares. A hand on his shoulder pulled him out and he felt himself taking a gulp of air he was sure everyone could hear. He turned and saw Paul regarding him with fatherly concern. Rizal shook his head, lowering his eyes ashamedly. Miss Liao nodded once, neither pleased nor annoyed. When Rizal looked to her again he found her face matched the surrounding walls, each caked in a white foundation a degree's rise away from melting. She spoke quickly again, handing a pen over to Mak.

"If you don't have any questions, you can sign your contracts and everything will be settled," Tala said.

Mak took the pen and scratched out his name with the same ambivalence with which he had taken in the entire proceeding. Without looking he handed the pen back over his shoulder to Rizal. Reaching out to take it, Rizal moved toward the desk and set the contract down at its edge, methodically meting out the strokes of each letter of his name, stopping to look them over slowly again when he was finished. Before he was finished checking, Miss Liao stood, reached out, and snatched the forms away from them both, filing them in a cabinet in the corner. She turned back to them and sat, clasped her hands neatly on the desk again, speaking to Tala.

"She wants to know if you know what they do here," Tala translated.

"Marble," Mak answered in English, pleased with himself.

Miss Liao nodded, showing the first hint of a smile. She went on speaking, Tala again struggling to keep up.

"Yes, this is a marble-processing facility. They receive raw shipments from the quarries and cut the rough blocks into tiles, then ship them all over the island. You will have a number of duties here. Some days you will run the machines. Others you will spend cleaning. You will learn as you go from the more experienced workers. They employ different nationalities here. Some Indonesians. A few Vietnamese and Thais. Mostly Filipino though." She paused, Miss Liao spitting out another quick succession of words, holding out her hands then placing them demurely on the desk.

"Miss Liao says if there are no further questions, she will take you to your dorm. It is nearly five o'clock, so the workers who will not be putting in overtime should return to their rooms soon. You can meet some of your coworkers and get settled in. Perhaps later you can also meet the shop foreman, Mr. Su. But before you do anything, are you sure you don't have any questions about your contract or the way things work here?" Rizal saw Mak shaking his head. He did the same. Miss Liao nodded, smiling wider now. She stood and held out a hand toward the door, moving to open it for them. Rizal turned toward the door and waited for Mak to rise and walk ahead so he could follow. Miss Liao led them down the hallway back to the lobby, then veered off toward a doorway by the west end of the building. When they got to the door they stopped, Miss Liao speaking to Tala and Paul. Tala nodded.

"Miss Liao says that the area beyond these doors is restricted. Employees only. Paul and I can't go with you."

Rizal eyed Mak with uncertainty. Mak shrugged his shoulders, extending a hand to Paul. He thanked him, bowing his head then to Tala. Rizal again followed suit. As he nodded to Tala she stepped toward him, drawing him into an embrace that flushed his cheeks.

"You still have the card I gave you?" she asked, "The one with the shelter number?" Rizal nodded as she squeezed him tighter. "If you have any problems, anything at all, no matter how small, you call that number, understand?" He nodded again and she released him, her eyes moist. She wiped at them and gave Mak and Rizal another long look each before a touch on the arm from Paul told her it was time to go. They turned and walked back toward the entrance, Tala looking back over her shoulder once, then again.

Rizal gave a halfhearted wave before turning back to Miss Liao, the smile she had shown in the office gone. She pulled open the door leading to a paving stone path, the path pointing toward another building. "This way," she said in English. Rizal felt Mak brush by him and followed him through, Miss Liao closing the door behind them.

The path took them to the employee dorm, a building that looked less permanent than the one they had just left. It was two stories, walls gleaming white, thin even at the most furtive glance. Square protrusions, air-conditioning units, poked out at intervals every few feet, windows not far from them. Miss Liao moved past the men and strode to the door ahead, swiping a key card through a machine that beeped, its red LED light turning green. The door buzzed open and she pulled it wide, motioning the two men inside. They stepped through into a hallway. Miss Liao stopped them there, pointing back to the door. She tapped her key card.

"Managers have key," she explained. "Workers no have key. You in dorm, you stay in. No out. When you work in factory, no go in dorm. No key card, no can go inside. Understand?"

Mak took on Datu's old role of translator and the

two men nodded obediently. Miss Liao returned the gesture and they moved down the hallway to a set of stairs and went up. Rizal found the silence unnerving, like they were intruders stepping someplace they shouldn't. On the second floor the planks beneath the loose gray carpet creaked, adding to the ominous feel of the building that even to his untrained eyes looked to have been hastily put up. White paint dried in rivulets left to slop down toward the floor. Electrical outlets hung loose from holes punched carelessly into the walls. Rizal shuddered at the thought of what might happen if there was a fire, remembering the spaghetti wiring back home that threatened to send up the whole slum from a single spark. Overhead lights blinkered on and off. Down the hallway they walked past closed doors spaced a few feet apart, looking more like entrances to storage closets than living quarters. When they reached a door near the end of the hall, Miss Liao swiped her key card through a sensor above the door handle. The light there turned from red to green and the door popped open. She bid them inside.

Mak went in first, Rizal following. A few steps was all it took to reach the far wall. On either side of the room were narrow beds, sheets folded neatly at the end of the mattress. A small dresser sat between the beds, opposite the door, a fan suspended in the upper corner of the room on the left. Miss Liao flipped the light switch by the door to no avail, an embarrassed smile turning quickly to a pursed set of lips.

"You sleep here," she said as though it required explanation. "After supper, man let you in. You stay until morning. Then breakfast, then work. Okay?"

Rizal wanted to ask questions. What time were the meals? Where was the bathroom? What if they had to use it during the night? What if they were sick? He held them, not wishing to jeopardize his job before it had even begun. He nodded instead, Mak doing the same as he took a seat on one of the beds, feeling the hard mattress beneath his backside. Miss Liao nodded to them both once more.

"Okay," she said flatly, lowering her chin to look at them both. "Rest now. You start work tomorrow."

With that she was gone. She left them there in their new home, two men, hardly better than strangers, now sharing a space not much bigger than the mausoleum Rizal had shared with his mother. At least here, though, there was a window. Taking in a breath of stale air Rizal stepped to the window to open it up, hoping a breeze from outside would chase some of the odor of paint and carpet glue from the room. When he got there, he froze. He studied the window for a time, looking for a latch to unlock it or a track along the bottom on which it would slide open and closed. Through the tinted glass with its dark plastic coating to keep out the sunlight, he looked down to the ground below and then to the view of the admin building beyond. He tapped the glass with his finger and it rattled in place, fixed, keeping the two men and the stuffy air within.

Chapter Twenty-Two

RIZAL heard the footsteps down the hallway, waking him just as they had the past two weeks. Next would come the knock on the door. His eyes blinked open and he heard the swipe of the key card, the beep of the sensor. The door popped open and was pushed wide. A uniformed security guard looked in and eyed Mak and Rizal, both sitting up slowly in their beds. The Taiwanese guard nodded and muttered something gruffly. Then he disappeared from the frame, moving on to the next room.

Rizal rose and waited for Mak to take his overalls off his corner of the dresser, laid over the edge so the sweat of the previous day's work could dry in the still air of the unventilated room. Mak gathered up his work clothes and moved silently around Rizal, he having to lean back over his bed so they could avoid touching one another. Then Rizal got his own overalls and stepped into them, buttoning them partway so he wouldn't have to undo them again when he got the chance to take his morning piss. The line at the second-floor bathroom was already building, the pair of stalls for the forty workers on floor two in high demand. Rizal contemplated waiting until after breakfast, sneaking off to the restroom in the warehouse when they were filing in for their shift.

Breakfast wouldn't wait and he'd missed it yesterday for a bout of irritable bowel brought on, he suspected, by the slop of greasy noodles and tough, cartilaginous meat served in the cafeteria the night before. He didn't want to miss breakfast again. The work would be hard and nonstop once it began. He would need fuel, however bland and tasteless it was going down.

Like everything else about the place, eating was a mechanical thing. A rote movement of the body's mechanisms with little in the way of purpose but preservation. Rizal left Mak to the bathroom line and went downstairs, passing the first floor, heading for the small basement cafeteria. The room was already filling up, the men segregated by nationality. Thai with Thai. Indonesian with Indonesian. Vietnamese with their countrymen and Pinoys with their own. Those who could speak some English might call out or say good morning to one from a country that wasn't theirs. But eat together? No. Breakfast was a time when the strain of conversation was to be kept to a minimum. If there were to be words, they would be in one's own language.

Rizal preferred his mornings as he did his afternoons and evenings: quiet. He found a table with a few empty chairs at the end and took the farthest one, leaving his hat with the company logo stitched above the bill on the seat while he went to grab a tray. When he returned with his bowl of congee and cup of coffee the hat was still there, wavy lines of sweat salt around the rim. He picked up the hat and sat down, staring into the bowl of watery rice porridge. Had he the energy, he might have sighed. As it was, he picked up his spoon and mindlessly went about shoveling the slop into his mouth, then guzzled his lukewarm coffee. As he finished, the work bell rang, the men rising in unison to bus their trays to the silver metal racks by the door. Then they filed out, headed back upstairs, bound for the factory floor.

It was Sunday. Supposedly a day off. But as Rizal had learned quickly, life at the factory in Zhubei was little different from that on the boat in Su'ao. Though the methods differed, the results were the same. The minders found ways to ensure the men were at work every day without fail. Rizal thought back to his first Friday on the job. The few days before were training. Moving from one machine to the next, learning how to operate them. Stern instructions from men warning of the dangers of severed fingers and lost limbs should he fail to pay the strictest attention. He watched as a man showed him how to program the CNC machine to cut the slabs to certain dimensions. One of the old-timers even let him have a few moments on the shapemill before shooing him away. Mostly, though, Rizal was on grunt duty. Menial work done by the low men on the roster. Shunting the pallets of heavy stone around the warehouse on a power jack that bucked and shorted its way about. Lifting slabs one by one onto the cutters and buffers so the skilled laborers could do their work. Rizal knew it could be years before he got on a machine. The only way would be for a man to quit or die. All around him were signs warning of the deadliness of their work. Now, nearing the end of his second week, Rizal was sure the only way he would meet his end in the plant would be to die of boredom.

At the end of that first Friday Mr. Su, the shop foreman, approached Rizal. Su mostly spent his days in the elevated office that rose above the factory floor near the loading dock. The men could feel his eyes watching them from his window, dreading the sound of heavy footsteps falling down the stairs – a sound that somehow managed to rise above the white noise of blades cutting stone cooled by high-pressure blasts of water and cutting fluid. Rizal watched from the corner of his eye as Su moved from one man to the next, speaking briefly then smiling as he scratched out something against the backing of his clipboard, finally patting each man on the shoulder. Soon he stood next to Rizal.

"Good week, my friend, yes?"

Rizal nodded.

"Good work, good pay."

Rizal slackened his grip on the accelerator of his jack. His feet ached as they hit the concrete floor, the steel toes of his company-provided work boots squeezing his feet.

"You want day off tomorrow, or you want to make more money?" Su asked, not waiting for a reply. "The others, they all work tomorrow. They work so hard. Earn big money. I think you are the same, yes?" Rizal felt his heart sink. Though he could not understand every word out of Su's mouth, he knew what was asked all the same, his English improving day by day. He was planning to use his days off to go to Zhongli to try and find Jasmine. Now Mr. Su stood in his way, eyes expectant. He raised up his clipboard. A list of names, each with a check next to it. Rizal nodded glumly and a check was placed next to his as well. Extra shifts. Extra pay. At least there *was* pay. In two more weeks he would have his first real paycheck. Enough to finally send some money home. He sighed and finished his shift, bringing loads of stone to the men on their machines that cut and polished, then toted the finished pieces in his rusty vehicle to the loading dock, where the drivers waited idly for their trucks to fill. The mechanical motions of the day fulfilled, there was nothing to do but slide into those of the night. Eating. Waiting in line for the shower. Washing off the day's sweat and grime, water pooling below, rising up his ankles, the drain blocked with the filth of other men. Then being let into his room, the door locking behind him, often finding Mak there ahead of him, leaning back on his pillow, staring at the ceiling or already asleep. Not the sleep of comfort that came after a hard day's work, but the numb rest of knowing the inevitable. That the day to come would be just as the one nearly ended.

Sunday, though, was cleaning day. A day when all men, whether they spent Monday to Saturday standing at a machine or riding a power jack, were equal. They filed in casually. Those who were wont to socialize did so freely. The managers were all at home, as was Mr. Su, enjoying their day off. Sundays the men in charge were *migrantes* like Rizal and Mak. So long as the place appeared clean on Monday, little else mattered.

"No need to break our backs today, *chupaleros*," one of the day's supervisors boomed. He was Pinoy. Rizal recognized him though he didn't know his name, just as he knew few of the others, aside from Mak. This one worked one of the shapemills, in charge of the artisan orders calling for special cuts and designs. An old-timer. On Sundays he made sure nothing went missing and the men didn't grow too lax in their duties. He called out tasks, putting groups of men on sweeping and dusting, others on cleaning the machines. He pointed Rizal toward a barrel of paraffin.

"Hey, *tado*," he said, pulling his hard hat up and sliding it back down, "you know how to use this stuff to clean the saw on the CNC?"

Rizal looked to the barrel. Normally on Sundays he got in fast and got himself a broom. It was easy to loll through the day with a broom in your hand, pushing piles of dust suppressor around in no particular hurry. Today his mind had been elsewhere. Back in Navotas, or maybe in Bagong Silangan. The man cocked an eyebrow at him. Rizal shook his head, embarrassed.

"Ah, it's easy. Even a *buset* like you can handle it. You see the torch over there?" The old-timer pointed to a blowtorch resting against a steel support rising up to the corrugated roof. "You use that to melt a block of the wax in a pail, then pour the wax on the blades and just wipe it off. Easy. Wear gloves so you don't get burned. Get yourself a couple of guys to help and you'll be done in no time. Then, I don't know ... dust patrol. No need to kill ourselves today, eh, *anak*?"

Rizal nodded, smiling in spite of his nerves playing havoc with his stomach. He went to pick up the torch, looking around to see who was free. A familiar face set him partly at ease.

"Mak!" he called out. Mak already had himself a broom. He was leaning on it, content to while away the hours that should have been his own anyway were it not for the enforced guilt that held them there. Mak's eyes were rimmed by dark rings. As it was in prison, there was an underground economy going at the factory. Mak was one of its steady buyers. Whiskey. Always whiskey. A small bottle to sip away the evening hours. Anything was better than all that time with nothing to do but stare at those four bare walls. Today Rizal could see the hangover written in the bags under Mak's eyes, the sheepish look of pain etched in the lines at the corners of his mouth.

"Come on, *kupal*," Rizal called to him again. "Help me clean this *paking* machine. I have no idea what I'm doing. Get another guy if you can. More hands, less work."

Rizal turned his attention back to the torch, picking it up, studying it. Trying to figure out how the thing worked. He hoped Mak knew more about it than he did. He brought it over to the container of paraffin and pried off the lid, leaning it on its edge on the ground against the barrel. He stared at the white blocks within, edges almost clear. He heard footsteps behind and was joined by Mak on his right. He turned to his left to see who Mak had recruited as the third man. When he saw who it was, he shot Mak a look. It was a Taiwanese member of the staff – one of the few locals employed there who wasn't management or in the admin building along with Ms. Liao. He was a young man, maybe a year or two older than Rizal. Most gave him space. There was something about him – the way his eyes drifted off to some faraway corner, seeing things no one else could see. And he was quiet. Hardly said a word. To Rizal he seemed – he didn't know the right word for it. Slow, maybe, like the kids who huffed too much shoe polish back home. Whenever Rizal saw him, he seemed to be laughing to himself. Giggling like a child, though he wasn't saying anything, nor had anything been said to him. Rizal smiled uneasily at the man, drawing no reaction at all. He turned his back to him, speaking to Mak.

"Him, *kuya*?" he hissed.

Mak looked nervously back to the Taiwanese, then to Rizal.

"Easy, *anak*," he whispered. "You don't think *kuya* Mak knows what he's doing? This guy barely knows what day of the week it is. But he'll do anything you tell him. We can get him to do the whole job. The others are always having him do their chores for them. We get him to do this for us while we kick back and relax, understand?"

Rizal lowered his head, stealing a glance back. The man had his head down, staring at his shoes.

"I don't know, *kuya*...."

"Come on," said Mak, "I'll show you." He turned and snapped his fingers at the man. "Hey, my friend," he spoke in English. The man's head raised up, eyes widening in a look halfway between fear and surprise. "You want to help us, right? Be a good friend, yeah?"

The man nodded eagerly, though to Rizal it wasn't clear whether he understood or not. Mak seemed not to share his friend's concern.

"Good boy," said Mak. "Now come, come with *kuya* Mak and I'll show you what we're gonna do." He led the man to the container, pulling out a block of paraffin and dumping it into another pail, this one made of metal. "You see that?" he pointed to the block. The man nodded. Mak slapped him on the shoulder. "Now ... hey, what's your name, anyway?" The man looked at him wide-eyed again. Mak shook his head. "Never mind. We'll call you ... Fred, okay? Fred sound good to you? Yeah?" Mak nodded and the man nodded along with him. "All right, Fred. Here, take this." Mak picked up the torch and fished a pack of matches out of his pocket, turned on the gas and lit it. "All you have to do is hold this to the block, okay? Just hold the flame there until the whole thing melts, got it? Like this."

Mak held the torch to the block and it started to melt. "Just like that, see?"

Fred nodded.

"Good boy," said Mak, slowly transferring the torch to Fred's hands. Fred took it and squatted down, a smile breaking on his face. He laughed softly as Rizal had often seen him do, slowly melting the wax as Mak had shown him. Mak backed away, stifling his own laughter. He turned to Rizal, cocking a thumb at the man behind him.

"You see? Today will be the easiest money we ever made. We knock off behind the pallets over there. Come back when Fred's done melting the wax, then show him how to put it on the saw blade and wipe it off. Then we knock off the rest of the day too!"

Rizal looked past Mak to Fred. He sat stoically, eyes on his task. It looked like he had it under control, moving the flame from one corner of the block to the other, melting it evenly. Perhaps Fred wasn't as slow as he had thought. He shrugged.

"Okay, *kuya*," said Rizal. "You're right. Let's go relax."

They walked off behind the high stacks of unused pallets and Mak took out a twelve-ounce bottle of whiskey. He took a swig himself then offered Rizal one. Rizal declined bashfully. Mak shrugged and took another pull. They were alone, out of view of the men and the overhead security cameras. The drink seemed to dull Mak's usual glow. The brightness went out of his eyes, breath weighted and slowed. He gave Rizal a long look before he spoke – a look Rizal did his best to avoid. But there was no getting away. Not from his eyes, not from his words.

"Did you think it would be different, *anak*?" Mak asked.

"Different?"

"Working here, I mean. Did you think it would be ... I don't know. Not like this?"

"Maybe, *kuya*. I never really thought about it."

Mak pulled out a cigarette. The supervisors didn't care if the men smoked on Sundays, so long as the butts got swept up and the workers had the courtesy to light up out of sight. Mak lit a smoke and offered one to Rizal. Rizal shook his head and Mak shrugged and took a long drag, *tsk*-ing as he exhaled.

"Don't you think that's the problem?" he said. Seriousness was out of character for him, but he was deadly serious now. A frown creased the corners of his narrowed eyes. "Nobody thinks about it. Hardly *anybody* talks about it. Things just are the way they are. Jobs back home are scarce, the pay is low. So they say we can go overseas to work. Every year, millions of us. We get on airplanes, fly all over the world to do something we should be able to do at home. Leave our families behind, our kids. We're promised big money, at least enough to send some home every month to our parents, our partners, our children. Like that's supposed to make up for them growing up without a mother or a father. Then we find out that big money isn't so big after all. But it keeps going, *anak*. The cycle keeps on spinning. Guys like you and me – *migrantes* – even knowing what we know now, we'll do it again. We'll come back.

Because what else is there for us? What other hope do we have except to take the crumbs that fall to the floor while the men at the table eat their fill?"

Rizal felt the back of his neck grow hot. This talk made him ... uncomfortable. Embarrassed. Like he had failed to see something that had been in front of his face the whole time. He felt stupid then. Perhaps that's why he said what he said next.

"What are you complaining about, huh? Are you really that lazy, *kupal*? *Pakshet*, am I supposed to spend my Sunday standing here, listening to you whine? Here we have work. It's more than we would have back in the Philippines. *Susmaryosep*, I can't believe I have to spend my Sunday listening to this shit. You don't like it, *kuya*? Then quit. Stop being such a coward. Quit and go home. But when you get there, don't you dare moan about how hard it is to find a job or how corrupt everything is. Just remember what you had in Taiwan. A job. A bed. Three meals a day. Maybe we should be grateful, huh? Maybe we should be thankful for what we have. Ever think of that?"

As the words poured from his mouth Rizal felt sick to his stomach. They were not his own. He wasn't even sure he believed them. No, they were the words of his mother. Words born of the shame of subjugation. Words coming from poverty – from living in dust and dirt in a place where waves of garbage lapped at the shore and people plucked the plastic and junk from the water, salvaging a life from the world's castaways. Yes, that's what he felt like. A castaway of the world, shipped off to a foreign land. Boxed up and sent to place where he wasn't even a person. He was a commodity. A thing.

He felt sick, and he felt sorry. But it was too late. His words hung in the air like a bad smell. Rizal hoped Mak would be angry. Mak just looked sad. Ashamed. His cigarette hung limp between his fingers, down by his waist. He put his bottle away in his back pocket and sighed. Without looking at Rizal, he spoke.

"You're right, *anak*," he said. "You're right," he turned away, speaking over his shoulder. "Come on. We'd better get to work."

Mak shuffled off, back to the factory floor. Rizal stayed for a time behind the pallets, thinking. Wondering why he said all that, where it came from. How he could have been so heartless toward a man who had shown him nothing but kindness? This place – it had seeped into his body. Infected him with something dark and mean. That thing was slowly eating his soul, stealing away all those things he once was. Before long, he knew, everything he had been would be gone. He would be just another man. Not a man. A *migrante*, like the millions shipped like cargo from one place to another. A thing. A strong back useful only so long as he was able to stand and swing a hammer or haul up nets full of fish or sweep a floor or clean a bathroom or climb up a set of scaffolding or.... And when it would all be done, when his back was broken, when his hands were gnarled and useless, mind and body numb, he would be thrown away. Just another piece of garbage, slapping up against the steps in Navotas, like the doll – the pink plastic torso bobbing in a gasoline rainbow.

Rizal hung back, thinking such thoughts, mood flagging from bad to worse. The darkness in his mind took his ability to see the present, but it did not stop him from hearing it. And what he heard next sent him running out from behind the pallets, back onto the warehouse floor. That was where the terrible sound came from. The sound of Mak screaming in agony.

Chapter Twenty-Three

"How could this happen?"

The question came from Mr. Su in Mandarin, translated into Tagalog for Rizal by an interpreter – a *migrante* who had been working in Taiwan long enough to pick up much of the language. They were in Mr. Su's air-conditioned office, seated at the shop foreman's desk, angled so that it looked out over the warehouse floor through a large rectangular window. Rizal, his back to the window, stared down at his boots, splotched with dried paraffin wax. The wax had whorls of red in it. The sight sent a horrible image flashing through Rizal's mind. A face twisted in agony. Mak's face, skin a bubbling, bloody mess. A sound rang in Rizal's ears. The garbled noise of screams and laughter. A sound he would never forget as long as he lived.

"Well?" Mr. Su switched to English. Rizal's head jerked upward. He was afraid. Shaking. Unsure of what he should say and how he should say it. He hadn't seen what had happened. But it didn't take much to put it together. The question was, would Mr. Su believe him? Would anyone?

"Yes, sir?" Rizal asked. Already he had forgotten the question. Mr. Su sighed his impatience. The interpreter looked nervous – almost as nervous as Rizal himself.

Mr. Su spoke again in Mandarin. Again the interpreter spelled it out for Rizal in his own tongue.

"You were told to melt down the wax to clean the saw, yes or no?"

"Yes," Rizal answered, the word coming quiet and hesitant. Mr. Su stared at him, firing off another question. The interpreter gulped out the translation.

"You were told to melt the wax – you, and no one else. Correct?"

"Yes, but…." Rizal couldn't remember if he was told to do it alone or to get some help, or if he had found Mak because he was afraid to do it by himself.

"Correct?" Mr. Su spoke for himself. Rizal understood.

"Yes."

The answer, rather than placating the foreman, only served to enrage him. His anger sent him sputtering back into his own language. The interpreter swallowed and chose his translation carefully, omitting certain words for his countryman's sake.

"Then why, of all people, did you have such a … such a … simple man do your job for you?"

Rizal heard the laughter again, ricocheting through his skull. The screams. Mak's face and upper body covered in the melted paraffin. It fused with his clothing and skin, melting it into rivers and rising bubbles of malformed flesh. "Fred." Why had he done it? More than anything Rizal wanted the chance to ask him. Why had he thrown the bubbling wax in Mak's face? What had possessed him to injure the man so grievously? Had he snapped for some reason unknown, or was his mind simply gone as Rizal had thought? But Rizal had been taken away not long after the ambulance took

Mak. Fred had been led out the door, not by the police but by a man in plain clothes. A Taiwanese. A man, Rizal's interpreter had whispered to him on the way up the stairs to Mr. Su's office, who knew the owner of the company well — might even have been a relative. *Guanxi*, Rizal thought. Now he was alone. The last man left to take the blame.

"Of course," Mr. Su sighed again, tired of waiting for Rizal to reply, "there will be consequences." He spoke quickly from here on out, shifting in his seat more than once. "Someone will have to answer for Mak's injuries. Naturally the man you shirked your responsibilities on can't be held accountable for his actions. He's not right in the head. If you had just done what you were told, Rizal, all of this could have been avoided. I'm sorry to do this. I really am. But I'm afraid I have no choice but to...."

The sound of Mr. Su's words faded in Rizal's ears. They were replaced with another sound. The sound of seawater lapping against broken steps. The dull clunk of a pink plastic torso, pushed by the waves over and over again into barnacle-strewn concrete.

* * *

Three days later Rizal stood before a door, wondering if he should knock, unsure if it was the right one. He was in a place of wide streets and open sky — a world apart from Navotas, though it wasn't more than fifteen miles away, on the far side of Metro Manila. The door was painted a light shade of blue. Lighter even than the clear sky above, a blazing sun nearing its noonday height. Rizal was bleary-eyed; exhausted. Yet an intense energy radiated in his bones. On the flight from Taoyuan International Rizal had excused himself from his minder – a Pinoy official charged in dealing with deportations who hardly so much as introduced himself – to go to the bathroom. There he stood in front of the mirror, examining his face in the reflective glass, a face now foreign to its owner. He touched the skin beneath his eyes, rimmed with black rings. He held up an arm, thinner, he knew, than it had been before he left. He pulled at a ratty T-shirt, clothing looser than it was those few months ago. He eyed his curly locks – longer than Mama would ever have allowed them to get. He looked older, he thought. Much had changed in the time he had been away. Much had become different. And yet, much had stayed the same.

The door was set in the cinder block wall of a single-story home with a tin roof. It was like many in Bagong Silangan, the place named for hope. Here, as it did at Navotas, the city seemed to reach its end, doing so at empty, surveyed lots, while at Navotas it shrugged and gave up at the water's edge. Rizal stood in front of the door, wondering why he had come here first rather than face his mother at home. Why he had left the airport in the early-morning hours and walked mile after mile to a place where he might finally flag down a jeepney for a ride he couldn't pay for, all the way to the outskirts of Quezon. *Why?* he asked again and again. Of anyone who would give him the time he asked too where he might find the girl, Liezel, bearing his name or that of her mother. A girl of about four, he said, beautiful, with eyes that glowed though they were the darkest brown. Eyes that could light up the world.

The house Rizal stood before now, after following the directions of those kind enough to give them, backed on to the Marikina River, not far from the barangay hall where Manila met Calabarzon. Rizal could smell the sewage from the water, the fertilizer spread on the fields on the opposite bank. The odors of city and countryside – of rotting fruit, garbage, and diesel. The scent was both strange and reminiscent of home. But this was not his home. This was not his doorway. His, if it was where he had left it, was a piece of wood held in place with a cinder block, guarding the entryway of a mausoleum. His people were those who bedded down with the dead. Who sought refuge in small square tombs when the typhoon winds blew and the rains brought the floodwaters. His daughter and her mother – the woman who at one time had been foolish enough to want to call Rizal husband – this was their door, their home. They would decide whether or not it was open to him. At that moment Rizal couldn't decide which he hoped for more: an open door or one that remained closed.

It took several minutes to work up the courage to knock. Finally he raised a shaky hand and brought it down, the sound echoing in his ears like the pop of a homemade pistol. He thought of turning and walking away. *Why?* he asked himself still. Why put Liezel through this? Force her to see a man she would not remember, ask her to call him daddy? *Better she never knows you,* he told himself. *Best she grows up with her mother, her grandma, maybe even another man. A better man. One who doesn't have to go begging for work; a man who isn't fool enough to believe in something that's too good to be true. A real man.*

Rizal wanted to run. Instead he made himself stand there, waiting. Hearing the footsteps within. The rattle of the latch. The slow, pained creak as the door opened. And then, there she was. The little girl with eyes that could light up the world.

"Liezel?" he asked. His throat ached. She was so small. Impossibly small. He remembered holding her when she was a newborn, swaddled in an old towel. Those eyes. She had grown into their newborn beauty. A little person had formed from the aura of her innocent gaze. She looked at him, the man in her doorway. A man she didn't know. A stranger. But when this stranger said her name, she didn't question it. Didn't turn and run to fetch her mama. She nodded her head slowly, and waited for the man to speak again.

"Liezel, I...."

That was as far as Rizal got before the door opened wide and there standing before him was her, Liezel's mother. The woman whose name he couldn't bring himself to think, let alone say.

"Rizal?"

He nodded, much the same as his daughter. Slow, sheepish. Waiting to be sent away. Liezel's mother put a hand on her daughter's head.

"Liezel, honey, why don't you go and play with your dolls, okay?"

"Yes, Mama."

She waited until the little girl was gone. Rizal watched her go, entranced. He was drawn into her, his flesh and blood. A wave of guilt crashed down on him and he felt it shrink him into the crumbling footpath, gray chunks of cinder block felled from the walls towering above him. He wished one would topple and crush him. Take him from this world and rid him of the unshakable shame.

He heard the voice of his mother, scolding him and his childish ways. The voice was soon replaced by that of the woman standing in front of him.

"What are you doing here, Rizal?"

"Analyn, I...."

Saying her name for the first time in years felt strange. A weight was lifted, but the pain it bore onto him remained. Now, rather than pressing down, slumping his shoulders, holding his eyes to the ground, it surrounded him like an orb. A floating prison that would follow him as long as he lived.

"You think you can just show up like this? Not one word in four years, then suddenly here you are, knocking at our door like nothing happened? *Putang ina!* I should slam this door in your face, Rizal. And if Liezel asks who the strange, ugly man was, I'll tell her the truth. I'll tell her it was a useless, pitiful bum, and she should forget about him because he won't be coming back ever again."

Rizal wilted. The only grace was that Analyn's mother was not home. Had she been there, he would have been given both barrels. Blasted down to nothing and tossed into the river of sludge out back, like a salvage victim. Is that why he had come? To finally be broken down, all the way down? Working as a *migrante* had taken its piece of him. A chunk of his soul that might never grow back. But the piece that was missing before he left – it had been thrown away by *him*. There was only one person to blame, and he stood there, melting in the midday sun and the heat of the words of the mother of his child – a girl he knew he had no right to claim as his own. He sighed, and said the words he knew he had gone there to say.

"You're right, Analyn."

She folded her arms over her chest, glaring at him.

"What do you mean, 'You're right?'"

"I wasn't here for you and Liezel before. I don't deserve to be here now."

"That's right. You weren't. And you don't."

"I just...."

"You just what?" Analyn leaned against the door. *She looks tired*, Rizal thought. *Of course she does.*

"I just wanted you to know that I tried."

"You tried? Tried what, Rizal? What have you ever tried to do besides fetch water for your mama and the rest of your time running around with your useless friends?"

"I...." Rizal struggled to find the words. They were trapped somewhere inside, in a place he had yet to find. A place where he could describe what he was in the world; who he was trying to be. The man he might one day become, but then again may never be. "I ... I got a job," he stammered, "I mean, I had a job."

"Let me guess. You started running *shabu* like all the other gangster boys. They saw a *tanga* like you desperate for money and they let you spend all day in the sun selling poison to the *maganang kumain*. Then when it came time for you to be paid, they put a *baril* in your face and told you to get lost. Does that about cover it?"

Rizal felt something in him building behind his eyes. A thing that needed a target – whatever was standing in front of him. At that moment, it was Analyn.

"It's not my fault! You think I wanted this? You think this is how I want life to be? I know I haven't done everything right. But I saw a chance to do something, and I took it. And it was hell, Analyn. Every day I was over there it was hell. I wasn't a man. I was an animal. Less than human. I took it for as long as I could, and I would have taken more, just so I could make things right with you and Liezel and Mama. But they threw me away. Tossed me out like garbage because they needed someone to take the blame. To take their shit. That's what we *migrantes* do, Analyn. We take shit and we smile and we say, 'Thank you, sir, thank you,' while we shovel it up so rich people don't have to see it on their pretty sidewalks. I would have done that. For you and for my little girl. I would have done that to make things right. But they wouldn't let me have even that. I tried, Analyn," his voice quieted. "I just want you to know that I tried."

"*Migrante*? Rizal, what are you...."

Analyn's words faded into the heat of the day. They evaporated, mingling with the dust of the near countryside and the exhaust of the city. Back into the city and out of her and their daughter's lives disappeared Rizal, the father of the girl with the eyes that could light up the world. His anger turned inward expelled, there remained only the sorrow it had boiled down to. It was not a helpless sort of sadness, but a resigned one. A feeling that there was but one place for people like him. One place. One path. One destiny. The best a man born not just with a foot in the grave, but his entire being, could hope for.

Chapter Twenty-Four

It felt strange, coming back to his neighborhood – to set foot on the dirt footpaths of the Navotas City Cemetery – like this. To walk Maria Street, Diego Boulevard, Ruiz Avenue, with a wary eye, hoping not to be seen. He waited until dark to hop the iron fence, rather than walking through the front gate. It had taken him nearly until nightfall to get there anyway, traveling from the outskirts of Quezon City across the northern end of Metro Manila, all the way to Manila Bay. As dusk fell the leaves of the acacia trees rustled with the hint of an oncoming storm, a whispering wind strengthening hour by hour as it blew in off the bay. Rizal heard the familiar sounds and took in the familiar sights, now tinged with the weight he had felt before at Bagong Silangan – a force pushing him from all sides.

Rizal made his way toward the broken steps – the old boat launch. The place where the last boat owners of Navotas made their last trips out and back, leaving as captains, returning as the first generation of *migrantes.* There the sun's last rays still clung to the horizon. Rizal knew he would find his friend here, the one person he wanted to see, watching the light fade away. As Rizal neared the steps, he saw him lift a plastic bag to his mouth and nose, inhaling deeply. A wave splashed against the steps, droplets of water landing on the boy's head – the man's, rather. He seemed not to notice. Even when Rizal called out, the reaction was slow in coming.

"That stuff will turn you into a *tanga*, you know."

"Well," Kidlat's head turned slowly around, a shallow smile showing his grayed teeth in the last of the light, "what am I trying to be anyway?"

Rizal went and sat next to his friend, wincing as the uneven concrete dug into his backside. Kidlat did not seem at all surprised to see him; just stared out at the calm water, the last gasp of sunset wrapping distant cargo ships and barges in a wavering yellow-orange glow. Rizal thought back to his own time as a fisherman, the few months that became an eternity in the endless days spent wallowing on the deck of the boat, dying slow under the summer sun, and the nights that turned his hands to hunks of stone. He breathed in and smelled the salt water in the air mingled with the rubber-exhaust stench of the city; the piles of rotting garbage on the roadsides and those that burned in the slums, bales of cardboard moldering in the thick humidity. Lives coated in dust, choked by fumes, encased in concrete, awash in death. Everything around them was breaking down. Decayed or decaying. Rusted or rusting. Everything going in the same direction while politicians spoke of progress. Skyways and shopping malls. Better lives for the people.

Rizal looked to Kidlat, wondering if he would ask him how it had been. Where he had been. About the things he had seen. But there was only silence, and it was then that Rizal knew. Kidlat didn't ask because, in the end, what did it matter? If he had gone around the world and seen every sight there was to see, filled his pockets and seen them emptied, loved a woman in every port and left them all behind, he was right back where he started again, sitting in the same place he had sat as a boy. He had gone everywhere and nowhere. It was all the same – their lives were the same – now that they were again coated in the same dust, breathing the same smoggy air. Manila blackened their lungs, and so they would remain. The city, the country, the politicians and the powerful, the colonialists and the priests and the revolutionaries and counterrevolutionaries, had painted them with thick, indelible strokes just as the sun had scorched their brown skin. And just as their skin could not change its color, neither could they change who they were, where and what they came from, and where they would always wind up, no matter how far their travels might take them. This was how it would be, so long as the ways of the world continued as they were. Ways that were good only for some, murderous to the rest. Kidlat knew this, and so there was nothing to say. The silence between them was not a burden. It was a comfort, saving them from the pain of saying out loud all those things they knew. Though there was one question on Kidlat's mind.

"What will you do now, *kuya*?"

"*Hindi ko alam.*" I don't know.

"You should go and see your mother. She worries about you."

Rizal felt an ache in his heart. *Mama.* For all she knew, her only son was lost. Taken by the sea. Sold into slavery. Her worst fears come to life. He knew how she worried after him, even when he was near. *Yes*, he thought. *I should go to her now. Throw open the door and say, Here I am, Mama. Your baby boy, come home to take care of you.* How could he, though? How could he, when he had nothing? Nothing to show for all those months away. The ache was for his mother's pain, but also for his own shame. There was but one means of ridding himself of it, he knew. One path so he might someday return the way he had imagined he would, before he found out what the life of a *migrante* held. The path did not lead to his mother's doorstep. It led to an air-conditioned office, and a man – one of the powerful. A man he had once been naive enough to call *tiyo.*

Rizal stayed with Kidlat awhile. Together they watched the waves lapping against the steps in the dark. After a time, Rizal stood, saying goodbye to his friend. He lied to him without knowing exactly why, telling him he was going to see his mother. As he turned to leave, a figure, alone on the path, hidden by the darkness, startled him. Rizal squinted, and the figure moved forward, into a narrow swath of moonlight that cut through the clouds. There was Datu Death. For the first time he could remember, Rizal heard the old man speak. And for the first time he could remember, he stood before the man without fear.

"So," said Datu Death, "where will you go now, *anak*?"

* * *

Rizal did not go home to his mother. For the next few days he roamed the Navotas streets, looking for work that was not salvaging scraps – cardboard and bottles and cans to be sold at the junk shops for a few pesos a kilogram. The work of the young looking for change to spend at Internet cafes or on sweets, drugs, or alcohol, and the old who were desperate and hungry. There were Help Wanted signs in the windows of fast food restaurants – Jollibee and Mang Inasal. He walked into a Jollibee on M. Naval Street, asking about a job. A manager came to speak to him, eyes already nervous and darting. He asked if Rizal had a resume. Rizal told him no, looking around at the families eating at their tables, gobbling down French fries and hamburgers, spaghetti with ketchup and round pieces of hot dog. His belly rumbled with hunger. The manager sighed. Without a resume, he said, there was nothing he could do. And so Rizal took a deep, longing breath of the air filled with its scent of plenty, and went back to the streets of the poor. That night, he slept as he had the night before, on a cardboard mattress laid on the steps of a supermarket, in an entrance way blocked by the crisscross steel of a security door.

The next words Rizal would hear spoken toward him – words that were not asking him to move along or get out of the way or get out if he couldn't pay or wasn't going to buy anything – were these: "Tell me again, why is it that I should help you."

The words stung against Rizal's skin. He knew the question did not need an answer. The process was like life itself, a sentence to be endured, and so he did.

"You know you made a lot of trouble for *Tiyo* Benjie, ah? Mr. Chen was very angry. He called me many times. 'Why do your workers make so much trouble for me, Benjie? Why they don't want to work? Why do they always run away? Why, why, why, why, why?'" Benjie whirled his hands around his head like the questions were so many flies to be shooed away. "You did not last even a year, Rizal. You were sent back, and due to grave injuries suffered by a coworker no less. And yet you come to me and say what? That you wish to go back? That you want to be a *migrante* again? Then tell me why, Rizal. Why I should help you when I did everything for you already and it gave me nothing but headaches?"

Rizal's skin grew hot. Strangely he yearned to breathe in the warm city smog at that moment. To smell the culverts choked with trash and the sweet odor of mango peels and papayas and the sulfur scent of boiled *balut* from the roadside stands. The air in this room tasted stale, the smell of old sweat covered by cheap deodorant. He looked then to Benjie, leaning back in his chair, stains darkening his armpits. How could a man sitting still sweat so much, Rizal wondered. How could a man breathe so heavily when he seemed to do nothing at all?

"Well?" Benjie raised an eyebrow at the young man. Rizal knew the answer; the words sir Benjie expected him to say. Still he was reluctant to say them; to play the other man's game. There in the room was an invisible hoop, waiting for Rizal to jump through it. Rizal closed his eyes and jumped.

"We signed a contract, sir," said Rizal, looking the other man in the eye. "I owe you more than two years still. Two years of service fees. And the loan must be paid off. To pay you I need work. So I ask you to send me again. Let me be a *migrante*, like the ones you have helped before. I promise, sir Benjie, I won't let you down this time. I will put my head down. Keep my mouth shut. Work all day and all night if I have to. I'll make my money and pay you what I owe. But I can't do it without your help, sir. I can't do it on my own, and I can't do it in Manila, coming from the place I come from. So please, send me again. I will go anywhere. I will do whatever you say. Just give me a chance. One more is all I ask. It's all I need, sir."

Benjie leaned forward, a smile lightening his features. He scratched his nose, reaching for a pen. Opening a drawer, he pulled out a form. Then he began to scribble along the top of the page. From across the desk, Rizal watched as sir Benjie wrote a word, the meaning of which was yet to be decided. He watched as the other man gave form to *his* own name. And as he did, Rizal heard the words of his mother.

We are the nameless dead now.

CPSIA information can be obtained
at www.ICGtesting.com
Printed in the USA
LVHW051716181020
669109LV00035B/1366

9 781788 691932